# The Romance of a Mummy and Egypt

# The Romance of a Mummy and Egypt

## THÉOPHILE GAUTIER

*Translated by*

### F.C. DE SUMICHRAST

# ÆGYPAN PRESS

1901

Special thanks to Robert Cicconetti, Meredith Bach, and the
Online Distributed Proofreading Team (which can be found
at http://www.pgdp.net).

*The Romance of a Mummy and Egypt*
A publication of
ÆGYPAN PRESS

*www.aegypan.com*

# Table of Contents

# Introduction

*T*he subject of *The Romance of a Mummy* was possibly suggested to Théophile Gautier by Ernest Feydeau, the author of *Fanny* and other works of purely light literature, who published in 1858 a *General History of Funeral Customs and Burials among the Ancients.* This book was reviewed by Gautier when it appeared, and it is most likely that he had been previously made acquainted with its contents and had discussed Egyptian funeral rites and modes of sepulture with the author, for it was to Feydeau that he dedicated his novel when it was published in book form by Hachette in 1858. An omnivorous reader, Gautier had no doubt also perused the far more important works of Champollion, the decipherer of the inscriptions on the Rosetta stone, who first gave the learned world the key to the mysterious Egyptian hiero-glyphic alphabet. Champollion's *Monuments of Egypt and Nubia* had appeared in four volumes from 1835 to 1845, and a continuation by himself and the Vicomte Emmanuel de Rougé was completed in 1872. Champollion-Figeac's *Ancient Egypt* had been published in 1840, having been preceded by Lenormant's *The Museum of Egyptian Antiquities in the Louvre,* in 1830, and followed by Prisse d'Avennes' *Monuments of Egypt* in 1847. The explorations and discoveries of Mariette, summed up in that writer's *Selected Monuments and Drawings,* issued in 1856, and the steady growth of the Egyptian Museum in the Louvre, to which was added in 1852 the magnificent Clot-Bey collection, must have attracted the attention of Gautier, always keenly interested in art, literature, and erudition.

The account he gives, in his novel, of the ancient city of Thebes, of the great necropolis in the valley of Biban el Molûk, of the subterranean tombs, of the precautions taken by the designers to baffle curiosity, of the form and ornamentation of the sarcophagi, of the mummy-cases, of the mummy itself, of the manners, customs, dress, and beliefs of the ancient Egyptians, are marvelously accurate. Nothing is easier than to verify his descriptions by reference to the works of Champollion, Mariette, Wilkinson, Rawlinson, Erman, Edwards, and Maspero. Scarcely here and there will the reader find a possible error in his statements. It is evident that he has not trusted alone to what Feydeau told him, or to what he read in his book or in the works of Egyptologists; he examined the antiquities in the Louvre for himself; he noted carefully the scenes depicted on monuments and sarcophagi; he traced the ornamentation in all its details; he studied the poses, the attitudes, the expressions; he marked the costumes, the accessories; in a word, he mastered his subject, and then only did he, with that facility and certainty that amazed Balzac, write in swift succession the chapters of the novel which appeared in the numbers of the *Moniteur Universel* from March 11 to May 6, 1857.

His remark on Feydeau's book, "Picturesqueness in no wise detracts from accuracy," might well be applied to his own *Romance*, which fascinates the reader with its evocation of a long vanished past and its representation of a civilization buried for centuries in mystery. The weaving in of the wonders wrought by Moses and Aaron, of the overwhelming of the Pharaoh, whether Thotmes or Rameses, is skillfully managed, and imparts to the portions of the Biblical narrative used by him a verisimilitude and a sensation of actuality highly artistic. The purely erudite part of the work would probably not have interested the general public, indifferent to the discoveries of archæology, but the introduction of the human element of love at once captivated it; the erudite appreciated the accuracy of the restoration of ancient times and manners; the merely curious were pleased with a well told story, cleverly set in a framework whose strangeness appealed to their love of exoticism and novelty.

There have been added by the editor, as bearing upon the subject of the *Romance of a Mummy,* two or three chapters from the volume entitled *The Orient,* which is made up of a collection of sketches and letters of travel written at different times, and of reviews of books upon Eastern subjects, whether modern or ancient. The chapter describing a trip to Egypt was the result of a flying visit paid to that country on the occasion of the official opening of the Suez Canal in November, 1869. Gautier embarked on board the steamship *Moeris,* of the Messageries Impériales, at Marseilles. The very first night out he slipped and fell down the companion steps, and broke his left arm above the elbow. This painful accident did not prevent his fulfilling his promise to keep the *Journal Officiel,* with which he was then connected, fully supplied with accounts of the land and the inauguration ceremonies.

# The Romance of a Mummy

# The Romance of a Mummy

## PROLOGUE

"*I* have a presentiment that we shall find in the valley of Biban el Molûk a tomb intact," said to a highbred-looking young Englishman a much more humble personage who was wiping, with a big, blue-checked handkerchief, his bald head, on which stood drops of perspiration, just as if it had been made of porous clay and filled with water like a Theban water-jar.

"May Osiris hear you!" replied the English nobleman to the German scholar. "One may be allowed such an invocation in the presence of the ancient *Diospolis Magna*. But we have been so often deceived hitherto; treasure-seekers have always forestalled us."

"A tomb which neither the Shepherd Kings nor the Medes of Cambyses nor the Greeks nor the Romans nor the Arabs have explored, and which will give up to us its riches intact," continued the perspiring scholar, with an enthusiasm which made his eyes gleam behind the lenses of his blue glasses.

"And on which you will print a most learned dissertation which will give you a place by the side of Champollion, Rosellini, Wilkinson, Lepsius, and Belzoni," said the young nobleman.

"I shall dedicate it to you, my lord, for had you not treated me with regal munificence, I could not have backed up my system by an examination of the monuments, and I should have died in my little town in Germany without having beheld the marvels of this ancient land," replied the scholar, with emotion.

This conversation took place not far from the Nile, at the entrance to the valley of Biban el Molûk, between Lord Evandale, who rode an Arab horse, and Dr. Rumphius, more modestly perched upon an ass, the lean hind-quarters of which a fellah was belaboring. The boat which had brought the two travelers, and which was to be their dwelling during their stay, was moored on the other side of the Nile in front of the village of Luxor. Its sweeps were shipped, its great lateen sails furled on the yards. After having devoted a few days to visiting and studying the amazing ruins of Thebes, gigantic remains of a mighty world, they had crossed the river on a sandal, a light native boat, and were proceeding towards the barren region which contains within its depths, far down mysterious hypogea, the former inhabitants of the palaces on the other bank. A few men of the crew accompanied Lord Evandale and Dr. Rumphius at a distance, while the others, stretched out on the deck in the shadow of the cabin, were peacefully smoking their pipes and watching the craft.

Lord Evandale was one of those thoroughly irreproachable young noblemen whom the upper classes of Britain give to civilization. He bore everywhere with him the disdainful sense of security which comes from great hereditary wealth, a historic name inscribed in the "Peerage and Baronetage" — a book second only to the Bible in England — and a beauty against which nothing could be urged, save that it was too great for a man. His clear-cut and cold features seemed to be a wax copy of the head of Meleager or Antinoüs; his brilliant complexion seemed to be the result of rouge and powder, and his somewhat reddish hair curled naturally as accurately as an expert hairdresser or clever valet could have made it curl. On the other hand, the firm glance of his steel-blue eyes and the slightly sneering expression of his lower lip corrected whatever there might be of effeminate in his general appearance.

As a member of the Royal Yacht Squadron, the young nobleman indulged occasionally in a cruise on his swift yacht *Puck*, built of teak, fitted like a boudoir, and manned by a small crew of picked seamen. In the course of the preceding

year he had visited Iceland; in the present year he was visiting
Egypt, and his yacht awaited him in the roads of Alexandria.
He had with him a scholar, a physician, a naturalist, an artist,
and a photographer, in order that his trip might not be
unfruitful. He was himself highly educated, and his society
successes had not made him forget his triumphs at Cam-
bridge University. He was dressed with that accuracy and
careful neatness characteristic of the English, who traverse
the desert sands in the same costume which they would wear
when walking on the pier at Ramsgate or on the pavements
of the West End. A coat, vest, and trousers of white duck,
intended to repel the sun's rays, composed his costume,
which was completed by a narrow blue necktie with white
spots, and an extremely fine Panama hat with a veil.

Rumphius, the Egyptologist, preserved even in this hot
climate the traditional black coat of the scholar with its loose
skirts, its curled up collar, its worn buttons, some of which
had freed themselves of their silk covering. His black trousers
shone in places and showed the warp. Near the right knee an
attentive observer might have remarked upon the greyish
ground of the stuff a systematic series of lines of richer tone
which proved that he was in the habit of wiping his pen upon
this portion of his clothes. His muslin cravat, rolled in the
shape of a cord, hung loosely around his neck, on which stood
out strongly the Adam's apple. Though he was dressed with
scientific carelessness, Rumphius was not any the handsomer
on that account. A few reddish hairs, streaked with grey, were
brushed back behind his protruding ears, and were puffed up
by the high collar of his coat. His perfectly bald skull, shining
like a bone, overhung a prodigiously long nose, spongy and
bulbous at the end, so that with the blue discs of his glasses
he looked somewhat like an ibis, — a resemblance increased
by his head sunk between his shoulders. This appearance was
of course entirely suitable and most providential for one
engaged in deciphering hieroglyphic inscriptions and scrolls.
He looked like a bird-headed god, such as are seen on funeral
frescoes, who had transmigrated into the body of a scholar.

The lord and the doctor were traveling towards the cliffs
which encircle the somber valley of Biban el Molûk, the royal
necropolis of ancient Thebes, indulging in the conversation

of which we have related a part, when, rising like a Troglodyte from the black mouth of an empty sepulcher — the ordinary habitation of the fellahs — another person, dressed in somewhat theatrical fashion, abruptly entered on the scene, stood before the travelers, and saluted them with the graceful salute of the Orientals, which is at once humble, caressing, and noble.

This man was a Greek who undertook to direct excavations, who manufactured and sold antiquities, selling new ones when the supply of the old happened to fail. Nothing about him, however, smacked of the vulgar exploiter of strangers. He wore a red felt fez from which hung a long blue silk tassel; under the narrow edge of an inner linen cap showed his temples, evidently recently shaved. His olive complexion, his black eyebrows, his hooked nose, his eyes like those of a bird of prey, his big moustaches, his chin almost divided into two parts by a mark which looked very much like a saber-cut, would have made his face that of a brigand, had not the harshness of his features been tempered by the assumed amenity and the servile smile of a speculator who has many dealings with the public. He was dressed in very cleanly fashion in a cinnamon-colored jacket embroidered with silk of the same color, gaiters of the same stuff, a white vest adorned with buttons like chamomile flowers, a broad red belt, and vast bulging trousers with innumerable folds.

He had long since noted the boat at anchor before Luxor. Its size, the number of the oarsmen, the luxury of the fittings, and especially the English flag which floated from the stern, had led his mercantile instinct to expect a rich traveler whose scientific curiosity might be exploited, and who would not be satisfied with statuettes of blue or green enameled ware, engraved scarabæi, paper rubbings of hieroglyphic panels, and other such trifles of Egyptian art.

He had followed the coming and going of the travelers among the ruins, and knowing that they would not fail, after having sated their curiosity, to cross the stream in order to visit the royal tombs, he awaited them on his own ground, certain of fleecing them to some extent. He looked upon the whole of this funereal realm as his own property, and treated with scant courtesy the little subaltern jackals who ventured to scratch in the tombs.

With the swift perception characteristic of the Greeks, no sooner had he cast his eyes upon Lord Evandale than he quickly estimated the probable income of his lordship and resolved not to deceive him, reasoning that he would profit more by telling the truth than by lying. So he gave up his intention of leading the noble Englishman through hypogea traversed hundreds of times already, and disdained to allow him to begin excavations in places where he knew nothing would be found; for he himself had long since taken out and sold very dear the curiosities they had contained.

Argyropoulos (such was the Greek's name), while exploring the portion of the valley which had been less frequently sounded than others because hitherto the search had never been rewarded by any find, had come to the conclusion that in a certain spot, behind some rocks whose position seemed to be due to chance, there certainly existed the entrance to a passageway masked with peculiar care, which his great experience in this kind of search had enabled him to recognize by a thousand signs imperceptible to less clear-sighted eyes than his own, which were as sharp and piercing as those of the vultures perched upon the entablature of the temples. Since he had made that discovery, two years before, he had bound himself never to walk or look in that direction lest he might give a hint to the violators of tombs.

"Does your lordship intend to attempt excavations?" said he in a sort of cosmopolitan dialect which those who have been in the ports of the Levant and have had recourse to the services of the polyglot dragomans — who end by not knowing any language — are well acquainted with. Fortunately, both Lord Evandale and his learned companion knew the various tongues from which Argyropoulos borrowed. "I can place at your disposal," he went on, "some hundred energetic fellahs who, under the spur of whip and bakshîsh, would dig with their fingernails to the very center of the earth. We may try, if it pleases your lordship, to clear away a buried sphinx or a shrine, or to open up a hypogeum."

On seeing that his lordship remained unmoved by this tempting enumeration, and that a skeptical smile flitted across the doctor's face, Argyropoulos understood that he had not to deal with easy dupes, and he was confirmed in his intention to sell to the Englishman the discovery on which he reckoned to complete his fortune and to give a dowry to his daughter.

"I can see that you are scholars, not ordinary tourists, and that vulgar curiosity does not bring you here," he went on, speaking in English less mixed with Greek, Arabic, and Italian. "I will show you a tomb which has hitherto escaped all searchers, which no one knows of but myself. It is a treasure which I have carefully preserved for a person worthy of it."

"And for which you will have to be paid a high price," said his lordship, smiling.

"I am too honest to contradict your lordship; I do hope to get a good price for my discovery. Everyone in this world lives by his trade. Mine is to exhume Pharaohs and sell them to strangers. Pharaohs are becoming scarce at the rate at which they are being dug up; there are not enough left for everybody. They are very much in demand, and it is long since any have been manufactured."

"Quite right," said the scholar; "it is some centuries since the undertakers, dissectors, and embalmers have shut up shop, and the Memnonia, peaceful dwellings of the dead, have been deserted by the living."

The Greek, as he heard these words, cast a sidelong glance at the German, but fancying from his wretched dress that he had no voice in the matter, he continued to address himself exclusively to the young nobleman.

"Are a thousand guineas too much, my lord, for a tomb of the greatest antiquity, which no human hand has opened for more than three thousand years, since the priests rolled rocks before its mouth? Indeed, it is giving it away; for perhaps it contains quantities of gold, diamond, and pearl necklaces, carbuncle earrings, sapphire seals, ancient idols in precious metals, and coins which could be turned to account."

"You sly rascal!" said Rumphius, "you are praising up your wares, but you know better than anyone that nothing of the sort is found in Egyptian tombs."

Argyropoulos, understanding that he had to do with clever men, ceased to boast, and turning to Lord Evandale, he said to him, "Well, my lord, does the price suit you?"

"I will give a thousand guineas," replied the young nobleman, "if the tomb has not been opened; but I shall give nothing if a single stone has been touched by the crow-bar of the diggers."

"With the additional proviso," added Rumphius the prudent, "that we carry off everything we shall find in the tomb."

"Agreed!" said Argyropoulos, with a look of complete confidence. "Your lordship may get ready your bank-notes and gold beforehand."

"Dr. Rumphius," said Lord Evandale to his acolyte, "it strikes me that the wish you uttered just now is about to be realized. This man seems sure of what he says."

"Heaven will it may be so!" replied the scholar, shaking his head somewhat doubtfully; "but the Greeks are most bare-faced liars, *Cretæ mendaces,* says the proverb."

"No doubt this one comes from the mainland," answered Lord Evandale, "and I think that for once he has told the truth."

The Greek walked a few steps ahead of the nobleman and the scholar like a well-bred man who knows what is proper. He walked lightly and firmly, like a man who feels that he is on his own ground.

The narrow defile which forms the entrance to the valley of Biban el Molûk was soon reached. It had more the appearance of the work of man than of a natural opening in the mighty wall of the mountain, as if the Genius of Solitude had desired to make this realm of death inaccessible. On the perpendicular rocky walls were faintly discernible shapeless vestiges of weather-worn sculptures which might have been mistaken for the asperities of the stone imitating the worn figures of a half-effaced *basso-relievo.* Beyond the opening, the valley, which here widened somewhat, presented the most desolate sight. On either side rose steep slopes formed of huge masses of calcareous rock, rough, leprous-looking, worn, cracked, ground to sand, in a complete state of decomposition under the pitiless sun. They resembled bones calcined in the fire, and yawned with the weariness of eternity out of their deep crevices, imploring by their thousand cracks the drop of water which never fell. The walls rose almost vertically to a great height, and their dentelated crests stood out greyish-white against the almost black indigo of the sky, like the broken battlements of a giant ruined fortress. The rays of the sun heated to white heat one of the sides of the funeral valley, the other being bathed in that crude blue tint of torrid lands which strikes the people of the North as untruthful when it is reproduced by painters, and which stands out as sharply as the shadows on an architectural drawing.

The valley sometimes made sudden turns, sometimes narrowed into defiles as the boulders and cliffs drew closer or apart. The thoroughly dry atmosphere in these climates being perfectly transparent, there was no aërial perspective in this place of desolation. Every detail, sharp, accurate, bare, stood out, even in the background, with pitiless dryness, and the distance could only be guessed at by the smaller dimensions of objects. It seemed as though cruel nature had resolved not to conceal any wretchedness, any sadness of this bare land, deader even than the dead it contained. Upon the sun-lighted cliff streamed like a cascade of fire a blinding glare like that which is given out by molten metal; every rock face, transformed into a burning-glass, returned it more ardent still. These reflections, crossing and recrossing each other, joined to the flaming rays which fell from heaven and which were reflected by the ground, produced a heat equal to that of an oven, and the poor German doctor had hard work to wipe his face with his blue-checked handkerchief, which was as wet as if it had been dipped in water.

There was not a particle of loam to be found in the whole valley, consequently not a blade of grass, not a bramble, not a creeper, not even a patch of moss to break the uniformly whitish tone of the torrified landscape. The cracks and recesses of the rocks did not hold coolness enough for the thin, hairy roots of the smallest rock plant. The place looked as if it held the ashes of a chain of mountains, consumed in some great planetary conflagration, and the accuracy of the parallel was completed by great black strips looking like cauterized cicatrices which rayed the chalky slopes.

Deep silence reigned over this waste; no sign of life was visible; no flutter of wing, no hum of insect, no flash of lizard or reptile; even the shrill song of the cricket, that lover of burning solitudes, was unheard. The soil was formed of a micaceous, brilliant dust like ground sandstone, and here and there rose hummocks formed of the fragments of stone torn from the depths of the chain, which had been excavated by the persevering workmen of vanished generations, and the chisel of the Troglodyte laborers who had prepared in the shadow the eternal dwelling-places of the dead. The broken entrails of the mountain had produced other mountains, friable heaps of small rocks which might have been mistaken for the natural range.

On the sides of the cliffs showed here and there small openings surrounded with blocks of stone thrown in disorder: square holes flanked by pillars covered with hieroglyphs, the lintels of which bore mysterious cartouches on which could yet be made out in a great yellow disc the sacred scarabæus, the ram-headed sun, and the goddesses Isis and Nephthys standing or kneeling.

These were the tombs of the ancient kings of Thebes. Argyropoulos did not stop there, but led the travelers up a sort of steep slope, which at first glance seemed nothing but a break on the side of the mountain, choked in many places by fallen masses of rock, until they reached a narrow platform, a sort of cornice projecting over the vertical cliff on which the rocks, apparently thrown together by chance, nevertheless exhibited on close examination some symmetrical arrangement.

When the nobleman, who was a practiced athlete, and the doctor, who was much less agile, had succeeded in climbing up to him, Argyropoulos pointed with his stick to a huge stone and said with triumphant satisfaction, "There is the spot!"

He clapped his hands in Oriental fashion, and straightway from the fissures of the rocks, from the folds of the valley, hastened up pale, ragged fellahs, who bore in their bronze-colored arms crow-bars, pick-axes, hammers, ladders, and all necessary tools. They escaladed the steep slope like a legion of black ants; those who could not find room on the narrow

ledge on which already stood the Greek, Lord Evandale, and
Dr. Rumphius, hung by their hands and steadied themselves
with their feet against the projections in the rock. The Greek
signed to three of the most robust, who placed their crow-bars
under the edges of the boulder. Their muscles stood out upon
their thin arms, and they pressed with their whole weight on
the end of the levers. At last the boulder moved, tottered for
a moment like a drunken man, and, urged by the united
efforts of Argyropoulos, Lord Evandale, Rumphius, and a few
Arabs who had succeeded in climbing the ledge, bounded
down the slope. Two other boulders of less size went the same
way, one after another, and then it was plain that the belief
of the Greek was justified. The entrance to a tomb, which had
evidently escaped the investigations of the treasure-seekers,
appeared in all its integrity.

It was a sort of portico squarely cut in the living rock. On
the two side-walls a couple of pairs of pillars exhibited capitals
formed of bulls' heads, the horns of which were twisted like
the crescent of Isis. Below the low door, with its jambs flanked
by long panels covered with hieroglyphs, there was a broad,
emblematic square. In the center of a yellow disc showed by
the side of the scarabæus, symbol of successive new births,
the ram-headed god, the symbol of the setting sun. Outside
the disc, Isis and Nephthys, incarnations of the Beginning
and the End, were kneeling, one leg bent under the thigh, the
other raised to the height of the elbow, in the Egyptian
attitude, the arms stretched forward with an air of mysterious
amazement, and the body clothed in a close fitting gown
girdled by a belt with falling ends. Behind a wall of stone and
unbaked brick, that readily yielded to the pickaxes of the
workmen, was discovered the stone slab which formed the
doorway of the subterranean monument. On the clay seal
which closed it, the German doctor, thoroughly familiar with
hieroglyphs, had no difficulty in reading the motto of the
guardian of the funeral dwellings, who had closed forever this
tomb, the situation of which he alone could have found upon
the map of burial-places preserved in the priests' college.

"I begin to believe," said the delighted scholar to the young
nobleman, "that we have actually found a prize, and I with-

draw the unfavorable opinion which I expressed about this worthy Greek."

"Perhaps we are rejoicing too soon," answered Lord Evandale, "and we may experience the same disappointment as Belzoni, when he believed himself to be the first to enter the tomb of Menephtha Seti, and found, after he had traversed a labyrinth of passages, walls, and chambers, an empty sarcophagus with a broken cover; for the treasure-seekers had reached the royal tomb through one of their soundings driven in at another point in the mountain."

"Oh, no," answered the doctor; "the range is too broad here and the hypogeum too distant from the others for these wretched people to have carried their mines as far as this, even if they scraped away the rock."

While this conversation was going on, the workmen, urged by Argyropoulos, proceeded to lift the great stone slab which filled up the orifice of the passage. As they cleared away the slab in order to pass their crow-bars under it, for Lord Evandale had ordered that nothing should be broken, they turned up in the sand innumerable small statuettes a few inches in height, of blue and green enameled ware, of admirable workmanship, — tiny funeral statuettes deposited there as offerings by parents and friends, just as we place flowers on the thresholds of our funeral chapels; only, our flowers wither, while after more than three thousand years these witnesses of long bygone griefs are found intact, for Egypt worked for eternity only.

When the door was lifted away, giving for the first time in thirty-five centuries entrance to the light of day, a puff of hot air escaped from the somber opening as from the mouth of a furnace. The light, striking the entrance of the funeral passage, brought out brilliantly the coloring of the hieroglyphs engraved upon the walls in perpendicular lines upon a blue plinth. A reddish figure with a hawk's-head crowned with the *pschent*, the double crown of Upper and Lower Egypt, bore a disc containing a winged globe, and seemed to watch on the threshold of the tomb. Some fellahs lighted torches and preceded the two travelers, who were accompanied by Argyropoulos. The resinous flame burned with difficulty in the dense, stifling air which had been concentrated for so many thousands of years under the heated limestone of the mountain, in the labyrinths, passages, and blind ways of the hypogeum. Rumphius breathed hard and perspired in streams; the impassible Evandale turned hot and felt a moisture on his temples. As for the Greek, the fiery wind of the desert had long since dried him up, and he perspired no more than would a mummy.

The passage led directly to the center of the chain, following a vein of limestone of remarkable fineness and purity. At the end of the passageway a stone door, sealed as the other had been with a clay seal and surmounted by a winged globe, proved that the tomb had not been violated and pointed to the existence of another passageway sunk deeper still into the mountain.

The heat was now so intense that the young nobleman threw off his white coat, and the doctor his black one. These were soon followed by their vests and shirts. Argyropoulos, seeing that they were breathing with difficulty, whispered a few words to a fellah, who ran back to the entrance and brought two large sponges filled with fresh water, which the Greek advised the two travelers to place on their mouths so that they might breathe a fresher air through the humid pores, as is done in Russian baths when the steam heat is raised to excess.

The door was attacked and soon gave way. A steep staircase cut in the living rock was then seen descending. Against a green background edged with a blue line were ranged on either side of the passageway processions of symbolical statues, the colors of which were as bright and fresh as if the artist's brush had laid them on the day before. They would show for a second in the light of the torches, then vanish in the shadow like the phantoms of a dream. Below these narrow frescoes, lines of hieroglyphs, written perpendicularly like Chinese writing and separated by hollow lines, excited the erudite by the sacred mystery of their outlines. Along that portion of the walls which was not covered with hieratic signs, a jackal lying on its belly, with outstretched paws and pointed ears, and a kneeling figure wearing a miter, its hand stretched upon a circle, seemed to stand as sentries on either side of the door, the lintel of which was ornamented with two panels placed side by side, in which were figured two women wearing close-fitting gowns and extending their feathered arms like wings.

"Look here!" said the doctor, taking breath when he reached the foot of the staircase, and when he saw that the excavation sank deeper and deeper still. "Are we going down to the center of the earth? The heat is increasing to such a degree that we cannot be far from the sojourn of the damned."

"No doubt," answered Lord Evandale, "they followed the vein of limestone, which sinks in accordance with the law of geological undulations."

Another very steep passage came after the steps. The walls were lower, covered with paintings, in which could be made out a series of allegorical scenes, explained, no doubt, by the hieroglyphs inscribed below. This frieze ran all along the passage, and below it were small figures worshipping sacred scarabæi and the azure-colored symbolical serpent.

As he reached the end of the passage, the fellah who carried the torch threw himself back abruptly, for the path was suddenly interrupted by the mouth of a square well yawning black at the surface of the ground.

"There is a well, master," said the fellah, addressing himself to Argyropoulos; "what am I to do?"

The Greek took the torch, shook it to make it blaze up, and threw it into the small mouth of the well, bending cautiously over the opening. The torch fell, twisting and hissing. Soon a dull sound was heard, followed by a burst of sparks and a cloud of smoke, then the flame burned up bright and clear, and the opening of the well shone in the shadow like the bloodshot eye of a Cyclops.

"Most ingenious!" said the young nobleman. "This labyrinth, interrupted by oubliettes, must have cooled the zeal of robbers and scholars."

"Not at all," replied the doctor. "Those seek gold, these truth, which are the two most precious things in the world."

"Bring the knotted rope!" cried Argyropoulos to his Arabs. "We shall explore and sound the walls of the well, for the passage no doubt runs far beyond it."

Eight or ten men hung on to the rope, the end of which was let fall into the well. With the agility of a monkey or of an athlete, Argyropoulos caught hold of the swinging rope and let himself down some fifteen feet, holding on with his hands and striking with his heels the walls of the well. Wherever he struck the rock it gave out a dead, dull sound. Then Argyropoulos let himself fall to the bottom of the well and struck the ground with the hilt of his kandjar, but the compact rock did not resound. Lord Evandale and the doctor, burning with eager curiosity, bent over the edge at the risk of falling in headlong, and watched with intense interest the search undertaken by the Greek.

"Hold hard!" cried he at last, annoyed at finding nothing; and he seized the rope with his two hands to ascend.

The shadow of Argyropoulos, lighted from below by the torch which was still burning at the bottom of the well, was projected against the ceiling and cast on it a silhouette like that of a monstrous bird. His sunburned face expressed the liveliest disappointment, and under his moustache he was biting his lips.

"There is not a trace of a passage!" he cried; "and yet the excavation cannot stop here."

"Unless," said Rumphius, "the Egyptian who ordered this tomb died in some distant nome, on a voyage, or in battle, the work being then abandoned, as is known to have been the case occasionally."

"Let us hope that by dint of searching we shall find some secret issue," returned Lord Evandale; "otherwise we shall try to drive a transverse shaft through the mountain."

"Those confounded Egyptians were clever indeed at concealing the entrances to their tombs, — always trying to find out some way of putting poor people off the track. One would think that they laughed in anticipation at the disappointment of searchers," grumbled Argyropoulos. Drawing to the edge of the well, the Greek cast a glance, as piercing as that of a night-bird, upon the wall of the little chamber which formed the upper portion of the well. He saw nothing but the ordinary characters of psychostasia, — Osiris the judge seated on his throne in the regulation attitude, holding the crook in the one hand, the whip in the other, and the goddesses of Justice and Truth leading the spirit of the dead to the tribunal of Amenti. Suddenly he seemed to be struck with a new idea, and turned sharply around. His long experience as an excavator recalled to him a somewhat analogous case. In addition, the desire of earning the thousand guineas of his lordship spurred up his faculties. He took a pick-axe from the hands of a fellah, and began, walking backward, to strike sharply right and left on the surface of the rock, often at the risk of damaging some of the hieroglyphs or of breaking the beak or the wing-sheath of the sacred hawk or the scarabæus.

The wall, thus questioned, at last answered the hammer and sounded hollow. An exclamation of triumph broke from the Greek and his eyes flashed; the doctor and the nobleman clapped their hands.

"Dig here," said Argyropoulos, who had recovered his coolness, to his men.

An opening large enough to allow a man to pass through was made. A gallery running within the mountain around the obstacle which the well offered to the profane, led to a square hall, the blue vault of which rested upon four massive pillars ornamented by the red-skinned, white-garmented figures which so often show, in Egyptian frescoes, the full bust and the head in profile. This hall opened into another, the vault of which was somewhat higher and supported by two pillars only. Various scenes — the mystic bark, the bull Apis bearing the mummy towards the regions of the West, the judgment of the soul and the weighing of the deeds of the dead in the supreme scales, the offerings to the funeral divinities — adorned the pillars and the hall. They were carved in flat, low relief with sharp outline, but the painter's brush had not completed the work of the chisel. By the care and delicacy of the work might be judged the importance of the personage whose tomb it had been sought to conceal from the knowledge of men.

After having spent a few moments in examining these carvings, which were in the purest manner of the fine Egyptian style of the classical age, the explorers perceived that there was no issue from the hall, and that they had reached a sort of blind place. The air was becoming somewhat rarified, the torches burned with difficulty and further augmented the heat of the atmosphere, while the smoke formed a dense pall.

The Greek gave himself to the devil, but that did no good. Again the walls were sounded without any result. The mountain, thick and compact, gave back but a dead sound; there was no trace of a door, of a passage, or of any sort of opening.

The young nobleman was plainly discouraged, and the doctor let fall his arms by his side. Argyropoulos, who feared losing his thousand guineas, exhibited the fiercest despair. However, the party was compelled to retreat, for the heat had become absolutely suffocating.

They returned to the outer hall, and there the Greek, who could not make up his mind to see his golden dream vanish in smoke, examined with the most minute attention the shafts of the pillars to make certain that they did not conceal some artifice, that they did not mask some trap which might be discovered by displacing them; for in his despair he mingled the realism of Egyptian architecture with the chimerical constructions of the Arab tales. The pillars, cut out of the mountain itself, in the center of the hollowed mass, formed part of it, and it would have been necessary to employ gunpowder to break them down. All hope was gone.

"Nevertheless," said Rumphius, "this labyrinth was not dug for nothing. Somewhere or another there must be a passage like the one which goes around the well. No doubt the dead man was afraid of being disturbed by importunate persons and he had himself carefully concealed; but with patience and perseverance you can get anywhere. Perhaps a slab carefully concealed, the joint of which cannot be seen, owing to the dust scattered over the ground, covers some descent which leads, directly or indirectly, to the funeral hall."

"You are right, doctor," said Evandale; "those accursed Egyptians jointed stones as closely as the hinges of an English trap. Let us go on looking."

The doctor's idea struck the Greek as sound, and he made his fellahs walk about every part and corner of the hall, tapping the ground. At last, not far from the third pillar a dull resonance struck on the practiced ear of the Greek. He threw himself on his knees to examine the spot, brushing away with the ragged burnoose one of his Arabs had thrown him the impalpable dust of thirty-five centuries. A black, narrow, sharp line showed, and, carefully followed out, marked out on the ground an oblong slab.

"Did I not tell you," cried the enthusiastic doctor, "that the passage could not end in this way?"

"I am really troubled," said Lord Evandale, in his quaint, phlegmatic British fashion, "at disturbing the last sleep of the poor unknown body which did expect to rest in peace until the end of the world. The dweller below would willingly dispense with our visit."

"The more so that a third party is lacking to make the presentation formal," replied the doctor. "But do not be anxious, my lord, I have lived long enough in the days of the Pharaohs to present you to the illustrious personage who inhabits this subterranean passage."

Crow-bars were applied to the narrow fissure, and after a short time the stone moved and was raised. A staircase with high, steep steps, sinking into darkness, awaited the impatient travelers, who rushed down pell-mell. A sloping gallery painted on both walls with figures and hieroglyphs came next, then at the end of the gallery some more steps leading to a short corridor, a sort of vestibule to a hall in the same style as the first one, but larger and upborne by six pillars cut out of the living rock. The ornamentation was richer, and the usual motives of funeral paintings were multiplied on a yellow background. To the right and to the left opened in the rock two small crypts or chambers filled with funeral statuettes of enameled ware, bronze, and sycamore wood.

"We are in the antechamber of the hall where the sarcophagus is bound to be!" cried Rumphius, his clear grey eyes flashing with joy from below his spectacles, which he had pushed back over his forehead.

"Up to the present," said Lord Evandale, "the Greek has kept his word. We are the first living men who have penetrated so far since the dead, whoever he may be, was left with eternity and the unknown in this tomb."

"Oh, he must be some great personage," replied the doctor; "a king or a king's son, at the very least. I shall tell you later when I have deciphered his cartouche. But first let us enter this hall, the finest, the most important, which the Egyptians called the Golden Hall."

Lord Evandale walked ahead, a few steps before the less agile scholar, though perhaps the latter deferentially wished to leave the pleasure of the discovery to the young nobleman.

As he was about to step across the threshold, Lord Evandale bent forward as if something unexpected had struck him. Though accustomed not to manifest his emotions, he was unable to repress a prolonged and thoroughly British "Oh!" On the fine grey powder which covered the ground showed very distinctly, with the imprint of the toes and the great bone of the heel, the shape of a human foot, — the foot of the last priest or the last friend who had withdrawn, fifteen hundred years before Christ, after having paid the last honors to the dead. The dust, which in Egypt is as eternal as granite, had molded the print and preserved it for more than thirty centuries, just as the hardened diluvian mud has preserved the tracks of the animals which last traversed it.

"See," said Evandale to Rumphius, "that human footprint which is directed towards the exit from the hypogeum! In what narrow passage of the Libyan chain rests the mummified body that made it?"

"Who knows?" replied the scholar. "In any case, that light print, which a breath would have blown away, has lasted longer than empires, than religions and monuments believed eternal. The noble dust of Alexander was used perhaps to stop a bunghole, as Hamlet says, but the footprint of this unknown Egyptian remains on the threshold of a tomb."

Urged by a curiosity which did not allow them much time for recollection, the nobleman and the doctor entered the hall, taking care, nevertheless, not to efface the wondrous footprint. On entering, the impassible Evandale felt a strange emotion; it seemed to him, as Shakespeare says, that the time was out of joint. The feeling of modern life vanished, he forgot Great Britain and his name inscribed on the rolls of the peerage, his seat in Lincolnshire, his mansion in the West End, Hyde Park, Piccadilly, the Queen's Drawing-Room, the Yacht Squadron, and all that constituted his English existence. An invisible hand had turned upside down the sand-glass of eternity, and the centuries which had fallen one by one, like the hours, in the solitude of the night, were falling once more. History was as if it were not: Moses was living,

Pharaoh was reigning, and he, Lord Evandale, felt embarrassed because he did not wear his beard in ringlets, and had not an enameled neck-plate and a narrow vestment wrinkling in folds upon his hips, — the only suitable dress in which to be presented to a royal mummy. A sort of religious horror filled him, although there was nothing sinister about the place, as he violated this palace of death so carefully protected against profanation. His attempt seemed to him impious and sacrilegious, and he said to himself, "Suppose this Pharaoh were to rise on his couch and strike me with his scepter." For one moment he thought of letting fall the shroud half lifted from the body of this antique, dead civilization, but the doctor, carried away by scientific enthusiasm, and not a prey to such thoughts, shouted in a loud voice, "My lord, my lord, the sarcophagus is intact!"

These words recalled Lord Evandale to reality. By swift projection of his thought he traversed the thirty-five hundred years which he had gone back in his reverie, and he answered, "Indeed, dear doctor, intact?"

"Oh, unexpected luck! oh, marvelous chance! oh, wondrous find!" continued the doctor, in the excitement of a scholarly joy.

Argyropoulos, on beholding the doctor's enthusiasm, felt a pang of remorse, — the only kind of remorse that he could feel, — at not having asked more than twenty-five thousand francs. "I was a fool!" he said to himself. "This shall not happen again. That nobleman has robbed me."

In order to enable the strangers to enjoy the beauty of the spectacle, the fellahs had lighted all their torches. The sight was indeed strange and magnificent. The galleries and halls which led to the sarcophagus hall were flat-ceiled and not more than eight or ten feet high; but the sanctuary, the one to which all these labyrinths led, was of much greater proportions. Lord Evandale and Dr. Rumphius remained dumb with admiration, although they were already familiar with the funereal splendors of Egyptian art. Thus lighted up, the Golden Hall flamed, and for the first time, perhaps, the colors of the paintings shone in all their brilliancy. Red and blue, green and white, of virginal purity, brilliantly fresh and amazingly clear, stood out from the golden background of

the figures and hieroglyphs, and attracted the eye before the
subjects which they formed could be discerned. At first glance
it looked like a vast tapestry of the richest stuffs. The vault,
some thirty feet high, formed a sort of azure velarium bordered with long yellow palm-leaves. On the walls the symbolical globe spread its mighty wings and the royal cartouches
showed around. Farther on, Isis and Nephthys waved their
arms furnished with feathers like wings; the uræus swelled its
blue throat, the scarabæus unfolded its wings, the animal-
headed gods pricked up their jackal ears, sharpened their
hawk's-beaks, wrinkled their baboon faces, and drew into
their shoulders their vulture or serpent necks as if they were
endowed with life. Mystical consecrated boats (baris) passed
by on their sledges drawn by figures in attitudes of sadness,
with angular gestures, or propelled by half-naked oarsmen,
they floated upon symbolical undulating waves. Mourners
kneeling, their hand placed on their blue hair in token of
grief, turned towards the catafalques, while shaven priests,
leopard-skin on shoulder, burned perfumes in a spatula ter-
minating in a hand bearing a cup under the nose of the
godlike dead. Other personages offered to the funeral genii
lotus in bloom or in bud, bulbous plants, birds, pieces of
antelope, and vases of liquors. Acephalous figures of Justice
brought souls before Osiris, whose arms were set in inflexible
contour, and who was assisted by the forty-two judges of
Amenti, seated in two rows and bearing an ostrich-plume on
their heads, the forms of which were borrowed from every
realm of zoölogy.

All these figures, drawn in hollowed lines in the limestone
and painted in the brightest colors, were endowed with that
motionless life, that frozen motion, that mysterious intensity
of Egyptian art, which was hemmed in by the priestly rule,
and which resembles a gagged man trying to utter his secret.

In the center of the hall rose, massive and splendid, the
sarcophagus, cut out of a solid block of black basalt and
closed by a cover of the same material, carved in the shape
of an arch. The four sides of the funeral monolith were
covered with figures and hieroglyphs as carefully engraved as
the intaglio of a gem, although the Egyptians did not know
the use of iron, and the grain of basalt is hard enough to

blunt the best-tempered steel. Imagination loses itself when it tries to discover the process by which that marvelous people wrought on porphyry and granite as with a style on wax tablets.

At the angles of the sarcophagus were set four vases of oriental alabaster, of most elegant and perfect outline, the carved covers of which represented the man's head of Amset, the monkey head of Hapi, the jackal head of Tuamutef, and the hawk head of Kebhsnauf. The vases contained the viscerae of the mummy enclosed in the sarcophagus. At the head of the tomb an effigy of Osiris with plaited beard seemed to watch over the dead. Two colored statues of women stood right and left of the tomb, supporting, with one hand a square box on their head, and holding in the other a vase for ablutions which they rested on their hip. The one was dressed in a simple white skirt clinging to the hips and held up by crossed braces; the other, more richly costumed, was wrapped in a sort of narrow shift, covered with scales alternately red and green. By the side of the first there were three water-jars, originally filled with Nile water, which, as it evaporated, had left its mud, and a plate holding some alimentary paste, now dried up. By the side of the second, two small ships, like the model ships made in seaports, which reproduced accurately, the one the minutest details of the boats destined to bear the bodies from Diospolis to Memnonia, the other the symbolical boat in which the soul is carried to the regions of the West. Nothing was forgotten, — neither the masts, nor the rudder formed of one long sweep, nor the pilot, nor the oarsmen, nor the mummy surrounded by mourners and lying under the shrine on a bed with feet formed of lion's claws, nor the allegorical figures of the funeral divinities fulfilling their sacred functions. Both the boats and the figures were painted in brilliant colors, and on the two sides of the prow, beaklike as the poop, showed the great Osiris' eye, made longer still by the use of antimony. The bones and skull of an ox scattered here and there showed that a victim had been offered up as a scapegoat to the Fate which might have disturbed the repose of the dead. Coffers painted and bedizened with hieroglyphs were placed on the tomb; reed tables yet bore the final offerings. Nothing had been touched in this palace of death since the day when the mummy in its cartonnage and its two coffins had been placed upon its basalt couch. The worm of the sepulcher, which can find a way through the closest biers, had itself retreated, driven back by the bitter scent of the bitumen and the aromatic essences.

"Shall I open the sarcophagus?" said Argyropoulos, after Lord Evandale and Doctor Rumphius had had time to admire the beauty of the Golden Hall.

"Unquestionably," replied the nobleman; "but take care not to chip the edges of the cover as you put in your crow-bars, for I propose to carry off the tomb and present it to the British Museum."

The whole company bent their efforts to displacing the monolith. Wooden wedges were carefully driven in, and presently the huge stone was moved and slid down the props prepared to receive it. The sarcophagus having been opened, showed the first bier hermetically sealed. It was a coffer adorned with paintings and gilding, representing a sort of shrine with symmetrical designs, lozenges, quadrilles, palm leaves, and lines of hieroglyphs. The cover was opened, and Rumphius, who was bending over the sarcophagus, uttered a cry of surprise when he discovered the contents of the coffin, having recognized the sex of the mummy by the absence of the Osiris beard and the shape of the cartonnage. The Greek himself appeared amazed. His long experience in excavations enabled him to understand the strangeness of such a find. The valley of Biban el Molûk contains the tombs of kings only: the necropolis of the queens is situated farther away, in another mountain gorge. The tombs of the queens are very simple, and usually consist of two or three passage-ways and one or two rooms. Women in the East have always been considered as inferior to men, even in death. Most of these tombs, which were broken into at a very distant period, were used as receptacles for shapeless mummies carelessly embalmed, which still exhibit traces of leprosy and elephantiasis. How did this woman's coffin come to occupy this royal sarcophagus, in the center of this cryptic palace worthy of the most illustrious and most powerful of the Pharaohs?

"This," said the doctor to Lord Evandale, "upsets all my notions and all my theories. It overthrows the system most carefully built upon the Egyptian funeral rites, which never-theless have been so carefully followed out during thousands of years. No doubt we have come upon some obscure point, some forgotten mystery of history. A woman did ascend the throne of the Pharaohs and did govern Egypt. She was called Tahoser, as we learn from the cartouches engraved upon older inscriptions hammered away. She usurped the tomb as she usurped the throne. Or perhaps some other ambitious woman, of whom history has preserved no trace, renewed her attempt."

"No one is better able to solve this difficult problem than you," said Lord Evandale. "We will carry this box full of secrets to our boat, where you will, at your leisure, decipher this historic document and read the riddle set by these hawks, scarabæi, kneeling figures, serrated lines, winged uræus, and spatula hands, which you read as readily as did the great Champollion."

The fellahs, under the orders of Argyropoulos, carried off the huge coffer on their shoulders, and the mummy, perform-ing in an inverse direction the funeral travel it had accom-plished in the days of Moses, in a painted and gilded bari preceded by a long procession, was embarked upon the sandal which had brought the travelers, soon reached the vessel moored on the Nile, and was placed in the cabin, which was not unlike, so little do forms change in Egypt, the shrine of the funeral boat.

Argyropoulos, having arranged about the box all the ob-jects which had been found near it, stood respectfully at the cabin door and appeared to be waiting. Lord Evandale un-derstood, and ordered his valet to pay him the twenty-five thousand francs.

The open bier was placed upon rests in the center of the cabin; it shone as brilliantly as if the colors had been put on the day before, and framed in the mummy, molded within its cartonnage, the workmanship of which was remarkably fine and rich. Never had ancient Egypt more carefully wrapped up one of her children for the eternal sleep. Al-though no shape was indicated by the funeral Hermes, ending in a sheath from which stood out alone the shoulders and the head, one could guess there was under that thick envelope a young and graceful form. The gilded mask, with its long eyes outlined with black and brightened with enamel, the nose with its delicate nostrils, the rounded cheekbones, the half-open lips smiling with an indescribable, sphinxlike smile, the chin somewhat short in curve but of extreme beauty of contour, presented the purest type of the Egyptian ideal, and testified by a thousand small, characteristic details which art cannot invent, to the individual character of the portrait. Numberless fine plaits of hair, tressed with cords and separated by bandeaux, fell in opulent masses on either side of the face. A lotus stem, springing from the back of the neck, bowed over the head and opened its azure calyx over the dead, cold brow, completing with a funeral cone this rich and elegant headdress.

A broad necklace, composed of fine enamels cloisonnés with gold and formed of several rows, lay upon the lower portion of the neck, and allowed to be seen the clean, firm contour of two virgin breasts like two golden cups.

The sacred ram-headed bird, bearing between its green horns the red disc of the setting sun and supported by two serpents wearing the pschent and swelling out their hoods, showed on the bosom of the figure its monstrous form full of symbolic meaning. Lower down, in the spaces left free by the crossed zones, and rayed with brilliant colors representing bandages, the vulture of Phra, crowned with a globe, with outspread wings, the body covered with symmetrically arranged feathers, and the tail spread out fanwise, held in its talons the huge Tau, emblem of immortality. The funeral gods, green-faced, with the mouths of monkeys or jackals, held out with a gesture hieratic in its stiffness the whip, the crook, and the scepter. The eye of Osiris opened its red ball outlined with antimony. Celestial snakes swelled their hoods around the sacred discs; symbolical figures projected their feathered arms; and the two goddesses of the Beginning and the End, their hair powdered with blue dust, bare down to below the breasts and the rest of the body wrapped in a close-fitting skirt, knelt in Egyptian fashion on green and red cushions adorned with heavy tufts.

A longitudinal band of hieroglyphs, springing from the belt and running down to the feet, contained no doubt some formal funeral ritual, or rather, the names and titles of the deceased, a problem which Dr. Rumphius promised himself to solve later.

The character of the drawing, the boldness of the lines, the brilliancy of the colors in all these paintings denoted in the plainest manner to a practiced eye that they belonged to the finest period of Egyptian art. When the English nobleman and his companion had sufficiently studied this outer case, they drew the cartonnage from the box and set it up against the side of the cabin, where the funeral form, with its gilded mask, presented a strange spectacle, standing upright like a materialized specter and with a seeming attitude of life, after having preserved so long the horizontal attitude of death on a basalt bed in the heart of the mountain, opened up by impious curiosity. The soul of the deceased, which had reckoned on eternal rest and which had taken such care to preserve its remains from violation, must have been moved, beyond the worlds, in the circuit of its travels and transmigrations.

Dr. Rumphius, armed with a chisel and a hammer, to separate the two parts of the cartonnage of the mummy, looked like one of those funeral genii which wear a bestial mask and which are seen in the paintings of the hypogea crowding around the dead in the performance of some frightful and mysterious rite; the clean profile of Lord Evandale, calm and attentive, made him look like the divine Osiris awaiting the soul to be judged.

The operation having been at length completed — for the doctor wished not to scale off the gilding, — the box, resting on the ground, was separated into two parts like the casing of a cast, and the mummy appeared in all the brilliancy of its death toilet, coquettishly adorned as if it had wished to charm the genii of the subterranean realms. On opening the case, a faint, delightful, aromatic odor of cedar liquor, of sandal powder, of myrrh and cinnamon spread through the cabin of the vessel; for the body had not been gummed up and hardened with the black bitumen used in embalming the bodies of ordinary persons, and all the skill of the embalmers, the former inhabitants of Memnonia, seemed to have been directed to the preservation of these precious remains.

The head was enveloped in a network of narrow bands of fine linen, through which the face showed faintly. The essences in which they had been steeped had dyed the tissue a beautiful tawny tint. Over the breast a network of fine tubes of blue glass, very like the long jet beads which are used to embroider Spanish bodices, with little golden drops wherever the tubes crossed, fell down to the feet and formed a pearly shroud worthy of a queen. The statuettes of the four gods of Amenti in hammered gold shone brilliantly, and were symmetrically arranged along the upper edge of the network, which ended below in a fringe of most tasteful ornaments. Between the statuettes of the funeral gods was a golden plate, above which a lapis-lazuli scarabæus spread out its long golden wings. Under the mummy's head was placed a rich mirror of polished metal, as if it had been desired to give the dead soul an opportunity of beholding the specter of its beauty during the long night of the tomb. By the mirror lay a coffer of enameled ware, of most precious workmanship, which contained a necklace composed of ivory rings alternating with beads, gold, lapis-lazuli, and cornelian. By the side of the beauty had been placed also a narrow, square sandalwood basin in which, during her lifetime, the dead woman had performed her perfumed ablutions. Three vases of wavy alabaster fastened to the bier, as was also the mummy, by a layer of natron, contained, the first two, essences, the scent of which could still be noticed, and the third, antimony powder and a small spatula for the purpose of coloring the edge of the eyelids and extending the outer angle according to the antique Egyptian usage, still practiced at the present time by Eastern women.

"What a touching custom!" said Dr. Rumphius, excited by the sight of these treasures; "what a touching custom it was to bury with a young woman all her pretty toilet articles! For it is a young woman unquestionably that these linen bands, yellow with time and with essences, envelop. Compared with the Egyptians, we are downright barbarians; hurried on by our brutal way of living, we have lost the delicate sense of death. How much tenderness, how much regard, how much love do not these minute cares reveal, these infinite precautions, these useless caresses bestowed upon a senseless body,

— that struggle to snatch from destruction an adored form and to restore it intact to the soul on the day of the supreme reunion!"

"Perhaps," replied Lord Evandale, very thoughtful, "our civilization, which we think so highly developed, is, after all, but a great decadence which has lost even the historical remembrance of the gigantic societies which have disappeared. We are stupidly proud of a few ingenious pieces of mechanism which we have recently invented, and we forget the colossal splendors and the vast works impossible to any other nation, which are found in the ancient land of the Pharaohs. We have steam, but steam is less powerful than the force which built the Pyramids, dug out hypogea, carved mountains into the shapes of sphinxes and obelisks, sealed halls with one great stone which all our engines could not move, cut out monolithic chapels, and saved frail human remains from annihilation, — so deep a sense of eternity did it already possess."

"Oh, the Egyptians," said Dr. Rumphius, smiling, "were wonderful architects, amazing artists, and great scholars. A priest of Memphis and of Thebes could have taught even our German scholars; and as regards symbolism, they were greater than any symbolists of our day. But we shall succeed eventually in deciphering their hieroglyphs and penetrating their mysteries. The great Champollion has made out their alphabet; we shall easily read their granite books. Meanwhile, let us strip, as delicately as possible, this young beauty who is more than three thousand years of age."

"Poor woman!" murmured the young lord. "Profane eyes will now behold the mysterious charms which love itself perhaps never saw. Truly, under the empty pretext of scientific pursuit, we are as barbarous as the Persians of Cambyses, and if I were not afraid of driving to despair this worthy scholar, I should enclose you again, without having stripped off your last veil, within the triple box of your bier."

Dr. Rumphius raised from the casing the mummy, which was no heavier than a child's body, and began to unwrap it with motherly skill and lightness of touch. He first of all undid the outer envelope of linen, sewed together and impregnated with palm wine, and the broad bands which here and there girdled the body. Then he took hold of the end of a thin, narrow band, the infinite windings of which enclosed the limbs of the young Egyptian. He rolled up the band on itself as cleverly as the most skillful embalmer of the City of the Dead, following it up in all its meanderings and circumvolutions. As he progressed in his work, the mummy, freed from its envelope, like a statue which a sculptor blocks out of the marble, appeared more slender and exquisite in form. The bandage having been unrolled, another narrower one was seen, intended to bind the body more closely. It was of such fine linen, and so finely woven, that it was comparable to modern cambric and muslin. This bandage followed accurately every outline, imprisoning the fingers and the toes, molding like a mask the features of the face, which was visible through the thin tissue. The aromatic balm in which it had been steeped had stiffened it, and as it came away under the fingers of the doctor, it gave out a little dry sound like that of paper that is being crushed or torn. There remained but one turn to be taken off, and familiar though he was with such work, Dr. Rumphius stopped for a moment, either through respect for the dead, or through that feeling which prevents a man from breaking open a letter, from opening a door, from raising a veil which hides a secret that he burns to learn. He ascribed his momentary pause to fatigue, and as a matter of fact, the perspiration was dripping from his forehead without his thinking of wiping it with his great blue-checked handkerchief; but fatigue had nothing to do with it. Meanwhile the dead form showed through the fine, gauzelike stuff, and some gold work shone faintly through it as well.

The last wrapping taken off, the young woman showed in the chaste nudity of her lovely form, preserving, in spite of so many centuries that had passed away, the fullness of her contours, and the easy grace of her pure lines. Her pose, an infrequent one in the case of mummies, was that of the Venus of Medici, as if the embalmers had wished to save this beautiful body from the set attitude of death and to soften the inflexible rigidity of the cadaver.

A cry of admiration was uttered at the same time by Rumphius and Evandale at the sight of the marvel. Never did a Greek or Roman statue present a more beautiful appearance. The peculiar characteristics of the Egyptian ideal gave indeed to this lovely body, so miraculously preserved, a slenderness and a grace lacking in antique marbles, — the long hands, the highbred, narrow feet, the nails shining like agate, the slender waist, the shape of the breasts, small and turned up like a sandal beneath the veil which enveloped it, the slightly protruding contour of the hip, the roundness of the thigh, the somewhat long leg recalling the slender grace of the musicians and dancers represented on the frescoes of funeral repasts in the Thebes hypogea. It was a shape still childish in its gracefulness, yet possessing already all the perfections of a woman which Egyptian art expresses with such tender suavity, whether it paints the walls of the passages with a brush, or whether it patiently carves the hard basalt.

As a general rule mummies which have been filled with bitumen and natron resemble black simulacra carved in ebony; corruption cannot attack them, but the appearance of life is wholly lacking; the bodies have not returned to the dust whence they came, but they have been petrified in a hideous shape, which one cannot contemplate without disgust and terror. In this case, the body, carefully prepared by surer, longer, and more costly processes, had preserved the elasticity of the flesh, the grain of the skin, and almost its natural color. The skin, of a light brown, had the golden tint of a new Florentine bronze, and the amber, warm tone which is admired in the paintings of Giorgione and Titian covered with a smoky varnish, was not very different from what must have been the complexion of the young Egyptian during her lifetime. She seemed to be asleep rather than dead. The eyelids, still fringed with their long lashes, allowed eyes lustrous with the humid gleam of life to shine between their lines of antimony. One could have sworn they were about to shake off, as a light dream, their sleep of thirty centuries. The nose, delicate and fine, preserved its pure outline; no depression deformed the cheeks, which were as round as the side of a vase; the mouth, colored with a faint blush, had preserved its imperceptible lines, and on the lips, voluptuously molded, fluttered a melancholy and mysterious smile, full of gentleness, sadness, and charm, — that tender and resigned smile which pouts so prettily the lips of the adorable heads which surmount the Canopean vases in the Louvre.

Around the forehead, low and smooth in accordance with the laws of antique beauty, was massed jet-black hair divided and plaited into a multitude of fine tresses which fell on either shoulder. Twenty golden pins stuck into the tresses, like flowers in a ball headdress, studded with brilliant points the thick dark hair which might have been thought artificial, so abundant was it. Two great earrings, round discs resembling small bucklers, shimmered with yellow light by the side of the brown cheeks. A magnificent necklace, composed of three rows of divinities and amulets in gold and precious stones, encircled the neck of the coquettish mummy, and lower down upon her breast hung two other collars, the pearl, gold, lapis-lazuli, and cornelian rosettes of which alternated symmetrically with the most perfect taste. A girdle of nearly the same design enclosed her waist with a belt of gold and gems. A double bracelet of gold and cornelian beads adorned her left wrist, and on the index of the left hand shone a very small scarabæus of golden cloisonné enamel, which formed a seal ring and was held by a gold thread most marvelously plaited.

Strange were the sensations of the two men as they found themselves face to face with a human being who had lived in the days when history was yet young and was collecting the stories told by tradition; face to face with a body contemporary with Moses, which yet preserved the exquisite form of youth; as they touched the gentle little hand impregnated with perfumes, which a Pharaoh perhaps had kissed; as they fingered the hair, more durable than empire, more solid than granite monuments. At the sight of the lovely dead girl, the young nobleman felt the retrospective desire often inspired by the sight of a statue or a painting representing a woman of past days famous for her beauty. It seemed to him that he would have loved, had he lived three thousand years earlier, that beauty which nothingness had refused to destroy; and the sympathetic thought perhaps reached the restless soul that fluttered above its profaned frame.

Far less poetic than the young nobleman, Dr. Rumphius was making the inventory of the gems, without, however, taking them off; for Evandale had ordered that the mummy should not be deprived of this last frail consolation. To take away gems from a woman, even dead, is to kill her a second time. Suddenly a papyrus roll concealed between the side and arm of the mummy caught the doctor's eye.

"Oh!" said he, "this is no doubt a copy of the funeral ritual placed in the inner coffin and written with more or less care according to the wealth and rank of the person."

He unrolled the delicate band with infinite precautions. As soon as the first lines showed, he exhibited surprise, for he did not recognize the ordinary figures and signs of the ritual. In vain he sought in the usual places for the vignettes representing the funeral, which serve as a frontispiece to such papyri, nor did he find the Litany of the Hundred Names of Osiris, nor the soul's passport, nor the petition to the gods of Amenti. Drawings of a peculiar kind illustrated entirely different scenes connected with human life, and not with the voyage of the shade to the world beyond. Chapters and paragraphs seemed to be indicated by characters written in red, evidently for the purpose of distinguishing them from the remainder of the text, which was in black, and of calling the attention of the reader to interesting points. An inscription placed at the head appeared to contain the title of the work, and the name of the grammat who had written or copied it, — so much, at least, did the sagacious intuition of the doctor make out at the first glance.

"Undoubtedly, my lord, we have robbed Master Argyropoulos," said he to Evandale, as he pointed out the differences between the papyrus and the usual ritual. "This is the first time that an Egyptian manuscript has been found to contain anything else than hieratic formulæ. I am bound to decipher it, even if it costs me my sight, even if my beard grows thrice around my desk. Yes, I shall ferret out your secret, mysterious Egypt! Yes, I shall learn your story, you lovely dead; for that papyrus pressed close to your heart by your lovely arm surely contains it. And I shall be covered with glory, become the equal of Champollion, and make Lepsius die of jealousy."

The nobleman and the doctor returned to Europe. The mummy, wrapped up again in all its bandages and replaced within its three cases, rests within Lord Evandale's park in

Lincolnshire, in the basalt sarcophagus which he brought at great expense from Biban el Molûk and which he did not give to the British Museum. Sometimes Lord Evandale leans upon the sarcophagus, sinks into a deep reverie, and sighs.

After three years of unflagging application, Dr. Rumphius succeeded in deciphering the mysterious papyrus, save in some damaged parts, and in others which contained unknown signs. And it is his translation into Latin — which we have turned into French — that you are about to read, under the name, "The Romance of a Mummy."

I

Oph (that is the name of the city which antiquity called Thebes of the Hundred Gates, or Diospolis Magna), seemed asleep under the burning beams of the blazing sun. It was noon. A white light fell from the pale sky upon the baked earth; the sand, shimmering and scintillating, shone like burnished metal; shadows there were none, save a narrow, bluish line at the foot of buildings, like the inky line with which an architect draws upon papyrus; the houses, whose walls sloped well inwards, glowed like bricks in an oven; every door was closed, and no one showed at the windows, which were closed with blinds of reeds.

At the end of the deserted streets and above the terraces stood out in the hot, transparent air the tips of obelisks, the tops of pylons, the entablatures of palaces and temples, whose capitals, formed of human faces or lotus flowers, showed partially, breaking the horizontal lines of the roofs and rising like reefs amid the mass of private buildings. Here and there above a garden wall shot up the scaly trunk of a palm tree ending in a plume of leaves, not one of which stirred, for never a breath blew. Acacias, mimosas, and Pharaoh fig trees formed a cascade of foliage that cast a narrow blue shadow upon the dazzling brilliancy of the ground. These green spots refreshed and enlivened the solemn aridity of the picture, which but for them would have been that of a dead city.

A few slaves of the Nahasi race, black complexioned, monkey-faced, with bestial gait, alone braving the heat of the day, were bearing to their masters' homes the water drawn from the Nile in jars that were hung from a stick placed on their shoulder. Although they wore nothing but striped drawers wrinkling on their hips, their torsos, brilliant and polished like basalt, streamed with perspiration as they quickened their pace lest they should scorch the thick soles of their feet on the pavements, which were as hot as the floor of a vapor bath. The boatmen were asleep in the cabins of their boats moored to the brick wall of the river quay, sure that no one would waken them to cross to the other bank, where lay the Memnonia quarter. In the highest heaven wheeled vultures, whose shrill call, that at any other time would have been lost in the rumor of the city, could be plainly heard in the general silence. On the cornices of the monuments two or three ibises, one leg drawn up under their body, their long bill resting on their breast, seemed to be meditating deeply, and stood out against the calcined, whitish blue which formed the background.

And yet all did not sleep. From the walls of a great palace whose entablature, adorned with palmettos, made a long, straight line against the flaming sky, there came a faint murmur of music. These bursts of harmony spread now and then through the diaphanous shimmer of the atmosphere, and the eye might almost have followed their sonorous undulations. Deadened by the thickness of the walls, the music was strangely sweet. It was a song voluptuously sad, wearily languorous, expressing bodily fatigue and the discouragement of passion. It was full of the eternal weariness of the luminous azure, of the indescribable helplessness of hot countries. As the slave passed by the wall, forgetting the master's lash he would suspend his walk and stop to breathe in that song, impregnated with all the secret homesickness of the soul, which made him think of his far distant country, of his lost love, and of the insurmountable obstacles of fate. Whence came that song, that sigh softly breathed in the silence of the city? What restless soul was awake when all around was asleep?

The straight lines and the monumental appearance of the façade of the palace, which looked upon the face of the square, were typical of the civil and religious architecture of Egypt. The dwelling could belong to a princely or a priestly family only. So much was readily seen from the materials of which it was built, the careful construction, and the richness of the ornamentation.

In the center of the façade rose a great building flanked by two wings surmounted by a roof in the form of a truncated triangle. A broad, deeply cut molding of striking profile ended the wall, in which was visible no opening other than a door placed, not symmetrically in the center, but in the corner of the building, no doubt to allow ample space for the staircase within. A cornice in the same style as the entablature surmounted this single door. The building projected from a wall on which rested like balconies two stories of galleries, resembling open porticoes, composed of pillars singularly fantastic in style. The bases of these pillars represented huge lotus-buds, from the capsule of which, as it opened its dentelated rim, sprang the shaft like a giant pistil, swelling below, more slender at the top, girdled under the capital by a collar of moldings, and ending in a half-blown flower. Between the broad bays were small windows with their sashes in two parts filled with stained glass. Above ran a terraced roof flagged with huge slabs of stone.

On the outer galleries great clay vases, rubbed inside with bitter almonds and closed with leaves, resting upon wooden pedestals, cooled the Nile water in the drafts of air. Tables bore pyramids of fruits, sheaves of flowers and drinking-cups of different shapes; for the Egyptians love to eat in the open air, and take their meals, so to speak, upon the public street. On either side of the main building stretched others rising to the height of one story only, formed of a row of pillars engaged halfway up in a wall divided into panels in such a manner as to form around the house a shelter closed to the sun and the gaze of the outer world. All these buildings, enlivened by ornamental paintings, — for the capitals, the shafts, the cornices, and the panels were colored, — produced a delightful and superb effect.

The door opened into a vast court surrounded by a quad-rilateral portico supported by pillars, the capitals of which showed on each face a woman's head, with the ears of a cow, long, narrow eyes, slightly flattened noses, and a broad smile; each wore a thick red cushion and supported a cap of hard sandstone. Under the portico opened the doors of the apart-ments, into which the light came softened by the shade of the galleries. In the center of the court sparkled in the sun-shine a pool of water, edged with a margin of Syêné granite. On the surface of the pond spread the heart-shaped leaves of the lotus, the rose and blue flowers of which were half closed as if overcome by the heat in spite of the water in which they were plunged. In the flower-beds around the pool were planted flowers arranged fanlike upon small hillocks, and along the narrow walks laid out between the beds walked carefully two tame storks, which from time to time snapped their bills and fluttered their wings as if about to take flight. At the angles of the court the twisted trunks of four huge persæas exhibited a mass of metallic green foliage. At the end a sort of pylon broke the portico, and its large bay, framing in the blue air, showed at the end of a long avenue a summer kiosk of rich and elegant design. In the compartments traced on the right and on the left of the arbor by dwarf trees cut into the shape of cones, bloomed pomegranates, sycamores, tamarinds, periplocas, mimosas, and acacias, the flowers of which shone like colored lights on the deep green of the foliage which overhung the walls.

The faint, sweet music of which we have spoken proceeded from one of the rooms which opened into the interior por-tico. Although the sun shone full into the court, the ground of which blazed in the flood of light, a blue, cool shadow, transparently intense, filled the apartment, in which the eye, blinded by the dazzling reverberation, sought to distinguish shapes and at last made them out when it had become accustomed to the semi-light. A tender lilac tone overspread the walls of the room, around which ran a cornice painted in brilliant tones and enriched with small golden palm-branches. Architectural designs skillfully combined formed on the plain spaces panels which framed in ornaments, sheaves of flowers, birds, diapers of contrasted colors, and scenes of domestic life.

At the back, near the wall, stood a strangely shaped bed, representing an ox wearing ostrich-feathers with a disc between its horns, broadening its back to receive the sleeper upon a thin red mattress, and stiffening by way of feet its black legs ending in green hoofs, while its curled-up tail was divided into two tufts. This quadruped bed, this piece of animal furniture, would have seemed strange in any other country than Egypt, where lions and jackals are also turned into beds by the fancy of the workmen.

In front of the couch was placed a stool with four steps, which gave access to it: at the head, a pillow of Oriental alabaster, destined to support the neck without deranging the headdress, was hollowed out in the shape of a half moon. In the center a table of precious wood carved with exceeding care, stood upon a richly carved pedestal. A number of objects were placed upon it: a pot of lotus flowers, a mirror of polished bronze on an ivory stand, a vase of moss agate filled with antimony powder, a perfume spatula of sycamore wood in the shape of a woman bare to the waist stretching out as if she were swimming, and appearing to attempt to hold her box above the water.

Near the table, on an armchair of gilded wood picked out with red, with blue feet, and with lions for arms, covered with a thick cushion of purple stuff starred with gold and crossed with black, the end of which fell over the back, was seated a young woman, or rather, a young girl of marvelous beauty, in a graceful attitude of nonchalance and melancholy.

Her features, of ideal delicacy, were of the purest Egyptian type, and sculptors must have often thought of her as they carved the images of Isis and Hathor, even at the risk of breaking the rigorous hieratic laws. Golden and rosy reflections colored her warm pallor, in which showed her long black eyes, made to appear larger by lines of antimony, and full of a languorous, inexpressible sadness. Those great dark eyes, with the eyebrows strongly marked and the eyelids colored, gave a strange expression to the dainty, almost childish face. The half-parted lips, somewhat thick, of the color of a pomegranate flower, showed a gleam of polished white and preserved the involuntary and almost painful smile which imparts so sympathetic a charm to the Egyptian face. The nose, slightly depressed at the root, where the eyebrows melted one into another in a velvety shadow, rose in such pure lines, such delicate outlines, and with such well-cut nostrils that any woman or goddess would have been satisfied with it in spite of its slightly African profile. The chin was rounded with marvelous elegance and shone like polished ivory. The cheeks, rather rounder than those of the beauties of other nations, added to the face an expression of extreme sweetness and gracefulness.

This lovely girl wore for headdress a sort of helmet formed of a Guinea fowl, the half-closed wings of which fell upon her temples, and the pretty, small head of which came down to the center of her brow, while the tail, marked with white spots, spread out on the back of her neck. A clever combination of enamel imitated to perfection the plumage of the bird. Ostrich-feathers, planted in the helmet like an aigrette, completed this headdress, which was reserved for young virgins, as the vulture, the symbol of maternity, is worn only by women. The hair of the young girl, of a brilliant black, plaited into tresses, hung in masses on either side of her smooth, round cheeks, and fell down to her shoulders. In the shadowy masses of the hair shone, like suns in a cloud, great discs of gold worn as earrings. From the headdress hung gracefully down the back two long bands of stuff with fringed ends. A broad pectoral ornament, composed of several rows of enamels, gold and cornelian beads, and fishes and lizards of stamped gold, covered her breast from the lower part of the neck to the upper part of the bosom, which showed pink and white through the thin warp of the calasiris. The dress, of a large checkered pattern, was fastened under the bosom with a girdle with long ends, and ended in a broader border of transverse stripes edged with a fringe. Triple bracelets of lapis-lazuli beads, divided here and there by golden balls, encircled her slender wrists, delicate as those of a child; and her lovely, narrow feet with long, supple toes, were shod with sandals of white kid stamped with designs in gold, and rested on a cedar stool incrusted with red and green enamel.

Near Tahoser (for this was the name of the young Egyptian) knelt, one leg drawn back under the thigh and the other forming an obtuse angle, in the attitude which the painters love to reproduce on the walls of hypogea, a female harpist placed upon a sort of low pedestal, destined no doubt to increase the resonance of the instrument. A piece of stuff striped with colored bands, the ends of which, thrown back, hung in fluted lappets, bound her hair and framed in her face, smiling mysteriously like that of a sphinx. A narrow dress, or rather sheath, of transparent gauze outlined closely the youthful contours of her elegant, slender form. Her dress, cut below the breast, left her shoulders, chest, and arms free in their chaste nudity. A support, fixed to the pedestal on which was placed the player, and traversed by a bolt in the shape of a key, formed a rest for the harp, the weight of which, but for that, would have borne wholly upon the shoulders of the young woman. The harp, which ended in a sort of keyboard, rounded like a shell and covered with ornamental paintings, bore at its upper end a sculptured head of Hathor surmounted by an ostrich-plume. The nine cords were stretched diagonally and quivered under the long, slender hands of the harpist, who often, in order to reach the lower notes, bent with a sinuous motion as if she were about to float on the waves of music and accompany the vanishing harmony.

Behind her stood another musician, who might have been thought nude but for the faint white haze which toned the bronze color of her body. She played on a sort of guitar with an exceedingly long handle, the three cords of which were coquettishly adorned at their extremity with colored tufts. One of her arms, slender yet round, grasped the top of the handle with a sculptural pose, while the other upheld the instrument and touched the strings.

A third young woman, whose enormous mass of hair made her look all the more slender, beat time upon a tympanum formed of a wooden frame slightly curved inward, on which was stretched an onager-skin.

The harpist sang a plaintive melody, accompanied in unison, inexpressibly sad. The words breathed vague aspirations, vague regrets, a hymn of love to the unknown, and timid plaints of the rigor of the gods and the cruelty of fate. Tahoser, leaning upon one of the lions of her armchair, her hand under her cheek and her finger curved against her temple, listened with inattention more apparent than real, to the song of the musician. At times a sigh made her breast heave and raised the enamels of her necklace. Sometimes a moist light caused by a growing tear shone in her eye between the lines of antimony, and her tiny teeth bit her lower lip as if she were fighting her own emotion.

"Satou," she said, clapping her delicate hands together to silence the musician, who at once deadened with her palm the vibrations of the harp, "your song enervates me, makes me languid, and would make me giddy like overpowerful perfumes. The strings of your harp seem to be twisted with the vibrations of my heart and sound painfully within my breast. You make me almost ashamed, for it is my soul that mourns in your music. Who can have told you my secrets?"

"Mistress," replied the harpist, "the poet and the musician know everything; the gods reveal hidden things to them; they express in their rhythm what the thought scarcely conceives and what the tongue confusedly stammers. But if my song saddens you, I can, by changing its mode, bring brighter ideas to your mind." And Satou struck the cords of her harp with joyous energy, and with a quick measure which the tympanum marked with more rapid strokes.

After this prelude she began a song praising the charms of wine, the intoxication of perfumes, and the delight of the dance. Some of the women, who, seated upon folding-stools formed of the necks of blue swans, whose yellow bills clasped the frame of the seat, or kneeling upon scarlet cushions filled with the down of thistles, had assumed under the influence of Satou's music poses of utter languor, shivered; their nostrils swelled; they breathed in the magic rhythm; they rose to their feet, and, moved by an irresistible impulse, began to dance. A headdress, in the shape of a helmet cut out around the ear, enclosed their hair, some locks of which escaped and fell upon their brown cheeks, which the ardor of the dance soon turned rosy. Broad golden circles beat upon their necks, and through their long gauze shifts, embroidered at the top with pearls, showed their golden bronze bodies which moved with the ease of an adder. They twisted, turned, swayed their hips, bound with a narrow black girdle, threw themselves back, bowed down, inclined their heads to right and left as if they found a secret voluptuousness in touching their polished chins with their cold, bare shoulders, swelled out their breasts like doves, knelt and rose, pressed their hands to their bosom or voluptuously outspread their arms, which seemed to flutter as the wings of Iris or Nephthys, dragged their limbs, bent the knee, displayed their swift feet with little staccato movements, and followed every undulation of the music. The maids, standing against the wall to leave free space for the evolutions of the dancers, marked the rhythm by snapping their fingers or clapping their hands together. Some of these maids, absolutely nude, had no other raiment than a bracelet of enameled ware; others wore a narrow cloth held by straps, and a few sprays of flowers twisted in their hair. It was a strange and graceful sight. The buds and the flowers, gently moving, shed their perfume through the hall, and these young women, thus wreathed, might have suggested fortunate comparisons to poets.

But Satou had overestimated the power of her art. The joyous rhythm seemed to increase Tahoser's melancholy. A tear rolled down her fair cheek like a drop of Nile water on a nymphoea, and hiding her face in the breast of her favorite maid, who leaned upon the armchair of her mistress, she uttered with a sob, dovelike in its sadness, "Oh, my dear Nofré, I am very sad and very unhappy!"

## II

Nofré, anticipating some confidence, made a sign, and the harpist, the two musicians, the dancers, and the maids silently withdrew one by one, like the figures painted on frescoes. When the last had gone, the favorite said to her mistress in a petting, sympathetic tone, like a young mother soothing her child's tender grief, —

"What is the matter, dear mistress, that you are sad and unhappy? Are you not young, so fair that the loveliest envy you, and free to do what you please? And did not your father, the high priest Petamounoph, whose mummy rests concealed within a rich tomb, — did he not leave you great wealth to do with as you please? Your palace is splendid, your gardens vast and watered by transparent streams, your coffers of enameled ware and sycamore wood are filled with necklaces, pectorals, neck-plates, anklets, finely wrought seal-rings. Your gowns, your calasiris, your headdresses are greater in number than the days of the year. Hopi, the father of waters, regularly covers with his fertilizing mud your domains, which a vulture flying at top speed could scarce traverse from sunrise to sunrise. And yet your heart, instead of opening joyously like a lotus bud in the month of Hathor or of Choeak, closes and contracts painfully."

Tahoser answered Nofré: —

"Yes, indeed, the gods of the higher zones have treated me favorably. But what matter one's possessions if one lacks the one thing desired? An unsatisfied wish makes the rich as poor, in his gilded, brightly painted palace, in the midst of his heaps of grain, of perfumes and precious things, as the most wretched workman of the Memnonia, who sops up with sawdust the blood of the bodies, or the semi-nude Negro driving on the Nile his frail papyrus-boat under the burning midday sun."

Nofré smiled, and said with a look of imperceptible raillery, —

"Is it possible, O mistress, that a single one of your fancies has not been fulfilled at once? If you want a jewel, you give the workman an ingot of pure gold, cornelians, lapis-lazuli, agates, and hematite, and he carries out the wished-for design. It is the same way with gowns, cars, perfumes, flowers, and musical instruments. From Philæ to Heliopolis your slaves seek out for you what is most beautiful and most rare; and if Egypt does not hold what you want, caravans bring it to you from the ends of the world."

The lovely Tahoser shook her pretty head and seemed annoyed at her confidante's lack of intelligence.

"Forgive me, mistress," said Nofré, changing her tone as she understood that she had made a mistake. "I had forgotten that it will soon be four months since the Pharaoh left on his expedition to Upper Ethiopia, and that the handsome oëris (general), who never passed under the terrace without looking up and slowing his steps, accompanies His Majesty. How well he looked in his uniform, how handsome, young, and bold!"

Tahoser's rosy lips half parted, as if she were about to speak, but a faint, rosy flush spread over her cheeks, she bowed her head, and the words ready to issue forth did not unfold their sonorous wings.

The maid thought she had guessed right, and continued, —

"In that case, mistress, your grief will soon end, for this morning a breathless runner arrived, announcing the triumphal return of the king before sundown. Have you not already heard innumerable rumors buzzing confusedly over the city, which is awakening from its midday torpor? List! The wheels of the cars sound upon the stone slabs of the streets, and already the people are hurrying in compact bodies to the riverbank, to cross it and reach the parade ground. Throw off your languor and come also to see that wondrous spectacle. When one is sad, one ought to mingle with the crowd, for solitude feeds somber thoughts. From his chariot Ahmosis will smile graciously upon you, and you will return happier to your palace."

"Ahmosis loves me, but I do not love him," answered Tahoser.

"You speak as a maid," replied Nofré, who was very much smitten with the handsome officer, and who thought that the disdainful nonchalance of Tahoser was assumed. In point of fact, Ahmosis was a very handsome fellow. His profile resembled that of the images of the gods carved by the most skillful sculptors. His proud, regular features equaled in beauty those of a woman; his slightly aquiline nose, his brilliant black eyes lengthened with antimony, his polished cheeks, smooth as Oriental alabaster, his well-shaped lips, his tall, handsome figure, his broad chest, his narrow hips, his strong arms on which, however, no muscle stood out in coarse relief, were all that were needed to seduce the most difficult to please; but Tahoser did not love him, whatever Nofré might think. Another idea, which she refrained from expressing, for she did not believe Nofré capable of understanding her, helped the young girl to make up her mind. She threw off her languor, and rose from her armchair with a vivacity quite unexpected after the broken-down attitude she had preserved during the singing and the dancing.

Nofré, kneeling before her, fastened on her feet sandals with turned-up ends, cast scented powder on her hair, drew from a box several bracelets in the shape of serpents, and a few rings with sacred scarabæi for gems, put on her cheeks a green powder which immediately turned rose-color as it touched the skin, polished her nails with a cosmetic, and adjusted the somewhat rumpled folds of her calasiris like a zealous maid who means that her mistress shall show to the greatest advantage. Then she called two or three servants, and ordered them to make ready the boat and transport to the other side of the river the chariot and oxen.

The palace, or if this name seems too pompous, the dwelling of Tahoser, rose close to the Nile, from which it was separated by gardens only. Petamounoph's daughter, her hand resting on Nofré's shoulder, and preceded by her servants, walked down to the water-gate through the arbor, the broad leaves of which, softening the rays of the sun, flecked with light shadows her lovely face. She soon reached the wide brick quay, on which swarmed a mighty multitude, awaiting the departure or return of the boats.

The vast city held now only the sick, the invalids, old people unable to move, and the slaves left in charge of the houses. Through the streets, the squares, the dromos (temple avenues), down the sphinx avenues, through the pylons, along the quays, flowed streams of human beings all bound for the Nile. The multitude exhibited the strangest variety. The Egyptians were there in largest numbers, and were recognizable by their clean profile, their tall, slender figures, their fine linen robes or their carefully pleated calasiris. Some, their heads enveloped in striped green or blue cloth, with narrow drawers closely fitting to their loins, showed to the belt their

bare torsos the color of baked clay. Against this mass of
natives stood out divers members of exotic races: Negroes
from the Upper Nile, as black as basalt gods, their arms
bound round with broad ivory rings, their ears adorned with
barbaric ornaments; bronzed Ethiopians, fierce-eyed, uneasy,
and restless in the midst of this civilization, like wild beasts
in the glare of day; Asiatics with their pale-yellow complexion
and their blue eyes, their beard curled in spirals, wearing a
tiara fastened by a band, and draped in heavily embroidered,
fringed robes; Pelasgi, dressed in wild beasts' skins fastened
on the shoulder, showing their curiously tattooed legs and
arms, wearing feathers in their hair, with two long love-locks
hanging down. Through the multitude gravely marched
shaven-headed priests with a panther's-skin twisted around
their body in such a way that the head of the animal formed
a sort of belt-buckle, byblos shoes on their feet, in their hand
a tall acacia-stick on which were engraved hieroglyphic characters; soldiers, their silver-studded daggers by their side, their
bucklers on their backs, their bronze axes in their hands;
distinguished personages, their breasts adorned with neck-
plates of honor, to whom the slaves bowed low, bringing their
hands close to the ground; and sliding along the walls with
humble and sad mien, poor, half-nude women traveling along
bowed under the weight of their children suspended from
their neck in rags of stuff or baskets of espartero; while
handsome girls, accompanied by three or four maids, passed
proudly with their long, transparent dresses knotted under
their breasts with long, floating scarves, sparkling with enamels, pearls, and gold, and giving out a fragrance of flowers
and aromatic essences.

Among the foot-passengers went litters borne by Ethiopians running rapidly and rhythmically; light carts drawn by
spirited horses with plumed headgear; ox chariots moving
slowly along and bearing a whole family. Scarcely did the
crowd, careless of being run over, draw aside to make room,
and often the drivers were forced to strike with their whips
those who were slow or obstinate in moving away.

The greatest animation reigned on the river, which, notwithstanding its breadth, was so covered with boats of all
kinds that the water was invisible along the whole stretch of

the city; all manner of craft, from the bark with raised poop and prow and richly painted and gilded cabin to the light papyrus skiff, — everything had been called into use. Even the boats used to ferry cattle and to carry freight, and the reed rafts kept up by skins, which generally carried loads of clay vessels, had not been disdained. The waters of the Nile, beaten, lashed, and cut by oars, sweeps, and rudders, foamed like the sea, and formed many an eddy that broke the force of the current.

The build of the boats was as varied as it was picturesque. Some were finished off at each end with a great lotus flower curving inwards, the stem adorned with fluttering flags; others were forked at the poop which rose to a point; others again were crescent-shaped, with horns at either end; others bore a sort of a castle or platform on which stood the pilots; still others were composed of three strips of bark bound with cords, and were driven by a paddle. The boats for the transport of animals and chariots were moored side by side, supporting a platform on which rested a floating bridge to facilitate embarking and disembarking. The number of these was very great. The horses, terrified, neighed and stamped with their sounding hoofs; the oxen turned restlessly towards the shore their shining noses whence hung filaments of saliva, but grew calmer under the caresses of their drivers. The boatswains marked time for the rowers by striking together the palms of their hands; the pilots, perched on the poop or walking about on the raised cabins, shouted their orders, indicating the maneuvers necessary to make way through the moving labyrinth of vessels. Sometimes, in spite of all precautions, boats collided, and crews exchanged insults or struck at each other with their oars. These countless crafts, most of them painted white and adorned with ornaments of green, blue, or red, laden with men and women dressed in many-colored costumes, caused the Nile to disappear entirely over an extent of many miles, and presented under the brilliant Egyptian sun a spectacle dazzling in its changefulness. The water, agitated in every direction, surged, sparkled, and gleamed like quicksilver, and resembled a sun shattered into millions of pieces.

Tahoser entered her barge, which was decorated with won-drous richness. In the center stood a cabin, its entablature surmounted with a row of uræus-snakes, the angles squared to the shape of pillars, and the walls adorned with designs. A binnacle with pointed roof stood on the poop, and was matched at the other end by a sort of altar enriched with paintings. The rudder consisted of two huge sweeps, ending in heads of Hathor, that were fastened with long strips of stuff and worked upon hollow posts. On the mast shivered — for the east wind had just risen — an oblong sail fastened to two yards, the rich stuff of which was embroidered and painted with lozenges, chevrons, birds, and chimerical ani-mals in brilliant colors; from the lower yard hung a fringe of great tufts.

The moorings cast off and the sail braced to the wind, the vessel left the bank, sheering with its sharp prow between the innumerable boats, the oars of which became entangled and moved about like the legs of a scarabæus thrown over on its back. It sailed on carelessly amidst a stream of insults and shouts. Its greater power enabled it to disdain collisions which would have run down frailer vessels. Besides, Tahoser's crew were so skillful that their vessel seemed endowed with life, so swiftly did it obey the rudder and avoid in the nick of time serious obstacles. Soon it had left behind the heavily laden boats with their cabins filled with passengers inside, and on the roof three or four rows of men, women, and children crouching in the attitude so dear to the Egyptian people. These individuals, so kneeling, might have been mis-taken for the assistant judges of Osiris, had not their faces, instead of bearing the expression of meditation suited to funeral councilors, expressed the most unmistakable delight. The fact was that the Pharaoh was returning victorious, bringing vast booty with him. Thebes was given up to joy, and its whole population was proceeding to welcome the favorite of Ammon Ra, Lord of the Diadem, the Emperor of the Pure Region, the mighty Aroëris, the Sun God and the Subduer of Nations.

Tahoser's barge soon reached the opposite bank. The boat bearing her car came alongside almost at the same moment. The oxen ascended the flying bridge, and in a few minutes were yoked by the alert servants who had been landed with them.

The oxen were white spotted with black, and bore on their heads a sort of tiara which partly covered the yoke; the latter was fastened by broad leather straps, one of which passed around the neck of the oxen, and the other, fastened to the first, passed under their belly. Their high withers, their broad dewlaps, their clean limbs, their small hoofs, shining like agate, their tails with the tuft carefully combed, showed that they were thorough-bred and that hard field-work had never deformed them. They exhibited the majestic placidity of Apis, the sacred bull, when it receives homage and offerings.

The chariot, extremely light, could hold two or three persons standing. The semicircular body, covered with ornaments and gilding arranged in graceful curved lines, was supported by a sort of diagonal stay, which rose somewhat beyond the upper edge and to which the traveler clung with his hand when the road was rough or the speed of the oxen rapid. On the axle, placed at the back of the body in order to diminish the jolting, were two six-spoked wheels held by keyed bolts. On top of a staff planted at the back of the vehicle spread a parasol in the shape of palm leaves.

Nofré, bending over the edge of the chariot, held the reins of the oxen, bridled like horses, and drove the car in the Egyptian fashion, while Tahoser, motionless by her side, leaned a hand, studded with rings from the little finger to the thumb, on the gilded molding of the shell. These two lovely maidens, the one brilliant with enamels and precious stones, the other scarcely veiled in a transparent tunic of gauze, formed a charming group on the brilliantly painted car. Eight or ten men-servants, dressed in tunics with transverse stripes, the folds of which were massed in front, accompanied the equipage, keeping step with the oxen.

On this side of the river the crowd was not less great. The inhabitants of the Memnonia quarters and of the neighboring villages were arriving in their turn, and every moment the boats, landing their passengers on the brick quay wall, brought additional sight-seers to swell the multitude. The wheels of innumerable chariots, all driving towards the parade ground, flashed like suns in the golden dust which they raised. Thebes at that moment must have been as deserted as if a conqueror had carried away its people into captivity.

The frame, too, was worthy of the picture. In the midst of green fields whence rose the aigrettes of the dôm palms, showed in bright colors houses of pleasaunce, palaces, and summer homes surrounded by sycamores and mimosas. Pools of water sparkled in the sunshine, the festoons of vines climbed on the arched arbors, and in the background stood out the gigantic pylons of the palace of Rameses Meïamoun, with its huge pylons, its enormous walls, its gilded and painted flagstaffs from which the colors blew out in the wind; and further to the north the two colossi sitting in postures of eternal immobility, mountains of granite in human shape, before the entrance to the Amenophium, showed through a bluish haze, half masking the still more distant Rhamesseium, and beyond it the tomb of the high priest, but allowing the palace of Menephta to be seen at one of its angles.

Nearer the Lybian chain, from the Memnonian quarter inhabited by the undertakers, dissectors, and embalmers, went up into the blue air the red smoke of the natron boilers, for the work of death never ceased; in vain did life spread tumultuously around, the bandages were being prepared, the cases molded, the coffins carved with hieroglyphs, and some cold body was stretched out upon the funeral bed, with feet of lion or jackal, waiting to have its toilet made for eternity.

On the horizon, but, owing to the transparency of the air, seeming to be much nearer, the Libyan mountains showed against the clear sky their limestone crests and their barren slopes hollowed out into hypogea and passages.

Looking towards the other bank the prospect was no less wondrous. Against the vaporous background of the Arabian chain, the gigantic pile of the Northern Palace, which distance itself could scarce diminish, reared above the flat-roofed dwellings its mountains of granite, its forest of giant pillars, rose-colored in the rays of the sunshine. In front of the palace stretched a vast esplanade reaching down to the river by a staircase placed at the angles; in the center an avenue of ram-headed sphinxes perpendicular to the Nile, led to a huge pylon, in front of which stood two colossal statues and a pair of obelisks, the pyramidions of which, rising above the cornice, showed their flesh-colored points against the uniform blue of the sky. Beyond and above the boundary wall rose the side façade of the temple of Ammon. More to the right were the temples of Khons and Oph. A giant pylon, seen in profile and facing to the south, and two obelisks sixty cubits in height, marked the beginning of that marvelous avenue of two thousand sphinxes with lions' bodies and rams' heads, which reached from the Northern Palace to the Southern Palace. On the pedestals could be seen swelling the huge quarters of the first row of these monsters, that turned their backs to the Nile. Farther still, there showed faintly in the rosy light cornices on which the mystic globe outspread its vast wings, heads of placid-faced colossi, corners of mighty buildings, needles of granite, terraces rising above terraces, columns of palm trees growing like tufts of grass amid these vast constructions; and the Palace of the South uprose, with high painted walls, flag-adorned staffs, sloping doors, obelisks, and herds of sphinxes. Beyond, as far as the eye could reach, Oph stretched out with its palaces, its priests' colleges, its houses, and in the dimmest distance the crests of its walls and the summits of its gates showed as faint blue lines.

Tahoser gazed upon the prospect which was so familiar to her, but her glance expressed no admiration; however, as she passed a house almost buried amid luxuriant vegetation, she lost her apathy, and seemed to seek on the terraces and on the outer gallery some well-known form.

A handsome young man, carelessly leaning against one of the slender pillars of the building, appeared to be watching the crowd, but his dark eyes, with their dreamy look, did not rest on the chariot which bore Tahoser and Nofré.

Meanwhile the hand of the daughter of Petamounoph clung nervously to the edge of the car; her cheeks turned pale under the light touch of rouge which Nofré had put on, and as if she felt herself fainting, she breathed in rapidly and often the scent of her nosegay of lotus.

III

*I*n spite of her usual perspicacity, Nofré had not noticed
the effect produced on her mistress by the sight of the careless
stranger. She had observed neither her pallor, followed by a
deep blush, nor the brighter gleam of her glance nor the
rustling of the enamels and pearls of her necklace rising and
falling with her bosom. It is true that her whole attention was
given to the management of the equipage, which presented a
good deal of difficulty in view of the ever denser masses of
sight-seers crowding to be present at the triumphal entrance
of the Pharaoh.

At last the car reached the parade ground, a vast enclosure
carefully leveled for military displays. Great banks, which
must have cost thirty enslaved nations the labor of years,
formed a bold framework for the immense parallelogram.
Sloping revetment walls of unbaked bricks covered the banks,
and the crests were lined many files deep by hundreds of
thousands of Egyptians, whose white or brightly striped
costumes fluttered in the sun with that constant motion
characteristic of a multitude even when it seems to be motionless. Behind this ring of spectators the cars, chariots, and
litters watched by the coachmen, drivers, and slaves, seemed
to be the camp of a migrating nation, so great was their
number; for Thebes, the wonder of the ancient world, reckoned more inhabitants than do certain kingdoms. The fine,
smooth sand of the vast arena lined with a million people,
sparkled under the light, falling from a sky as blue as the
enamel of the Osiris statuettes.

On the southern side of the parade ground the revetment
wall was cut through by a road which ran towards Upper
Egypt along the foot of the Libyan chain. At the opposite
corner the revetment was again cut so that the road was
prolonged to the palace of Rameses Meïamoun through the
thick brick walls. Petamounoph's daughter and Nofré, for
whom the servants had made room, stood on this corner on

the top of the wall, so that they could see the whole procession pass at their feet.

A mighty rumor, low, deep, and powerful, like that of an advancing ocean, was heard in the distance and drowned the innumerable noises arising from the crowd, as the roar of a lion silences the yelping of a tribe of jackals. Soon the separate sounds of the instruments were heard amidst the thunderous noise produced by the driving of war chariots and the rhythmic marching of the soldiers. A sort of reddish mist like that raised by the desert wind filled the sky in that direction, and yet there was no breeze, — not a breath of air, — and the most delicate branches of the palms were as motionless as if they had been carved on granite capitals. Not a hair moved on the wet temples of the women, and the fluted lappets of their headdresses fell limp behind their backs. The dusty mist was produced by the army on the march, and hovered above it like a dun-colored cloud.

The roar increased, the cloud of dust opened, and the first files of musicians debouched into the vast arena, to the intense delight of the multitude, which, notwithstanding its respect for the majesty of the Pharaoh, was beginning to weary of waiting under a sunshine which would have melted any but Egyptian skulls.

The advance guard of musicians stopped for a few moments. Delegations of priests and deputations of the chief inhabitants of Thebes crossed the parade ground to meet the Pharaoh, and drew up in double line in attitudes of the deepest respect so as to leave a free passage for the procession.

The music, which alone might have formed a small army, was composed of drums, tambourines, trumpets, and sistra. The first squad passed, blowing a sounding blare of triumph through its short copper bugles that shone like gold. Everyone of these musicians carried a second bugle under his arm, as if the instrument were likely to be worn out before the man. The costume of the trumpeters consisted of a short tunic bound by a sash the broad ends of which fell in front. A narrow band upholding two ostrich-plumes fastened their thick hair. The plumes thus placed looked like the antennæ of a scarabæus, and imparted to those who wore them a quaint, insectlike appearance.

The drummers, clad in a mere pleated kilt and bare to the belt, struck with sycamore sticks the wild-ass-skin stretched over their kettledrums suspended from a leather baldric, keeping the time which the drum major marked by clapping his hands as he frequently turned towards them. Next to the drummers came the sistrum players, who shook their instruments with sharp, quick movements, and at regular intervals made the metal rings sound upon the four bronze bars. The tambourine players carried transversely before them their oblong instrument fastened by a scarf passed behind their neck, and struck with both fists the skin stretched on either end.

Each band numbered not less than two hundred men, but the storm of sound produced by the bugles, drums, sistra, and tambourines, which would have been deafening within the palace, was in no wise too loud or too tremendous under the vast cupola of the heavens, in the center of that immense space, amid buzzing multitudes, at the head of an army which baffles enumeration and which was advancing with the roar of great waters. Besides, were eight hundred musicians too many to precede the Pharaoh, beloved of Ammon Ra, represented by colossi of basalt and granite sixty cubits high, whose name was written on the cartouches of imperishable monuments, and whose story was carved and painted upon the walls of the hypostyle halls, on the sides of pillars, in endless *bassi-relievi* and innumerable frescoes? Was it too much indeed for a king who dragged a hundred conquered nations by their hair, and from the height of his throne ruled the nations with his whip? For the living Sun that flamed on dazzled eyes? For one who, save that he did not possess eternal life, was a god?

Behind the music came the captive barbarians, strange to look at, with bestial faces, black skins, woolly hair, as much like monkeys as men, and dressed in the costume of their country, — a skirt just above the hips held by a single brace, embroidered with ornaments in divers colors. An ingenious cruelty had directed the binding together of the prisoners. Some were bound by the elbows behind the back; others by their hands raised above their head, in the most uncomfortable position; others again had their wrists caught in stocks; others with their neck in an iron collar or held by a rope which fastened a whole file of them, with a loop for each victim. It seemed as if the object sought had been to thwart as much as possible natural attitudes in the fettering of these poor wretches, who marched before their conqueror awkwardly and with difficulty, rolling their big eyes and twisting and writhing in pain. Guards marched at their side, striking them with sticks to make them keep time.

Next came, bowed with shame, exposed in their wretched, deformed nudity, dark-complexioned women, with long hanging tresses, carrying their children in a piece of stuff fastened around their brow, — a vile herd intended for the meanest uses. Others, young, handsome and fairer, their arms adorned with broad bracelets of ivory, their ears pulled down by great metal discs, wrapped themselves in long, wide-sleeved tunics embroidered around the neck and falling in fine, close folds down to their ankles, on which rattled anklets, — poor girls, snatched from their country, their parents, their lovers perhaps; yet they smiled through their tears, for the power of beauty is boundless, strangeness gives birth to caprice, and perhaps the royal favor awaited some of these barbaric captives in the secret depths of the harem. Soldiers accompanied them and kept the multitude from crowding upon them.

The standard-bearers followed, bearing on high the golden staff of their ensigns, which represented mystic baris, sacred hawks, heads of Hathor surmounted by ostrich-plumes, winged ibex, cartouches bearing the king's name, crocodiles, and other warlike or religious symbols. Long white streamers spotted with black spots were tied to these standards, and fluttered gracefully on the march.

At the sight of the standards which announced the arrival of the Pharaoh, the deputations of priests and notables stretched out their hands in supplication towards him, or let them fall on their knees, the palms turned up. Some even prostrated themselves, their knees close to the body, their faces in the dust, in an attitude of absolute submission and deep adoration, while the spectators waved great palm-branches.

A herald or reader, holding in his hand a roll covered with hieroglyphic signs, marched along between the standard-bearers and the incense-burners, who preceded the king's litter.

He shouted, in a loud voice as sonorous as a brazen trumpet, the victories of the Pharaoh; he related the fortunes of the Pharaoh's battles, announced the number of captives and of war chariots taken from the enemy, the amount of the booty, the measures of gold-dust, the elephants' tusks, the ostrich-plumes, the quantities of balsamic gum, the giraffes, lions, panthers, and other rare animals. He named the barbaric chiefs who had been slain by the javelins of His Majesty the Almighty Aroëris, favorite of the gods. At each proclamation the people uttered a mighty shout, and from the top of the revetment banks threw down upon the conqueror's pathway long, green palm-branches.

At last the Pharaoh appeared. Priests, who turned and faced him at regular intervals, swung their censers, after having cast incense upon the coals lighted in a little bronze cup which was held by a hand at the end of a sort of scepter topped by a sacred animal's head. They marched respectfully backwards while the scented blue smoke rose to the nostrils of the triumphant sovereign, apparently as indifferent to these honors as if he were a god of bronze or basalt.

Twelve oëris, or military chiefs, their heads covered with a light helmet surmounted by an ostrich-plume, bare to the belt, their loins wrapped in a loin cloth of stiff folds, wearing their buckler hanging from their belt, supported a sort of daïs on which rested the throne of the Pharaoh. This was a chair with feet and arms formed of lions, with a high back provided with a cushion that fell over it, and adorned on its sides with a network of rose and blue flowers. The feet, the arms, and the edges of the throne were gilded, while brilliant colors filled the places left empty. On either side of the litter four fan-bearers waved huge feather fans, semicircular in form, carried at the end of long, gilded handles. Two priests bore a huge cornucopia richly ornamented, whence fell quantities of giant lotus-flowers.

The Pharaoh wore a helmet shaped like a miter and cut out around the ears, where it fell over the neck by way of a protection. On the blue ground of the helmet sparkled innumerable dots like birds' eyes, formed of three circles, black, white, and red. It was adorned with scarlet and yellow lines, and the symbolic uræus snake, twisting its golden scales on the fore part, rose and swelled above the royal brow. Two long, purple, fluted lappets fell upon his shoulders and completed this majestic headdress.

A broad necklace, of seven rows of enamels, gems, and golden beads, swelled on the Pharaoh's breast and shone in the sun. His upper garment was a sort of close-fitting jacket, of rose and black checkers, the ends of which, shaped like narrow bands, were twisted tightly several times around the bust. The sleeves, which came down to the biceps and were edged with transverse lines of gold, red, and blue, showed round, firm arms, the left provided with a broad wristlet of metal intended to protect it from the switch of the cord when the Pharaoh shot an arrow from his triangular bow. His right arm was adorned with a bracelet formed of a serpent twisted several times on itself, and in his hand he held a long golden scepter ending in a lotus-bud. The rest of the body was enveloped in the finest linen cloth with innumerable folds, held to the hips by a girdle inlaid with plates of enamel and gold. Between the jacket and the belt, the torso showed, shining and polished like rose granite worked by a skillful workman. Sandals with pointed upturned toes protected his long narrow feet, which were held close to one another like the feet of the gods on the walls of the temples. His smooth, beardless face with its great, regular features, which it seemed impossible for any human emotion to alter, and which the blood of vulgar life did not color, with its deathlike pallor, its closed lips, its great eyes made larger still by black lines, the eyelids of which never closed anymore than did those of the sacred hawk, — inspired through its very immobility respect and awe. It seemed as though those fixed eyes gazed upon eternity and the infinite only; surrounding objects did not appear to be reflected in them. The satiety of enjoyment, of will satisfied the moment it was expressed, the isolation of a demigod who has no fellow among mortals, the disgust of worship, and the weariness of triumph had forever marked that face, implacably sweet and of granitelike serenity. Not even Osiris judging the souls of the dead could look more majestic and more calm. A great tame lion, lying by his side upon the litter, stretched out its enormous paws like a sphinx upon a pedestal, and winked its yellow eyes. A rope fixed to

the litter, fastened to the Pharaoh the chariots of the conquered chiefs. He dragged them behind him like animals in
a leash. These vanquished chiefs, in gloomy, fierce attitudes,
whose elbows, drawn together by their points, formed an ugly
angle, staggered awkwardly as they were dragged by the cars
driven by Egyptian coachmen.

Next came the war chariots of the young princes of the
royal family, drawn by pairs of thorough-bred horses of noble
and elegant shape, with slender legs and muscular quarters,
their manes cut close and short, shaking their heads adorned
with red plumes, frontlets, and headgear of metal bosses. A
curved pole, adorned with scarlet squares, pressed down on
their withers, and supported two small saddles surmounted
with balls of polished brass held together by a light yoke, with
curved ends. Girths and breast-harnesses richly embroidered,
and superb housings rayed with blue or red and fringed with
tufts, completed their strong, graceful, and light harness.

The body of the car, painted red and green, and ornamented with plates and bosses of bronze like the boss on the
bucklers, had on either side two great quivers placed diagonally in opposite directions, the one containing javelins, and
the other arrows. On either side a carved and gilded lion, its
face wrinkled with a dreadful grin, seemed to roar, and to be
about to spring at the foe.

The young princes wore for a headdress a narrow band
which bound their hair and in which twisted, as it swelled its
hood, the royal asp. For dress they wore a tunic embroidered
around the neck and the sleeves with brilliant embroidery
and bound at the waist with a leather belt fastened with a
metal plate on which were engraved hieroglyphs. Through
the belt was passed a long, triangular, brazen-bladed poniard,
the handle of which, fluted transversely, ended in a hawk's-
head. On the car, by the side of each prince, stood the driver,
whose business it was to drive during the battle, and the
equerry charged with warding off with a buckler the blows
directed at the fighter, while he himself shot his arrows or
hurled the javelins which he took from the quivers at the
sides.

Behind the princes came the chariots which formed the
Egyptian cavalry, to the number of twenty thousand, each

drawn by two horses and carrying three men. These chariots
came ten abreast, with wheels almost touching yet never
meeting, so skillful were the drivers. Some lighter cars, intended for skirmishes and reconnaissances came foremost,
bearing a single warrior, who in order to have his hands free
while fighting, passed the reins around his body. By leaning
to the right, to the left or backwards, he directed and stopped
his horses, and it was truly marvelous to see these noble
animals, which seemed left to themselves, guided by imperceptible movements and preserving an unchangingly regular
gait.

On one of these chariots the elegant Ahmosis, Nofré's
protégé, showed his tall figure and cast his glance over the
multitude, trying to make out Tahoser.

The trampling of the horses held in with difficulty, the
thunder of the bronze-bound wheels, the metallic justling of
weapons, imparted to the procession an imposing and formidable character well calculated to strike terror into the bravest
souls. Helmets, plumes, corselets covered with green, red, and
yellow scales, gilded bows, brazen swords, flashed and
gleamed fiercely in the sun shining in the heavens above the
Libyan chain like a great Osiris eye, and one felt that the
charge of such an army must necessarily sweep the nations
before it even as the storm drives the light straw. Under these
numberless wheels the earth resounded and trembled as if in
the throes of an earthquake.

Next to the chariots came the infantry battalions marching
in order, the men carrying their shields on the left arm, and
a lance, a javelin, a bow, a sling, or an axe in the right hand.
The soldiers wore helmets adorned with two horse-hair tails.
Their bodies were protected by a cuirass of crocodile-skin;
their impassible look, the perfect regularity of their motions,
their coppery complexion, deepened still more by the recent
expedition to the burning regions of Upper Egypt, the desert
dust which lay upon their clothes, inspired admiration for
their discipline and courage. With such soldiers Egypt could
conquer the world.

Then came the troops of the allies, easily known by the
barbarous shape of their helmets, like miters cut off, or else
surmounted with a crescent stuck on a point. Their broad-

bladed swords, their saw-edged axes, must have inflicted incurable wounds.

Slaves carried the booty announced by the herald on their shoulders or on stretchers, and belluaria led panthers, wildcats, crawling as if they sought to hide themselves, ostriches flapping their wings, giraffes overtopping the crowd with their long necks, and even brown bears taken, it was said, in the Mountains of the Moon.

The King had long since entered his palace, yet the defile was still proceeding. As he passed the revetment on which stood Tahoser and Nofré, the Pharaoh, whose litter, borne upon the shoulders of oëris, placed him above the crowd on a level with the young girl, had slowly fixed upon her his dark glance. He had not turned his head, not a muscle of his face had moved, and his features had remained as motionless as the golden mask of a mummy, yet his eyes had turned between his painted eyelids towards Tahoser, and a flash of desire had lighted up their somber discs, an effect as terrific as if the granite eyes of a divine simulacrum, suddenly lighted up, were to express a human thought. He had half raised one of his hands from the arm of his throne, a gesture imperceptible to everyone, but which one of the servants marching near the litter noticed, and at once looked towards the daughter of Petamounoph.

Meanwhile night had suddenly fallen, for there is no twilight in Egypt, — night, or rather a blue day, treading close upon the yellow day. In the azure of infinite transparency gleamed unnumbered stars, their twinkling light reflected confusedly in the waters of the Nile, which was stirred by the boats that brought back to the other shore the population of Thebes; and the last cohorts of the army were still tramping across the plain, like a gigantic serpent, when the barge landed Tahoser at the gate of her palace.

## IV

*T*he Pharaoh reached his palace, situated a short distance from the parade ground on the left bank of the Nile. In the bluish transparency of the night the mighty edifice loomed more colossal still, and its huge outlines stood out with terrifying and somber vigor against the purple background of the Libyan chain. The feeling of absolute power was conveyed by that mighty, immovable mass, upon which eternity itself could make no more impression than a drop of water on marble. A vast court surrounded by thick walls, adorned at their summits with deeply cut moldings, lay in front of the palace. At the end of the court rose two high columns with palm-leaf capitals, marking the entrance to a second court. Behind these columns rose a giant pylon, consisting of two huge masses enclosing a monumental gate, intended rather for colossi of granite than for mere flesh and blood. Beyond these propylæa, and filling the end of a third court, the palace proper appeared in its formidable majesty. Two buildings projected squarely forward, like the bastions of a fortress, exhibiting on their faces low *bassi-relievi* of vast size, which represented, in the consecrated manner, the victorious Pharaoh scourging his enemies and trampling them under foot; immense pages of history carved with a chisel on colossal stone books which the most distant posterity was yet to read. These buildings rose much higher than the pylons. The cornices, curving outwards and topped with great stones so arranged as to form battlements, showed superbly against the crest of the Libyan Mountains, which formed the background of the picture.

The façade of the palace connected these buildings and filled up the whole of the intervening space. Above its giant gateway, flanked with sphinxes, showed three rows of square windows, through which streamed the light from the interior and which formed upon the dark wall a sort of luminous

checker-board. From the first story projected balconies, supported by statues of crouching prisoners.

The officers of the king's household, the eunuchs, the
servants, and the slaves, informed of the approach of His
Majesty by the blare of the trumpets and the roll of the drums,
had proceeded to meet him, and waited, kneeling and prostrate, in the court paved with great stone slabs. Captives, of
the despised race of Scheto, bore urns filled with salt and olive
oil, in which was dipped a wick, the flame of which crackled
bright and clear. These men stood ranged in line from the
basalt gate to the entrance of the first court, motionless like
bronze lamp-bearers.

Soon the head of the procession entered the pylon and the
bugles and the drums sounded with a din which, repeated by
the echoes, drove the sleeping ibises from the entablatures.
The bearers stopped at the gate in the façade between the two
pavilions; slaves brought a footstool with several steps and
placed it by the side of the litter. The Pharaoh rose with
majestic slowness and stood for a few moments perfectly
motionless. Thus standing on a pedestal of shoulders, he
soared above all heads and appeared to be twelve cubits high.
Strangely lighted, half by the rising moon, half by the light
of the lamps, in a costume in which gold and enamels
sparkled intermittently, he resembled Osiris, or Typhon
rather. He descended the steps as if he were a statue, and at
last entered the palace.

A first inner court, framed in by a row of huge pillars
covered with hieroglyphs, that bore a frieze ending in volutes,
was slowly crossed by the Pharaoh in the midst of a crowd of
prostrate slaves and maids.

Then appeared another court surrounded by a covered
cloister, and short columns, the capitals of which were formed
of a cube of hard sandstone, on which rested the massive
architrave. The imprint of indestructibility marked the
straight lines and the geometric forms of this architecture
built with pieces of mountains. The pillars and the columns
seemed to strike firmly into the ground in order to upbear
the weight of the mighty stones placed on the cubes of their
capitals, the walls to slope inwards so as to have a firmer
foundation, and the stones to join together so as to form but

one block; but polychromous decorations and *bassi-relievi* hollowed out and enriched with more brilliant tints added, in the daytime, lightness and richness to these vast masses, which when night had fallen, recovered all their imposing effect.

Under the cornice, in the Egyptian style, the unchanging lines of which formed against the sky a vast parallelogram of deep azure, quivered, in the intermittent breath of the breeze, lighted lamps placed at short distances apart. The fishpond in the center of the court mingled, as it reflected them, their red flashes with the blue gleams of the moon. Rows of shrubs planted around the basin gave out a faint, sweet perfume. At the back opened the gate of the harem and of the private apartments, which were decorated with peculiar magnificence.

Below the ceiling ran a frieze of uræus snakes, standing on their tails and swelling their hoods. On the entablature of the door, in the hollow of the cornice, the mystic globe outspread its vast, imbricated wings; pillars ranged in symmetrical lines supported heavy sandstone blocks forming soffits, the blue ground of which was studded with golden stars. On the walls vast pictures, carved in low, flat relief and colored with the most brilliant tints, represented the usual scenes of the harem and of home life. The Pharaoh was seen on his throne, gravely playing at drafts with one of his women who stood nude before him, her head bound with a broad band from which rose a mass of lotus flowers. In another the Pharaoh, without parting with any of his sovereign and sacerdotal impassibility, stretched out his hand and touched the chin of a young maid dressed in a collar and bracelet, who held out to him a bouquet of flowers. Elsewhere he was seen undecided and smiling, as if he had slyly put off making a choice, in the midst of the young queens, who strove to overcome his gravity by all sorts of caressing and graceful coquetries.

Other panels represented female musicians and dancers, women bathing, flooded with perfumes and massaged by slaves, — the poses so elegant, the forms so youthfully suave, and the outlines so pure, that no art has ever surpassed them.

Rich and complicated ornamental designs, admirably carried out in harmonious green, blue, red, yellow, and white, covered the spaces left empty. On cartouches and bands in the shape of stelæ were inscribed the titles of the Pharaoh and inscriptions in his honor.

On the shafts of the huge columns were decorative or symbolical figures wearing the pschent, armed with the tau, following each other in procession, and whose eyes, showing full upon a side face, seemed to look inquisitively into the hall. Lines of perpendicular hieroglyphs separated the zones of personages. Among the green leaves carved on the drum of the capital, buds and lotus flowers stood out in their natural colors, imitating baskets of bloom.

Between each pair of columns an elegant table of cedar bore on its platform a bronze cup filled with scented oil, from which the cotton wicks drew an odoriferous light. Groups of tall vases, bound together with wreaths, alternated with the lamps and held at the foot of each pillar sheaves of golden grain mingled with field grasses and balsamic plants.

In the center of the hall a round porphyry table, the disc of which was supported by the statue of a captive, disappeared under heaped-up urns, vases, flagons, and pots, whence rose a forest of gigantic artificial flowers; for real flowers would have appeared mean in the center of that vast hall, and nature had to be proportioned to the mighty work of man. These enormous calyxes were of the most brilliant golden yellow, azure, and purple.

At the back rose the throne, or chair, of the Pharaoh, the feet of which, curiously crossed and bound by encircling ribbing, had in their reentering angles four statuettes of barbaric Asiatic or African prisoners recognizable by their beards and their dress. These figures, their elbows tied behind their backs, and kneeling in constrained attitudes, their bodies bowed, bore upon their humbled heads the cushion, checkered with gold, red, and black, on which sat their conqueror. Faces of chimerical animals from whose mouths fell, instead of a tongue, a long red tuft, adorned the crossbars of the throne.

On either side of it were ranged, for the princes, less splendid, though still extremely elegant and charmingly fanciful chairs; for the Egyptians are no less clever at carving cedar, cypress, and sycamore wood, in gilding, coloring, and inlaying it with enamels, than in cutting in the Philoe or Syêné quarries monstrous granite blocks for the palaces of the Pharaohs and the sanctuaries of the gods.

The King crossed the hall with a slow, majestic step, without his painted eyelids having once moved; nothing indicated that he heard the cries of love that welcomed him, or that he perceived the human beings kneeling or prostrate, whose brows were touched by the folds of the calasiris that fell around his feet. He sat down, placing his ankles close together and his hands on his knees in the solemn attitude of the gods.

The young princes, handsome as women, took their seats to the right and left of their father. The servants took off their enameled necklaces, their belts, and their swords, poured flagons of scent upon their hair, rubbed their arms with aromatic oils, and presented them with wreaths of flowers, cool, perfumed collars, odorous luxuries better suited to the festival than the heavy richness of gold, of precious stones and pearls, which, for the matter of that, harmonize admirably with flowers.

Lovely nude slaves, whose slender forms showed the graceful transition from childhood to youth, their hips circled with a narrow belt that concealed none of their charms, lotus flowers in their hair, flagons of wavy alabaster in their hands, timidly pressed around the Pharaoh and poured palm oil over his shoulders, his arms, and his torso, polished like jasper. Other maids waved around his head broad fans of painted ostrich-feathers on long ivory or sandalwood handles, that, as they were warmed by their small hands, gave forth a delightful odor. Others placed before the Pharaoh stalks of nymphoea that bloomed like the cup of the censers. All these attentions were rendered with a deep devotion, and a sort of respectful awe, as if to a divine, immortal personage, called down by pity from the superior zones to the vile tribe of men; for the king is the Son of the gods, the favored of Phré, the protégé of Ammon Ra.

The women of the harem had risen from their prostrate attitude, and seated themselves on superb, carved and gilded chairs, with red-leather cushions filled with thistle-down. Thus ranged, they formed a line of graceful, smiling heads which a painter would have loved to reproduce. Some were dressed in tunics of white gauze with stripes alternately opaque and transparent, the narrow sleeves of which left bare the delicate, round arms covered with bracelets from the wrist to the elbow: others, bare to the waist, wore a skirt of pale lilac rayed with darker stripes, and covered with a fillet of little rose beads which showed in the diaper the cartouche of the Pharaoh traced on the stuff; others wore red skirts with black-pearl fillets; others again, draped in a tissue as light as woven air, as transparent as glass, wound the folds around them, and managed to show off coquettishly the shape of their lovely bosoms; others were enclosed in a sheath covered with blue, green, or red scales which molded their forms accurately; and others again had their shoulders covered with a sort of pleated cape, and their fringed skirts were fastened below the breast with a scarf with long, floating ends.

The headdresses were no less varied. Sometimes the plaited hair was spun out into curls; sometimes it was divided into three parts, one of which fell down the back and the other two on either side of the cheeks. Huge periwigs, closely curled, with numberless cords maintained transversely by golden threads, rows of enamels, or pearls, were put on like helmets over young and lovely faces, which sought of art an aid which their beauty did not need.

All these women held in their hands a flower of the blue or white lotus, and breathed amorously, with a fluttering of their nostrils, the penetrating odor which the broad calyx exhaled. A stalk of the same flower, springing from the back of their necks, bowed over their heads and showed its bud between their eyebrows darkened with antimony.

In front of them black or white slaves, with no other garment than a waist girdle, held out to them necklaces of flowers made of crocuses, the blooms of which, white outside, are yellow inside, purple safflowers, golden-yellow chrysanthemums, red-berried nightshade, myosotis whose flowers seemed made of blue enamel of the statues of Isis, and nepenthes whose intoxicating odor makes one forget everything, even the far-distant home.

These slaves were followed by others, who on the upturned palm of their right hands bore cups of silver or bronze full of wine, and in the left held napkins with which the guests wiped their lips.

The wines were drawn from amphoræ of clay, glass, or metal held in elegant woven baskets placed on four-footed pedestals made of a light, supple wood interlaced in ingenious fashion. The baskets contained seven sorts of wines: date wine, palm wine, and wine of the grape, white, red, and green wines, new wine, Phoenician and Greek wines, and white Mareotis wine with a bouquet of violets.

The Pharaoh also took a cup from the hands of his cup-bearer standing near his throne, and put to his royal lips the strengthening drink.

Then sounded the harps, the lyres, the double flutes, the lutes, accompanying a song of triumph which choristers, ranged opposite the throne, one knee on the ground, accentuated as they beat time with the palms of their hands.

The repast began. The dishes, brought by Ethiopians from the vast kitchens of the palace, where a thousand slaves were busy preparing the feast in a fiery atmosphere, were placed on tables close by the guests. The dishes, of scented wood admirably carved, of bronze, of earthenware or porcelain enameled in brilliant colors, held large pieces of beef, antelope legs, trussed geese, siluras from the Nile, dough drawn out into long tubes and rolled, cakes of sesamum and honey, green watermelons with rosy meat, pomegranates full of rubies, grapes the color of amber or of amethyst. Wreaths of papyrus crowned these dishes with their green foliage. The cups were also wreathed in flowers, and in the center of the table, amid a vast heap of golden-colored bread stamped with designs and marked with hieroglyphs, rose a tall vase whence emerged, spraying as it fell, a vast sheaf of persolutas, myrtles, pomegranates, convolvulus, chrysanthemums, heliotropes, seriphiums, and periplocas, a mingling of colors and of scents. Under the tables, around the supporting pillar, were arranged pots of lotus. Flowers, flowers everywhere, even under the seats of the guests! The women wore them on their arms, round their necks, on their heads in the shape of bracelets, necklaces, and crowns; the lamps burned amid huge bouquets, the dishes disappeared under leaves, the wines sparkled amid violets and roses. It was a most characteristic, gigantic debauch of flowers, a colossal orgy of scents, un-known to other nations.

Slaves constantly brought from the gardens, which they plundered without diminishing their wealth, armfuls of rose laurel, of pomegranate, of lotus, to renew the flowers which had faded, while servants cast grains of nard and cinnamon upon the red-hot coals of the censers.

When the dishes and the boxes carved in the shape of birds, fishes, and chimeras, which held the sauces and condiments, had been cleared away, as well as the ivory, bronze, or wooden spatulæ, and the bronze and flint knives, the guests washed their hands, and cups of wine and fermented drinks kept on passing around.

The cup-bearer drew with a long-handled ladle the dark wine and the transparent wine from two great, golden vases adorned with figures of horses and rams, which were held in equilibrium in front of the Pharaoh by means of tripods on which they were set.

Female musicians appeared — for the orchestra of male musicians had withdrawn. A wide gauze tunic covered their slender, youthful bodies, veiling them no more than the pure water of a pool conceals the form of the bather who plunges into it. Papyrus wreaths bound their thick hair and fell to the ground in long tendrils; lotus flowers bloomed on top of their heads; great golden rings sparkled in their ears, necklaces of enamel and pearl encircled their necks, and bracelets clanked and rattled on their wrists. One played on the harp, another on the lute, a third on the double flute, crossing her arms and using the right for the left flute and the left for the right flute; a fourth placed horizontally against her breast a five-stringed lyre; a fifth struck the onager-skin of a square drum; and a little girl seven or eight years of age, with flowers in her hair and a belt drawn tight around her, beat time by clapping her hands.

The dancers came in. They were slight, slender, and as lithe as serpents; their great eyes shone between the black lines of their lids, their pearly teeth between the red bars of their lips. Long curls floated down on their cheeks. Some wore full tunics striped white and blue, which floated around them like a mist; others wore mere pleated short skirts falling over the hips to the knees, which allowed their beautiful, slender legs and round muscular thighs to be easily seen. They first assumed poses of languid voluptuousness and indolent grace, then, waving branches of bloom and clinking castanets, shaped like the head of Hathor, striking tambourines with their little closed hands, or making the tanned skin of drums resound under their thumbs, they gave themselves up to swifter steps and to bolder postures; they pirouetted, they whirled with ever-increasing ardor. But the Pharaoh, thoughtful and dreamy, did not condescend to bestow a glance of satisfaction upon them; his fixed gaze did not even fall upon them.

They withdrew, blushing and confused, pressing their palpitating breasts with their hands.

Dwarfs with twisted feet, with swollen and deformed bodies, whose grimaces were fortunate enough at times to bring a smile to the majestic, stony face of the Pharaoh, were no more successful; their contortions did not bring a single smile to his lips, the corners of which remained obstinately fixed.

To the sound of strange music produced by triangular harps, sistra, castanets, cymbals, and bugles, Egyptian clowns wearing high, white miters of ridiculous shape advanced, closing two fingers of their hand and stretching out the other three, repeating their grotesque gestures with automatic accuracy, and singing extravagant songs full of dissonances. His Majesty never changed countenance.

Women wearing a small helmet from which depended three long cords ending in a tassel, their wrists and ankles bound with black leather bands, and wearing close fitting drawers suspended by a single brace passed over their shoulders, performed tricks of strength and contortions each more surprising than another; posturing, throwing themselves back, bending their supple bodies like willow branches, and touching the ground with their necks without displacing their heels, supporting in that impossible attitude the weight of their companions; others juggled with a ball, two balls, three balls, before, behind, their arms crossed, astride of or standing upon the loins of one of the women of the company. One, indeed, the cleverest, put on blinkers like Tmei, the goddess of justice, and caught the globes in her hands without letting a single one fall. The Pharaoh was not moved by these marvels.

He cared no more either for the prowess of two combatants who, wearing a cestus on the left arm, fought with sticks. Men throwing at a block of wood knives which struck with miraculous accuracy the spot indicated did not interest him either. He even refused the draft-board which the lovely Twea, whom he looked upon usually with favor, presented to him as she offered herself as an adversary. In vain Amense, Taïa, Hont-Reché ventured upon timid caresses. He rose and withdrew to his apartments without having uttered a word.

Motionless on the threshold stood the servant who, during the triumphal procession, had noticed the imperceptible gesture of His Majesty.

He said: "O King, loved of the gods! I left the procession, crossed the Nile on a light papyrus-bark and followed the vessel of the woman on whom your hawk glance deigned to fall. She is Tahoser, the daughter of the priest Petamounoph."

The Pharaoh smiled and said: "It is well. I give thee a chariot and its horses, a pectoral ornament of beads of lapis-lazuli and cornelian, with a golden circle weighing as much as the green basalt weight."

Meanwhile the sorrowing women pulled the flowers from their hair, tore their gauze robes, and sobbed, stretched out upon the polished stone floors which reflected, mirrorlike, the image of their beautiful bodies, saying, "One of these accursed barbaric captives must have stolen our master's heart."


# V


On the left bank of the Nile stood the villa of Poëri, the young man who had filled Tahoser with such emotion when, proceeding to view the triumphal return of the Pharaoh, she had passed in her ox-drawn car under the balcony whereon leaned carelessly the handsome dreamer.

It was a vast estate, having something of the farm and something of the house of pleasaunce, which stretched between the banks of the river and the foothills of the Libyan chain, over an immense extent of ground, covered during the inundation by the reddish waters laden with fertilizing mud, and which during the rest of the year was irrigated by skillfully planned canals.

A wall, built of limestone drawn from the neighboring mountains, enclosed the garden, the store-houses, the cellars, and the dwelling. The walls sloped slightly inwards and were surmounted by an acroter with metal spikes, capable of stopping whosoever might attempt to climb over. Three doors, the leaves of which were hung on massive pillars, each adorned with a giant lotus-flower planted on top of the capital, were cut in the wall on three of the sides. In place of the fourth door rose a building which looked out into the garden from one of its façades, and on the road from the other.

The building in no respect resembled the houses in Thebes. The architect had not sought to reproduce either the heavy foundations, the great monumental lines, or the rich materials of city buildings, but had striven to attain elegant lightness, refreshing simplicity, and pastoral gracefulness in harmony with the verdure and the peacefulness of the country.

The lower courses of the building, which the Nile reached in times of high flood, were of sandstone, and the rest of the building of sycamore wood. Tall, fluted columns, extremely slender and resembling the staffs of the standards before the king's palace, sprang from the ground and rose unbroken to the palm-leaved cornice, where swelled out, under a simple cube, their lotus-flowered capitals.

The single story built above the ground-floor did not rise as high as the moldings which bordered the terraced roof, and thus left an empty space between the ceiling and the flat roof of the villa. Short, small pillars, with flowery capitals, divided into groups of four by the tall columns, formed an open gallery around this aërial apartment open to every wind.

Windows broader at the base than at the top of the opening, in accordance with the Egyptian style, and closed with
double sashes, lighted the first story. The ground-floor was
lighted by narrower windows placed closer to each other.

Above the door, which was adorned with deep moldings,
was a cross planted in a heart and framed in a parallelogram
cut in the lower part to allow the sign of favorable omen to
pass; the meaning being, as everyone knows, "A good house."

The whole building was painted in soft, pleasant colors;
the lotus of the capitals showed alternately red and blue in
the green capsules; the gilded palm-leaves of the cornices
stood out upon a blue background; the white walls of the
façades set off the painted framework of the windows, and
lines of red and green outlined panels and imitated the joints
of the stone.

Outside the enclosing wall, which was built flush with the
dwelling, stood a row of trees cut to a point, which formed a
screen against the dusty southern wind, always laden with the
desert heat.

In front of the building grew a vast vineyard. Stone shafts
with lotus capitals placed at symmetrical distances outlined,
through the vineyard, walks cutting each other at right angles.
Boughs of vine leaves joined one plant to another and formed
a succession of leafy arches under which one could walk erect.
The ground, carefully raked and heaped up at the foot of each
plant, contrasted by its brown color with the bright green of
the leaves, amid which played the sunbeams and the breeze.

On either side of the building two oblong pools bore upon
their transparent surface aquatic birds and flowers. At the
corners of these pools four great palm trees spread out fanwise
their green wreath of leaves at the top of their scaly trunks.

Compartments, regularly traced by narrow paths, divided
the garden around the vineyard, marking the place of each
different crop. Along a sort of belt walk which ran entirely
around the enclosure dôm palms alternated with sycamores,
squares of ground were planted with fig, peach, almond, olive,
pomegranate and other fruit trees; others, again, were planted
with ornamental trees only: the tamarisk, the cassia, the
acacia, the myrtle, the mimosa, and some still rarer gum trees
found beyond the cataracts of the Nile, under the Tropic of

Cancer, in the oases of the Libyan Desert, and upon the shores of the Erythrean Gulf; for the Egyptians are very fond of cultivating shrubs and flowers, and they exact new species as a tribute from the peoples they have conquered.

Flowers of all kinds, and many varieties of watermelons, lupines, and onions adorned the beds. Two other pools of greater size, fed by the covered canal leading from the Nile, each bore a small boat to enable the master of the estate to enjoy the pleasure of fishing. Fishes of divers forms and brilliant colors played in the limpid waters among the stalks and the broad leaves of the lotus. Banks of luxuriant vegetation surrounded these pools and were reflected in their green mirror.

Near each pool rose a kiosk formed of slender columns bearing a light roof and surrounded by an open balcony whence one could enjoy the sight of the waters and breathe the coolness of the morning and the evening while reclining on a rustic seat of wood and reeds.

The garden, lighted by the rising sun, had a bright, happy, restful look. The green of the trees was so brilliant, the colors of the flowers so splendid, air and light filled so joyously the vast enclosure with breeze and sunbeams, the contrast of the rich greenness with the bare whiteness of the chalky sterility of the Libyan chain, the crest of which was seen above the walls cutting into the blue sky, was so marked that one felt the wish to stop and set up one's tent there. It looked like a nest purposely built for a longed-for happiness.

Along the walks traveled servants bearing on their shoulders a yoke of bent wood, from the ends of which hung by ropes two clay jars filled at the reservoirs, the contents of which they poured into small basins dug at the foot of each plant. Others, handling a jar suspended from a pole working on a post, filled with water a wooden gutter which carried it to the parts of the garden that needed irrigating. Gardeners were clipping the trees to a point or into an elliptical shape. With the help of a hoe formed of two pieces of hardwood bound by a cord and thus making a hook, other workmen were preparing the ground for planting.

It was a delightful sight to see these men with their black, woolly hair, their bodies the color of brick, dressed only in a

pair of white drawers, going and coming amid the greenery
with orderly activity, singing a rustic song to which their steps
kept time. The birds perched on the trees seemed to know
them, and scarcely to fly off when, as they passed, they rubbed
against the branches.

The door of the building opened, and Poëri appeared on
the threshold. Though he was dressed in the Egyptian fashion, his features were not in accordance with the national
type, and it took no long observation to see that he did not
belong to the native race of the valley of the Nile. He was
assuredly not a *Rot'en'no.* His thin aquiline nose, his flat
cheeks, his serious-looking, closed lips, the perfect oval of his
face, were essentially different from the African nose, the
projecting cheekbones, the thick lips, and broad face characteristic of the Egyptians. Nor was his complexion the same;
the copper tint was replaced by an olive pallor, which the
rich, pure blood flushed slightly; his eyes, instead of showing
black between their lines of antimony, were of a dark blue
like the sky of night; his hair, silkier and softer, curled in less
crisp undulations, and his shoulders did not exhibit that
rigid, transversal line which is the characteristic sign of the
race as represented on the statues of the temples and the
frescoes of the tombs.

All these characteristics went to form a remarkable beauty,
which Petamounoph's daughter had been unable to resist.
Since the day when Poëri had by chance appeared to her,
leaning upon the gallery of the building — which was his
favorite place when he was not busy with the farm work —
she had returned many times under pretext of driving, and
had made her chariot pass under the balcony of the villa; but
although she had put on her handsomest tunics, fastened
around her neck her richest necklaces and encircled her wrists
with her most wondrously chased bracelets, wreathed her hair
with the freshest lotus-flowers, drawn to the temples the black
line of her eyes, and brightened her cheeks with rouge, Poëri
had never seemed to pay the smallest attention to her.

And yet Tahoser was rarely beautiful, and the love which
the pensive tenant of the villa disdained, the Pharaoh would
willingly have purchased at a great price. In exchange for the
priest's daughter he would have given Twea, Taïa, Amense,

Hont-Reché, his Asiatic captives, his vases of gold and silver, his necklaces of gems, his war chariots, his invincible army, his scepter, — all, in a word, even his tomb, on which since the beginning of his reign had been working in the darkness thousands upon thousands of workmen.

Love is not the same in the hot regions swept by a fiery wind as on the icy shores where calm descends from heaven with the cold; it is not blood but fire that flows in the veins. So Tahoser languished and fainted, though she breathed perfumes, surrounded herself with flowers, and drank drafts that bring forgetfulness. Music wearied her or overexcited her feelings; she had ceased to take any pleasure in the dances of her companions; at night, sleep fled from her eyelids, and breathless, stifling, her breast heaving with sighs, she would leave her sumptuous couch and stretch herself out upon the broad slabs of the pavement, pressing her bosom against the hard granite as if she wished to breathe in its coolness.

On the night which followed the triumphal entry of the Pharaoh, Tahoser felt so unhappy and life seemed so empty that she determined not to die without having made at least one last effort.

She wrapped herself up in a piece of common stuff, kept on but a single bracelet of odoriferous wood, twisted a piece of striped gauze around her head, and with the first light of the dawn, without being heard by Nofré, who was dreaming of the handsome Ahmosis, she left her room, crossed the garden, drew the bolts of the water gate, proceeded to the quay, waked a waterman asleep in his papyrus boat, and had herself transported to the other bank of the stream.

Staggering and pressing her little hand to her heart to still its beating, she drew near Poëri's dwelling.

It was now broad daylight, and the gates were opening to give passage to the ox teams going to work, and to the flocks going forth to pasture.

Tahoser knelt on the threshold and placed her hand above her head with a supplicating gesture, more beautiful, perhaps, even in this humble attitude and in her mean dress. Her bosom rose and fell and tears streamed down her pale cheeks.

Poëri saw her and took her for what she was, indeed, a most unhappy woman.

"Enter," said he; "enter without fear. This house is hospitable."

## VI

*T*ahoser, encouraged by the friendly words of Poëri, abandoned her supplicating attitude and rose. A rich glow flushed her cheek but now so pale; shame came back to her with hope; she blushed at the strange action to which love had driven her; she hesitated to pass the threshold which she had crossed so often in her dreams. Her maidenly scruples, stifled for a time by passion, resumed their power in the presence of reality.

The young man, thinking that timidity, the companion of misfortune, alone prevented Tahoser from entering the house, said to her in a soft, musical voice marked by a foreign accent, —

"Enter, maiden, and do not tremble so. My home is large enough to shelter you. If you are weary, rest; if you are thirsty, my servants will bring you pure water cooled in porous clay-jars; if you are hungry, they will set before you wheaten bread, dates, and dried figs."

Petamounoph's daughter, encouraged by these hospitable words, entered the house, which justified the hieroglyph of welcome inscribed upon the gate.

Poëri took her to a room on the ground-floor, the walls of which were painted with green vertical bands ending in lotus flowers, making the apartment pleasant to the eye. A fine mat of reeds woven in symmetrical designs covered the floor. At each corner of the room great sheaves of flowers filled tall vases, held in place by pedestals, and scattered their perfume through the cool shade of the hall. At the back a low sofa, the wood-work of which was ornamented with foliage and chimerical animals, tempted with its broad bed the fatigued or idle guest. Two chairs, the seats made of Nile reeds, with sloping back, strengthened by stays, a wooden foot-stool cut in the shape of a shell and resting upon three legs, an oblong table, also three-legged, bordered with inlaid work and ornamented in the center with uræus snakes, wreaths, and agricultural symbols, and on which was placed a vase of rose and blue lotus, — completed the furniture of the room, which was pastoral in its simplicity and gracefulness.

Poëri sat down on the sofa. Tahoser, bending one leg under her thigh and raising one knee, knelt before the young man who fixed upon her a glance full of kindly questioning. She was most lovely in that attitude. The gauze veil in which she was enveloped exhibited, as it fell back, the rich mass of her hair bound with a narrow white ribbon, and revealed her gentle, sweet, sad face. Her sleeveless tunic showed her lovely arms bare to the shoulder and left them free.

"I am called Poëri," said the young man; "I am steward of the royal estates, and have the right to wear the gilded ram's-horns on my state headdress."

"And I am called Hora," replied Tahoser, who had arranged her little story beforehand. "My parents are dead, their goods were sold by their creditors, leaving me just enough to pay for their burial; so I have been left alone and without means. But since you are kind enough to receive me, I shall repay you for your hospitality. I have been taught the work of women, although my condition did not oblige me to perform it. I can spin and weave linen with thread of various colors; I can imitate flowers and embroider ornaments on stuffs; I can even, when you are tired by your work and overcome by the heat of the day, delight you with song, harp, or lute."

"Hora, you are welcome to my dwelling," said the young man. "You will find here, without taxing your strength, — for you seem to me to be delicate, — occupation suitable for a maiden who has known better days; among my maids are gentle and good girls who will be pleasant companions for you, and who will show you how we live in this pastoral home. So the days will pass, and perhaps brighter ones will dawn for you. If not, you can quietly grow old in my home in the midst of abundance and peace. The guest whom the gods send is sacred."

Having said these words, Poëri arose, as if to avoid the
thanks of the supposed Hora, who had prostrated herself at
his feet and was kissing them, as do wretches who have just
been granted a favor; but the lover in her had taken the place
of the suppliant, and her ripe, rosy lips found it hard to leave
those beautiful, clean, white feet that resembled the jasper feet
of the gods.

Before going out to superintend the work of the farm, Poëri
turned around on the threshold of the room and said, —

"Hora, remain here until I have appointed a room for you.
I shall send you some food by one of my servants."

And he walked away quietly, the whip which marked his
rank hanging from his wrist. The workmen saluted him,
placing one hand on their head and the other to the ground,
but by the cordiality of their salute it was easily seen that he
was a kind master. Sometimes he stopped to give an order or
a piece of advice, for he was greatly skilled in matters of
agriculture and gardening. Then he resumed his walk, looking
to the right and left and carefully inspecting everything.
Tahoser, who had humbly accompanied him to the door, and
had crouched on the threshold, her elbow on her knee and
her chin on the palm of her hand, followed him with her
glance until he disappeared under the leafy arches. She kept
on looking long after he had passed out by the gate into the
fields.

A servant, in accordance with an order which Poëri had
given when he went out, brought on a tray a goose-leg, onions
baked in the ashes, wheaten bread and figs, and a jar of water
closed with myrtle flowers.

"The master sends you this. Eat, maiden, and regain your
strength."

Tahoser was not very hungry, but her part required that
she should exhibit some appetite; the poor must necessarily
devour the food which pity throws them. So she ate, and
drank a long draft of the cool water. The servant having gone,
she resumed her contemplative attitude. Innumerable contra-
dictory thoughts filled her mind: sometimes with maidenly
shame she repented the step she had taken; at others, carried
away by her passion, she exulted in her own audacity. Then
she said to herself: "Here I am, it is true, under Poëri's roof;

I shall see him freely every day; I shall silently drink in his beauty, which is more that of a god than of a man; I shall hear his lovely voice, which is like the music of the soul. But will he, who never paid any attention to me when I passed by his home dressed in my most brilliant garments, adorned with my richest gems, perfumed with scents and flowers, mounted on my painted and gilded car surmounted by a sunshade, and surrounded like a queen with a retinue of servants, — will he pay more attention to the poor suppliant maiden whom he has received through pity and who is dressed in mean stuff? Will my wretchedness accomplish what my wealth could not do? It may be, after all, that I am ugly, and that Nofré flatters me when she maintains that from the unknown sources of the Nile to the place where it casts itself into the sea there is no lovelier maid than her mistress. Yet no, — I am beautiful; the blazing eyes of men have told me so a thousand times, and especially have the annoyed airs and the disdainful pouts of the women who passed by me confirmed it. Will Poëri, who has inspired me with such mad passion, never love me? He would have received just as kindly an old, wrinkled woman with withered breasts, clothed in hideous rags, and with feet grimy with dust. Anyone but he would at once have recognized, under the disguise of Hora, Tahoser the daughter of the high priest Petamounoph; but he never cast his eyes upon me anymore than does the basalt statue of a god upon the devotees who offer up to it quarters of antelope and baskets of lotus."

These thoughts cast down the courage of Tahoser. Then she regained confidence, and said to herself that her beauty, her youth, her love would surely at last move that insensible heart. She would be so sweet, so attentive, so devoted, she would use so much art and coquetry in dressing herself, that certainly Poëri would not be able to resist. Then she promised herself to reveal to him that the humble servant-maid was a girl of high rank, possessing slaves, estates, and palaces, and she foresaw, in her imagination, a life of splendid and radiant happiness following upon a period of obscure felicity.

"First and foremost, let me make myself beautiful," she said, as she rose and walked towards one of the pools.

On reaching it, she knelt upon the stone margin, washed her face, her neck, and her shoulders. The disturbed water showed her in its mirror, broken by innumerable ripples, her vague, trembling image which smiled up to her as through green gauze; and the little fishes, seeing her shadow and thinking that crumbs of bread were about to be thrown to them, drew near the edge in shoals. She gathered two or three lotus flowers which bloomed on the surface of the pool, twisted their stems around the band that held in her hair, and made thus a headdress which all the skill of Nofré could never have equaled, even had she emptied her mistress's jewel-caskets.

When she had finished and rose refreshed and radiant, a tame ibis, which had gravely watched her, drew itself up on its two long legs, stretched out its long neck, and flapped its wings two or three times as if to applaud her.

Having finished her toilet, Tahoser resumed her place at the door of the house and waited for Poëri. The heavens were of a deep blue; the light shimmered in visible waves through the transparent air; intoxicating perfumes rose from the flowers and the plants; the birds hopped amid the branches, pecking at the berries; the fluttering butterflies chased one another. This charming spectacle was rendered yet more bright by human activity, which enlivened it by the communication of a soul. The gardeners came and went, the servants returned laden with panniers of grass or vegetables; others, standing at the foot of the fig trees, caught in baskets the fruits thrown to them by monkeys trained to pluck them and perched on the highest branches.

Tahoser contemplated with delight this beautiful landscape, the peacefulness of which was filling her soul, and she said to herself, "How sweet it would be to be beloved here, amid the light, the scents, and the flowers."

Poëri returned. He had finished his tour of inspection, and withdrew to his room to spend the burning hours of the day. Tahoser followed him timidly, and stood near the door, ready to leave at the slightest gesture, but Poëri signed to her to remain.

She came forward timidly and knelt upon the mat.

"You tell me, Hora, that you can play the lute. Take that instrument hanging upon the wall, strike its cords and sing me some old air, very sweet, very tender, and very slow. The sleep which comes to one cradled by music is full of lovely dreams."

The priest's daughter took down the mandore, drew near the couch on which Poëri was stretched, leaned the head of the lute against the wooden bed-head hollowed out in the shape of a half-moon, stretched her arm to the end of the handle of the instrument, the body of which was pressed against her beating heart, let her hand flutter along the strings, and struck a few chords. Then she sang in a true, though somewhat trembling voice, an old Egyptian air, the vague sigh breathed by the ancestors and transmitted from generation to generation, and in which recurred constantly one and the same phrase of a sweet and penetrating monotony.

"In very truth," said Poëri, turning his dark blue eyes upon the maid, "you know rhythm as does a professional musician, and you might practice your art in the palaces of kings. But you give to your song a new expression; the air you are singing, one would think you are inventing it, and you impart to it a magical charm. Your voice is no longer that of mourning; another woman seems to shine through you as the light shines from behind a veil. Who are you?"

"I am Hora," replied Tahoser. "Have I not already told you my story? Only, I have washed from my face the dust of the road, I have smoothed out the folds in my crushed gown and put a flower in my hair. If I am poor, that is no reason why I should be ugly, and the gods sometimes refuse beauty to the rich. But does it please you that I should go on?"

"Yes. Repeat that air; it fascinates, benumbs me, it takes away my memory like a cup of nepenthe. Repeat it until sleep and forgetfulness fall upon my eyelids."

Poëri's eyes, fixed at first upon Tahoser, soon were half-closed, and then completely so. The maiden continued to strike the strings of the mandore, and sang more and more softly the refrain of her song. Poëri slept. She stopped and fanned him with a palm-leaf fan thrown on the table.

Poëri was handsome, and sleep imparted to his pure features an indescribable expression of languor and tenderness.
His long eyelashes falling upon his cheeks seemed to conceal
from him a celestial vision, and his beautiful, red, half-open
lips trembled as if they were speaking mute words to an
invisible being. After a long contemplation, emboldened by
silence and solitude, Tahoser, forgetting herself, bent over the
sleeper's brow, kept back her breath, pressed her heart with
her hand, and placed a timid, furtive, winged kiss upon it.
Then she drew back ashamed and blushing. The sleeper had
faintly felt in his dream Tahoser's lips; he uttered a sigh and
said in Hebrew, "Oh, Ra'hel, beloved Ra'hel!"

Fortunately these words of an unknown tongue conveyed
no meaning to Tahoser, and she again took up the palm-leaf
fan, hoping yet fearing that Poëri would awake.

## VII

W hen day dawned, Nofré, who slept on a cot at her
mistress's feet, was surprised at not hearing Tahoser call her
as usual by clapping her hands. She rose on her elbow and
saw that the bed was empty; yet the first beams of the sun,
striking the frieze of the portico, were only now beginning
to cast on the wall the shadow of the capitals and of the upper
part of the shafts of the pillars. Usually Tahoser was not an
early riser, and she rarely rose without the assistance of her
women. Neither did she ever go out until after her hair had
been dressed, and perfumed water had been poured over her
lovely body, while she knelt, her hands crossed upon her
bosom.

Nofré, feeling uneasy, put on a transparent gown, slipped
her feet into sandals of palm fiber, and set out in search of
her mistress. She looked for her first under the portico of the
two courts, thinking that, unable to sleep, Tahoser had per-

haps gone to enjoy the coolness of dawn in the inner cloisters; but she was not there.

"Let me visit the garden," said Nofré to herself; "perhaps she took a fancy to see the night dew sparkle on the leaves of the plants and to watch for once the awakening of the flowers."

Although she traversed the garden in every direction, she found it absolutely untenanted. Nofré looked along every walk, under every arbor, under every arch, into every grove, but unsuccessfully. She entered the kiosk at the end of the arbor, but she did not find Tahoser; she hastened to the pond, in which her mistress might have taken a fancy to bathe, as she sometimes did with her companions, upon the granite steps which led from the edge of the basin to the bottom of fine sand. The broad nymphoea-leaves floated on the surface, and did not appear to have been disturbed; the ducks, plunging their blue necks into the calm water, alone rippled it, and they saluted Nofré with joyous cries.

The faithful maid began to feel seriously alarmed; she roused the whole household. The slaves and the maids emerged from their cells, and informed by Nofré of the strange disappearance of Tahoser, proceeded to make most minute search. They ascended the terraces, rummaged every room, every corner, every place where she might possibly be. Nofré, in her agitation, even opened the boxes containing the dresses and the caskets holding the jewels, as if they could possibly have held her mistress. Unquestionably Tahoser was not within the dwelling.

An old and consummately prudent servant bethought himself of examining the sand of the walks in search of the footprints of his young mistress. The heavy bolts of the gate leading into the city were in place, and this proved that Tahoser had not gone out that way. It is true that Nofré had carelessly traversed every path, marking them with her sandals, but by bending close to the ground, old Souhem speedily noticed among Nofré's footprints a slight imprint made by a narrow, dainty sole belonging to a much smaller foot than the maid's. He followed this track, which led him, passing under the arbor, from the pylon in the court to the water gate. The bolts, as he pointed out to Nofré, had been drawn, and the two leaves of the door were held merely by their weight; therefore Petamounoph's daughter had gone out that way. Farther on the track was lost; the brick quay had preserved no trace; the boatman who had carried Tahoser across had not returned to his station; the others were asleep, and when questioned replied that they had seen nothing. One, however, did report that a woman, poorly dressed and belonging apparently to the lowest class, had been ferried over early to the other side of the river to the Memnonia quarter, no doubt to carry out some funeral rite. This description, which in no way tallied with the elegant Tahoser, completely upset the suppositions of Nofré and Souhem.

They returned to the house sad and disappointed. The men and women servants sat down on the ground in desolate attitudes, letting one of their hands hang down, its palm turned up, and placing the other on their head, all of them calling together in plaintive chorus, "Woe! woe! woe! Our mistress is gone!"

"By Oms, the dog of the lower regions, I shall find her," said old Souhem, "even if I have to walk living to the very confines of the Western Region to which travel the dead. She was a kind mistress; she gave us food in abundance, did not exact excessive labor, and caused us to be beaten only when we deserved it and in moderation. Her foot was not heavy on our bowed necks, and in her home a slave might believe himself free."

"Woe! woe! woe!" repeated the men and women as they cast dust upon their heads.

"Alas! dear mistress, who knows where you are now?" said her faithful maid, whose tears were flowing. "Perchance some enchanter compelled you to leave your palace through a spell in order to work his odious will on you. He will lacerate your fair body, will draw your heart out through a cut like that made by the dissectors, will throw your remains to the ferocious crocodiles, and on the day of reunion your mutilated soul will find shapeless remains only. You will not go to join, at the end of the passages of which the undertaker keeps the plan, the painted and gilded mummy of your father, the high priest Petamounoph, in the funeral chamber which has been cut out for you."

"Calm yourself, Nofré," said old Souhem; "let us not despair too soon. It may be that Tahoser will soon return. She has no doubt yielded to some fancy which we cannot guess, and presently we shall see her come back, gay and smiling, holding aquatic flowers in her hands."

Wiping her eyes with the corner of her dress, the maid nodded assent. Souhem crouched down, bending his knees like those of the dog-faced figures which are roughly carved out of a square block of basalt, and pressing his temples between his dry hands, seemed to reflect deeply. His face of a reddish brown, his sunken eyes, his prominent jaws, the deeply wrinkled cheeks, his straight hair framing in his face like bristles, made him altogether like the monkey-faced gods. He was certainly not a god, but he looked very much like a monkey.

The result of his meditations, anxiously awaited by Nofré, was thus expressed: "The daughter of Petamounoph is in love."

"Who told you?" cried Nofré, who thought that she was the only one who could read her mistress's heart.

"No one; but Tahoser is very beautiful; she has already beheld sixteen times the rise and fall of the Nile. Sixteen is the number symbolical of voluptuousness; and for some time past she has been calling at unaccustomed hours her players on the harp, the lute, and the flute, like one who seeks to calm the agitation of her heart by music."

"You speak sensibly, and wisdom dwells in your old bald head. But how have you learned to know women, — you who merely dig the earth in the garden and bear jars of water on your shoulders?"

The slave opened his lips with a silent smile and exhibited two rows of teeth fit to crush date-stones. The grin meant, "I have not always been old and a captive."

Enlightened by Souhem's suggestion, Nofré immediately thought of the handsome Ahmosis, the oëris of the Pharaoh, who so often passed below the terrace, and who had looked so splendid on his war chariot in the triumphal procession. As she was in love with him herself, though she was not fully aware of it, she assumed that her mistress shared her feelings. She put on a somewhat heavier dress and repaired to the officer's dwelling. It was there, she fancied, that Tahoser would certainly be found.

The young officer was seated on a low seat at the end of the room. On the walls hung trophies of different weapons: the leather tunic covered with bronze plates on which was engraved the cartouche of the Pharaoh; the brazen poniard, with the jade handle open-worked to allow the fingers to pass through; the flat-edged battle-axe, the falchion with curved blade; the helmet with its double plume of ostrich-feathers; the triangular bow; and the red-feathered arrows. His distinctive necklaces were placed upon pedestals, and open coffers showed booty taken from the enemy.

When he saw Nofré, whom he knew well, standing on the threshold, he felt quick pleasure, his brown cheeks flushed, his muscles quivered, his heart beat high. He thought Nofré brought him a message from Tahoser, although the priest's daughter had never taken notice of his glances; but the man to whom the gods have imparted the gift of beauty easily fancies that all women fall in love with him. He rose and took a few steps towards Nofré, whose anxious glance examined the corners of the room to make sure whether Tahoser was there or not.

"What brings you here, Nofré?" said Ahmosis, seeing that the young maid, full of her search, did not break silence. "Your mistress is well, I hope, for I think I saw her yesterday at the Pharaoh's entry."

"You should know whether my mistress is well better than anyone else," replied Nofré; "for she has fled from her home without informing anyone of her intentions. I could swear by Hathor that you know the refuge which she chose."

"She has disappeared! — what are you talking about?" cried Ahmosis, with a surprise that was unquestionably genuine.

"I thought she loved you," said Nofré, "and sometimes the best-behaved maidens lose their heads. So she is not here?"

"The god Phrah, who sees everything, knows where she is, but not one of his beams, which end in hands, has fallen on her within these walls. Look for yourself and visit every room."

"I believe you, Ahmosis, and I must go; for if Tahoser had come, you could not conceal it from her faithful Nofré, who would have asked nothing better than to serve your loves. You are handsome; she is very rich and a virgin; the gods would have beheld your marriage with pleasure."

Nofré returned to the house more anxious and more upset than before. She feared that the servants might be suspected of having killed Tahoser in order to seize on her riches, and that the judges would seek to make them confess under torture what they did not actually know.

The Pharaoh, on his part, was also thinking of Tahoser. After having made the libations and the offerings required by the ritual, he had seated himself in the inner court of the harem, and was sunk in thought, paying no attention to the gambols of his women, who, nude and crowned with flowers, were disporting themselves in the transparent waters of the piscina, splashing each other and uttering shrill, sonorous bursts of laughter, in order to attract the attention of the master, who had not made up his mind, contrary to his habit, which of them should be the favorite queen that week.

It was a charming picture which these beautiful women presented; in a framework of shrubs and flowers, in the center of the court, surrounded by columns painted in brilliant colors, in the clear light of an azure sky, across which flew from time to time an ibis with outstretched neck and trailing legs, their shapely bodies shone in the water like submerged statues of jasper.

Amense and Twea, weary of swimming, had emerged from the water, and kneeling on the edge of the basin, were spreading out to dry in the sun their thick black hair, the long locks of which made their white skins seem whiter still. A few last drops of water ran down their shining shoulders and their arms polished like jade. Maids rubbed them with aromatic oil and essences, while a young Ethiopian girl held out the calyx of a large flower so that they might breathe its perfume.

It might have been thought that the artist who had carved the decorative *bassi-relievi* of the rooms in the harem had taken these graceful groups as models; but the Pharaoh could not have looked with a colder glance at the designs cut in the stone. Perched on the back of his armchair the tame monkey was eating dates and cracking its jaws; against the master's legs the tame cat rubbed itself, arching its back; the deformed dwarf pulled the monkey's tail and the cat's moustaches, making the one scratch and the other chatter, a performance which usually caused His Majesty to smile; but His Majesty was not in a smiling mood on that day. He put the cat aside, made the monkey get off the armchair, smote the dwarf on the head, and walked toward the granite apartments.

Each of those rooms was formed of blocks of prodigious size, and closed by stone gates which no human power could have forced unless the secret of opening them were known. Within these halls were kept the riches of the Pharaoh, and the booty taken from conquered nations. They held ingots of precious metals, crowns of gold and silver, neckplates and bracelets of cloisonné enamel, earrings which shone like the disc of Moui, necklaces of seven rows of cornelian, lapis-lazuli, red jasper, pearls, agates, sardonyx, and onyx; exquisitely chased anklets, belts, with plates engraved with hieroglyphs, rings with scarabæi set in them; quantities of fishes, crocodiles, and hearts stamped out of gold, serpents in enamel twisted on themselves; bronze vases, flagons of wavy alabaster, and of blue glass on which wound white spirals; coffers of enameled ware; boxes of sandal wood of strange and chimerical forms; heaps of aromatic gums from all countries; blocks of ebony; precious stuffs so fine that a whole piece could have been pulled through a ring; white and black ostrich plumes, and others colored in various ways; monstrously huge elephant's-tusks, cups of gold, silver, gilded glass; statues marvelous both as regards the material and the workmanship.

In every room the Pharaoh caused to be taken a litter-load borne by two robust slaves of Kousch and Scheto, and clapping his hands, he called Timopht, the servant who had followed Tahoser, and said to him, "Have all these things taken to Tahoser, the daughter of the high priest Petamounoph, from the Pharaoh."

Timopht placed himself at the head of the procession, which crossed the Nile on a royal barge, and soon the slaves with their load reached Tahoser's house.

"For Tahoser, from the Pharaoh," said Timopht, knocking at the door.

At the sight of those treasures Nofré nearly fainted, half with fear, half with amazement. She dreaded lest the King should put her to death on learning that the priest's daughter was no longer there.

"Tahoser has gone," said she, tremulously, "and I swear by the four sacred geese, Amset, Sis, Soumauts, and Kebhsniv, which fly to the four quarters of the wind, that I know not where she is."

"The Pharaoh beloved of Phré, favorite of Ammon Ra, has sent these gifts, — I cannot take them back. Keep them until Tahoser is found. You shall answer for them on your head. Have them put away in rooms and guarded by faithful servants," replied the envoy of the King.

When Timopht returned to the palace and, prostrate, his elbows close to his sides, his brow in the dust, said that Tahoser had vanished, the King became very wroth, and he struck the slab of the flooring so fiercely with his scepter that the slab was split.

## VIII

*T*ahoser, nevertheless, scarce bestowed a thought on Nofré, her favorite maid, or on the anxiety which her absence would necessarily cause. The beloved mistress had completely forgotten her beautiful home in Thebes, her servants, and her ornaments, — a most difficult and incredible thing in a woman. The daughter of Petamounoph had not the least suspicion of the Pharaoh's love for her; she had not observed the glance full of desire which had fallen upon her from the heights of that majesty which nothing on earth could move. Had she seen it, she would have deposited the royal love as an offering, with all the flowers of her soul, at the feet of Poëri.

While driving her spindle with her toe to make it ascend along the thread, — for this was the task which had been set her, — she followed with her glance every motion of the young Hebrew, her looks enveloped him like a caress. She silently enjoyed the happiness of remaining near him in the building to which he had given her access.

If Poëri had turned towards her, he would no doubt have been struck by the moist brilliancy of her eyes, the sudden blushes which flushed her fair cheeks, the quick beating of her heart which might be guessed by the rising and falling of her bosom; but seated at a table, he bent over a leaf of papyrus on which, with the help of a reed, taking ink from a hollowed slab of alabaster, he inscribed accounts in demotic numbers.

Did Poëri perceive the evident love of Tahoser for him? Or for some secret reason, did he pretend not to perceive it? His manner towards her was gentle and kindly, but reserved, as if he sought to prevent or repel some importunate confession which it would have given him pain to reply to. And yet the sham Hora was very beautiful. Her charms, betrayed by the poverty of her dress, were all the more beautiful; and just as in the hottest hours of the day a luminous vapor is seen quivering upon the gleaming earth, so did an atmosphere of love shimmer around her. On her half-open lips her passion fluttered like a bird that seeks to take its flight; and softly, very softly, when she was sure that she would not be heard, she repeated like a monotonous cantilena, "Poëri, I love you."

It was harvest time, and Poëri went out to oversee the workmen. Tahoser, who could no more leave him than the shadow can leave the body, followed him timidly, fearing lest he should tell her to remain in the house; but the young man said to her in a voice marked by no accent of anger, —

"Grief is lightened by the sight of the peaceful work of agriculture, and if some painful remembrance of vanished prosperity weighs down your soul, it will disappear at the sight of this joyous activity. These things must be novel to you, for your skin, which the sun has never kissed, your delicate feet, your slender hands, and the elegance with which you drape yourself in the piece of coarse stuff which serves you for a vestment, prove to me that you have always inhabited cities, and have lived in the midst of refinement and luxury. Come, then, and sit down, while still turning your spindle, under the shadow of that tree, where the harvesters have hung up, to keep it cool, the skin which holds their drink."

Tahoser obeyed and sat down under the tree, her arms crossed on her knees and her knees up to her chin. From the garden wall, the plain stretched to the foot of the Libyan chain like a yellow sea over which the least breath of air drove waves of gold. The light was so intense that the golden tone of the grain whitened in places and became silvery. In the rich mud of the Nile the grain had grown strong, straight, and high like javelins, and never had a richer harvest, flaming and crackling with heat, been outspread in the sun. The crop was abundant enough to fill up to the ceiling the range of vaulted granaries which rose near the cellars.

The workmen had already been a long while at work, and here and there out of the waves of the corn showed their woolly or close-shaven heads covered with pieces of white stuff, and their naked torsos the color of baked brick. They bent and rose with a regular motion, cutting the grain just below the ear, as regularly as if they had followed a line marked out by a cord. Behind them in the furrows walked the gleaners with esparto bags, in which they placed the harvested ears, and which they then carried on their shoulders, or suspended from a cross-bar and with the help of a companion, to grinding-mills situated some distance apart. Sometimes the breathless harvesters stopped to take breath, and putting their sickles under their right arm drank a draft of water. Then they quickly resumed their work, fearing the foreman's stick.

The harvested grain was spread on the threshing-floor in layers evened with a pitchfork, and slightly higher on the edges on account of the additional basketfuls which were being poured on.

Then Poëri signed to the ox-driver to bring on his animals. They were superb oxen with long horns, curved like the headdress of Isis, with high withers, deep dewlaps, clean, muscular limbs; the brand of the estate, stamped with a red-hot iron, showed upon their flanks. They walked slowly, bearing a horizontal yoke which bore equally upon the heads of the four.

They were driven on to the threshing-floor; urged by the double-lashed whip, they began to trample in a circle, making the grain spring from the ear under their cloven hoofs; the sun shone on their lustrous coats, and the dust which they raised ascended to their nostrils, so that after going around about twenty times, they would lean one against another, and in spite of the hissing whip which lashed their flanks, they would unmistakably slacken their pace. To encourage them, the driver who followed them, holding by the tail the nearest animal, began to sing in a joyous, quick rhythm the old ox-song: "Turn for yourselves, O oxen, turn for yourselves; measures for you, and measures for your masters." And the team, with new spirit, started on and disappeared in a cloud of yellow dust that sparkled like gold.

The work of the oxen done, came servants who, armed with wooden scoops, threw the grain into the air and let it fall to separate it from the straw, the awn, and the shell. The grain thus winnowed was put into bags, the numbers of which were noted by a scribe, and carried to the lofts, which were reached by ladders.

Tahoser under the shadow of her tree enjoyed this animated and grandiose spectacle, and often her heedless hand forgot to spin the thread. The day was waning, and already the sun, which had risen behind Thebes, had crossed the Nile and was sinking towards the Libyan chain, behind which its disc sets every evening. It was the hour when the cattle returned from the fields to the stable. She watched near Poëri the long pastoral procession.

First was seen advancing the vast herd of oxen, some white, others red, some black with lighter spots, others piebald, others brindled. They were of all colors and all sizes. They passed by, lifting up their lustrous mouths whence hung filaments of saliva, opening their great, gentle eyes; the more impatient, smelling the stables, half raised themselves for a moment and peered above the horned multitude, with which, as they fell, they were soon confounded; the less skillful, outstripped by their companions, uttered long, plaintive bellows as if to protest. Near the oxen walked the herds with their whip and their rolled up cord.

On arriving near Poëri they knelt down, and, with their elbows close to their sides, touched the ground with their lips as a mark of respect. Scribes wrote down the number of heads of cattle upon tablets.

Behind the oxen came the asses, trotting along and kicking under the blows of the donkey drivers. These had smooth-shaven heads, and were dressed in a mere linen girdle, the end of which fell between their legs. The donkeys went past, shaking their long ears and trampling the ground with their little, hard hoofs. The donkey drivers performed the same genuflection as the ox-herds, and the scribes noted also the exact number of the animals.

Then it was the turn of the goats. They arrived, headed by the he-goat, their broken and shrill voices trembling with pleasure; the goat-herds had much difficulty in restraining their high spirits and in bringing back to the main body the marauding ones which strayed away. They were counted, like the oxen and the asses, and with the same ceremonial the goat-herds prostrated themselves at Poëri's feet.

The procession was closed by the geese, which, weary with walking on the road, balanced themselves on their web feet, flapped their wings noisily, stretched out their necks, and uttered hoarse cries. Their number was taken, and the tablets handed to the steward of the domain. Long after the oxen, the asses, the goats, and the geese had gone in, a column of dust which the wind could not sweep away still rose slowly into the heavens.

"Well, Hora," said Poëri to Tahoser, "has the sight of the harvest and the flocks amused you? These are our pastoral pleasures. We have not here, as in Thebes, harpists and danc-ers; but agriculture is holy; it is the nurse of man, and he who sows a grain of corn does a deed agreeable to the gods. Now come and take your meal with your companions. For my part, I am going back to the house to calculate how many bushels of wheat the ears have produced."

Tahoser put one hand to the ground and the other on her head as a mark of respectful assent, and withdrew.

In the dining-hall laughed and chattered a number of young servants as they ate their onions and cakes of doora and dates. A small earthenware vase full of oil, in which dipped a wick, gave them light, — for night had fallen, — and cast a yellow light upon their brown cheeks and bodies which no garment veiled. Some were seated on ordinary wooden seats, others leaned against the wall with one leg drawn up.

"Where does the master go like that every evening?" said a little, sly-looking maid, as she peeled a pomegranate with pretty, monkeylike gestures.

"The master goes where he pleases," replied a tall slave, who was chewing the petals of a flower. "Is he to tell you what he does? It is not you, in any case, who will keep him here."

"Why not I as well as another?" answered the child, piqued.

The tall slave shrugged her shoulders.

"Hora herself, who is fairer and more beautiful than any of us, could not manage it. Though he bears an Egyptian name and is in the service of the Pharaoh, he belongs to the barbarous race of Israel, and if he goes out at night, it is no doubt to be present at the sacrifices of children which the Hebrews perform in desert places, where the owl hoots, the hyena howls, and the adder hisses."

Tahoser quietly left the room without a word, and concealed herself in the garden behind the mimosa bushes. After waiting two hours, she saw Poëri issue forth into the country. Light and silent as a shadow, she started to follow him.


IX


*P*oëri, who was armed with a strong palm stick, walked towards the river along a causeway built over a field of submerged papyrus which, leafy at their base, sent up on either hand their straight stalks six and eight cubits high, ending in a tuft of fiber and looking like the lances of an army in battle array.

Holding in her breath and walking on tiptoe, Tahoser followed him on the narrow road. There was no moon that night, and the thick papyrus would in any case have been sufficient to conceal the young girl, who remained somewhat behind.

An open space had to be crossed. The sham Hora let Poëri go on first, bent down, made herself as small as she could, and crawled along the ground. Next they entered a mimosa wood, and, concealed by the clumps of trees, Tahoser was able to proceed without having to take as many precautions. She was so close to Poëri, whom she feared to lose sight of in the darkness, that very often the branches that he pushed aside slapped her in the face; but she paid no attention to this. A feeling of burning jealousy drove her to seek the solution of the mystery, which she did not interpret as did the servants in the house. Not for one moment had she believed that the young Hebrew went out thus every night to perform any infamous and profane rite; she believed that a woman was at the bottom of these nocturnal excursions, and she wanted to know who her rival was. The cold kindness of Poëri had proved to her that his heart was already won; otherwise, how could he have remained insensible to charms famous throughout Thebes and the whole of Egypt? Would he have pretended not to understand a love that would have filled with pride oëris, priests, temple scribes, and even princes of the royal blood?

On reaching the river shore, Poëri descended a few steps cut out of the slope of the bank, and bent down as if he were casting off a rope. Tahoser, lying flat on the summit of the bank, above which the top of her head alone showed, saw to her great despair that the mysterious stroller was casting off a light papyrus bark, narrow and long like a fish, and that he was making ready to cross the river. The next moment he sprang into the boat, shoved off with his foot, and sculled into the open with a single oar placed at the stern of the skiff.

The poor girl was plunged in grief and despair: she was going to lose track of the secret which it was so important that she should learn. What was she to do? Retrace her steps, her heart a prey to suspicion and uncertainty, the worst of evils? She summoned all her courage and soon made up her mind. It was useless to think of looking for another boat. She let herself down the bank, drew off her dress in a twinkling, and fastened it in a roll upon her head; then she boldly plunged into the river, taking care not to splash. As supple as a water-snake, she stretched out her lovely arms over the dark waves in which quivered the reflection of the stars, and began to follow the boat at a distance. She swam superbly, for every day she practiced with her women in the vast piscina in her palace, and no one cleaved the waters more skillfully than Tahoser.

The current, less swift at this point, did not greatly hinder her, but in the center of the stream she had to strike out in the boiling water and to swim faster in order to avoid being carried to leeward. Her breath came shorter and quicker, and yet she held it in lest the young Hebrew should hear her. Sometimes a higher wave lapped with its foam her half-open lips, wetted her hair, and even reached her dress rolled up in a bundle. Happily for her, — for her strength was beginning to give way, — she soon found herself in stiller water. A bundle of reeds coming down the river touched her as it passed, and filled her with quick terror. The dark, green mass looked in the darkness like the back of a crocodile; Tahoser thought she had felt the rough skin of the monster; but she recovered from her terror and said, as she swam on, "What matter if the crocodiles eat me up, if Poëri loves me not?"

There was real danger, especially at night. During the day the constant crossing of boats and the work going on along the quays drove away the crocodiles, which went to shores less frequented by man to wallow in the mud and to sun themselves; but at night they became bold again.

Tahoser did not think of them; love is no calculator, and even if she had thought of this form of peril, she would have braved it, timid though she was, and frightened by an obstinate butterfly that mistaking her for a flower kept fluttering around her.

Suddenly the boat stopped, although the bank was still some distance away. Poëri, ceasing to scull, seemed to cast an uneasy glance around him. He had perceived the whitish spot made on the water by Tahoser's rolled up dress. Thinking she was discovered, the intrepid swimmer bravely dived, resolved not to come to the surface, even were she to drown, until Poëri's suspicions had been dispelled.

"I could have sworn somebody was swimming behind me," said Poëri, as he went on sculling again; "but who would venture into the Nile at such a time as this? I must have been crazy. I mistook for a human head covered with linen a tuft of white reeds, or perhaps a mere flake of foam, for I can see nothing now."

When Tahoser, whose temples were beginning to beat violently, and who began to see red flashes in the dark waters of the river, rose hastily to fill her lungs with a long breath of air, the papyrus boat had resumed its confident way, and Poëri was handling the scull with the imperturbable phlegm of the allegorical personages who row the barge of Maut on the *bassi-relievi* and the paintings of the temples. The bank was only a few strokes off; the vast shadow of the pylons and the huge walls of the Northern Palace — the dark pile of which was faintly seen surmounted by the pyramidions of six obelisks through the violet blue of the night — spread immense and formidable over the river, and sheltered Tahoser, who could swim without fear of being noticed.

Poëri landed a little below the palace and fastened his boat to a post so as to find it on his return. Then he took his palm stick and ascended the slope of the quay with a swift step.

Poor Tahoser, almost worn out, clung with her stiffened hands to the first step of the stair, and with difficulty drew from the stream her dripping limbs, which the contact of the air made heavier as she suddenly felt the fatigue. But the worst of her task was over. She climbed the steps, one hand pressed to her quick-beating heart, the other placed on her head to steady her rolled up and soaked dress. After having noticed the direction in which Poëri was walking, she sat down on top of the bank, untied her dress, and put it on. The contact of the wet stuff made her shudder slightly, yet the night air was soft and the southern breeze blew warm; but she was stiff and feverish, and her little teeth were chattering. She summoned up her energy, and gliding close by the sloping walls of the giant buildings, she managed not to lose sight of the young Hebrew, who turned around the corner of the mighty brick walls of the palace and entered the streets of Thebes.

After walking for some fifteen minutes, the palaces, the temples, the splendid dwellings vanished, and were replaced by humbler houses; granite, sandstone, and limestone were replaced by unbaked bricks and by clay worked with straw. Architectural design disappeared; low huts showed around like blisters or warts upon lonely places, upon waste fields, and were changed by the darkness into monstrous shapes. Pieces of wood and molded bricks arranged in heaps obstructed the way. Out of the silence rose strange, troubling sounds: an owl whirled through the air, lean dogs, raising their long, pointed noses, followed with plaintive bay the erratic flight of a bat; scorpions and frightened reptiles scurrying by, made the dry grass rattle.

"Could Harphre have spoken the truth?" thought Tahoser, impressed by the sinister aspect of the place. "Is it possible that Poëri comes here to sacrifice a child to those barbarous gods who love blood and suffering? Never was anyplace better fitted for cruel rites."

Meanwhile, profiting by the shadow of corners, the ends of walls, the clumps of vegetation, and the unevenness of the ground, she kept at the same distance from Poëri.

"Even if I were to be present as an invisible witness at some scene as frightful as a nightmare, to hear the cries of the victim, to see the priest, his hands red with blood, draw from the little body the smoking heart, I should go on to the end," said Tahoser to herself, as she saw the young Hebrew enter a hut built of clay, through the crevices of which shone a few rays of yellow light.

When Poëri was fairly within, the daughter of Petamounoph approached, though not a pebble cracked under her light step, nor a dog marked her presence by a bark. She went around the hut, pressing her hand to her heart and holding in her breath, and discovered, by seeing it shine against the dark ground of the clay wall, a crack wide enough to allow her glance to penetrate the interior. A small lamp lighted the room, which was less bare than might have been supposed from the outward appearance of the cabin. The smooth walls were as polished as stucco. On wooden pedestals, painted in various colors, were placed vases of gold and silver; jewels sparkled in half-open coffers; dishes of brilliant metal shone on the wall; and a nosegay of rare flowers bloomed in an enameled jar in the center of a small table. But it was not these details which interested Tahoser, although the contrast of this concealed luxury with the external poverty of the dwelling had at first somewhat surprised her. Her attention was irresistibly attracted by another object.

On a low platform covered with matting was a marvelously beautiful woman of an unknown race. She was fairer than any of the maids of Egypt, as white as milk, as white as a lily, as white as the ewes which have just been washed. Her eyebrows were curved like ebony bows, and their points met at the root of the thin, aquiline nose, the nostrils of which were as rosy as the interior of a shell; her eyes were like doves' eyes, bright and languorous; her lips were like two bands of purple, and as they parted showed rows of pearls; her hair hung on either side of her rosy cheeks in black, lustrous locks like two bunches of ripe grapes. Earrings shimmered in her ears, and necklaces of golden plates inlaid with silver sparkled around a neck that was round and polished like an alabaster column. Her dress was peculiar. It consisted of a full tunic embroidered with stripes and symmetrical designs of various colors, falling from her shoulders halfway down her legs and leaving her arms free and bare.

The young Hebrew sat down by her on the matting, and spoke to her words which Tahoser could not understand, but the meaning of which she unfortunately guessed too well; for Poëri and Ra'hel spoke in the language of their country, so sweet to the exile and captive. Yet hope dies hard in the loving breast.

"Perhaps it is his sister," said Tahoser, "and he goes to see her in secret, being unwilling that it should be known that he belongs to that enslaved race."

Then she put her eye to the crevice and listened with painful and intense attention to the harmonious and rhythmic language, every syllable of which held a secret which she would have given her life to learn, and which sounded in her ears vague, swift, and unmeaning like the wind in the leaves and the water on the bank.

"She is very beautiful for a sister," she murmured, as she cast a jealous glance upon the strange and charming face with its red lips and its pale complexion that was set off by ornaments of exotic shapes, and the beauty of which had something fatally mysterious about it.

"Oh, Ra'hel, my beloved Ra'hel!" repeated Poëri often.

Tahoser remembered having heard him whisper that name while she was fanning him in his sleep.

"He thought of her even in his dreams. No doubt Ra'hel is her name." And the poor child felt in her breast a sharp pang as if all the uræus snakes of the entablatures, all the royal asps of the Pharaonic crowns, had struck their venomous fangs in her heart.

Ra'hel bowed her head on Poëri's shoulder like a flower overladen with sunshine and love; the lips of the young man touched the hair of the lovely Jewess, who fell back slowly, yielding her brow and half-closed eyes to his earnest and timid caress. Their hands, which had sought each other, were now clasped and feverishly pressed together.

"Oh, why did I not surprise him in some impious and mysterious ceremony, slaying with his own hands a human victim, drinking its blood in a cup of black ware, rubbing his face with it? It seems to me that I should have suffered less than at the sight of that lovely woman whom he embraces so timidly," murmured Tahoser in a faint voice as she sank on the ground in a corner by the hut.

Twice she strove to rise, but she fell back on her knees. Darkness came over her, her limbs gave way, and she fell in a swoon.

Meanwhile Poëri issued from the hut, giving a last kiss to Ra'hel.

## X

*T*he Pharaoh, raging and anxious on hearing of the disappearance of Tahoser, had given way to that desire for change which possesses a heart tormented by an unsatisfied passion. To the deep grief of Amense, Hont-Reché, and Twea, his favorites, who had endeavored to retain him in the Summer Palace by all the resources of feminine coquetry, he now inhabited the Northern Palace on the other side of the Nile. His fierce preoccupation was irritated by the presence and the chatter of his women; they displeased him because they were not Tahoser. He now thought ugly those beauties who had seemed to him formerly so fair; their young, slender, graceful bodies, their voluptuous attitudes, their long eyes brightened by antimony and flashing with desire, their purple lips, white teeth, and languishing smiles, — everything in them, even the perfume of their cool skin, as delicate as a bouquet of flowers or a box of scent, had become odious to him. He seemed to be angry with them for having loved them, and to be unable to understand how he could have been smitten by such vulgar charms. When Twea touched his breast with the slender, pink finger of her little hand, shaking with emotion, as if to recall the remembrance of former familiarities; when Hont-Reché placed before him the draft-board supported by two lions back to back, in order to play a game; when Amense presented him with a lotus-flower with respectful, supplicating grace, he could scarcely refrain from striking them with his scepter, and his royal eyes flashed with such disdain that the poor women who had ventured on such boldness, withdrew abashed, their eyes wet with tears, and leaned silently against the painted wall, trying by their motionlessness to appear to be part of the paintings on the frescoes.

To avoid these scenes of tears and violence, he had withdrawn to the palace of Thebes, alone, taciturn, and somber; and there, instead of remaining seated on his throne in the solemn attitude of the gods and of kings, who, being almighty, neither move nor make a gesture, he walked feverishly up and down through the vast halls. Strange was it to see that tall Pharaoh with imposing mien, as formidable as the granite colossi, his like, making the stone floors resound under his curved sandals. When he passed, the terrified guards seemed to be petrified and to turn to stone. They remained breathless, and not even the double ostrich-feather in their headgear dared tremble. When he had passed, they scarce ventured to whisper, "What is the matter today with the Pharaoh?"

Had he returned from his expedition a beaten man, he could not have been more morose and somber. If, instead of having won ten victories, slain twenty thousand enemies, brought back two thousand virgins chosen from among the fairest, a hundred loads of gold-dust, a thousand loads of ebony and elephants' tusks, without counting the rare products and the strange animals, — if, instead of all this, Pharaoh had seen his army cut to pieces, his war chariots overthrown and broken, if he had escaped alone from the rout under a shower of arrows, dusty, blood-covered, taking the reins from the hands of his driver dead by his side, — he certainly could not have appeared more gloomy and more desperate. After all, the land of Egypt produces soldiers in abundance; innumerable horses neigh and paw the ground in the palace stables; and workmen could soon bend wood, melt copper, sharpen brass. The fortune of war is changeable, but a disaster may be atoned for. To have, however, wished for a thing which did not at once come to him, to have met with an obstacle between his will and the carrying out of that will, to have hurled like a javelin a desire which had not struck its mark, — that was what amazed the Pharaoh who dwelt in the higher plane of almightiness. For one moment it occurred to him that he was only a man.

So he wandered through the vast courts, down the avenues of giant pillars, passed under the mighty pylons, between the lofty monolithic obelisks and the colossi which gazed upon him with their great, frightened eyes. He traversed the hypostyle hall and the maze of the granitic forest with its one hundred and sixty-two pillars tall and strong as towers. The figures of gods, of kings, and of symbolic beings painted on the walls seemed to fix upon him their great eyes, drawn in black upon their profile masks, the uræus snakes to twist and swell their hoods, the bird-faced divinities to stretch out their necks, the globes to spread over the cornices their fluttering wings of stone. A strange, fantastic life animated these curious figures, and peopled with living swarms the solitudes of the vast hall, which was as large as an ordinary palace. The divinities, the ancestors, the chimerical monsters, eternally motionless, were amazed to see the Pharaoh, ordinarily as calm as themselves, striding up and down as though he were a man of flesh, and not of porphyry and basalt.

Weary of roaming about that mysterious forest of pillars that upbore a granite heaven, like a lion which seeks the track of its prey and scents with its wrinkled nose the moving sand of the desert, the Pharaoh ascended one of the terraces of the palace, stretched himself on a low couch, and sent for Timopht.

Timopht appeared at once, and advanced from the top of the stairs to the Pharaoh, prostrating himself at every step. He dreaded the wrath of the master whose favor he had, for a moment, hoped he had gained. Would the skill he had shown in discovering the home of Tahoser be a sufficient excuse for the crime of losing track of the lovely maid?

Raising one knee and leaving the other bent, Timopht stretched out his arms with a supplicating gesture.

"O King, do not doom me to death or to be beaten beyond measure. The beauteous Tahoser, the daughter of Petamounoph, on whom your desire deigned to descend as the hawk swoops down upon the dove, will doubtless be found; and when, returned to her home, she sees your magnificent gifts, her heart will be touched, and she will come of herself to take, among the women that dwell in your harem, the place which you will assign to her."

"Did you question her servants and her slaves?" said the King. "The stick loosens the most rebellious tongue, and suffering makes men and women say what they would otherwise hide."

"Nofré and Souhem, her favorite maid and her oldest servant, told me that they had noticed the bolts of the garden gate drawn back, that probably their mistress had gone out that way. The gate opens on the river, and the water does not preserve the track of boats."

"What did the boatmen of the Nile say?"

"They had seen nothing. One man alone said that a poorly dressed woman crossed the stream with the first light of day; but it could not be the beautiful and rich Tahoser, whose face you have yourself noticed, and who walks like a queen in her superb garments."

Timopht's logic did not appear to convince the Pharaoh. He leaned his chin on his hand and reflected for a few moments. Poor Timopht waited in silence, fearing an explosion of fury. The King's lips moved as if he were speaking to himself.

"That mean dress was a disguise. Yes, it must have been. Thus disguised, she crossed to the other side of the river. Timopht is a fool, who cannot see anything. I have a great mind to have him thrown to the crocodiles or beaten to death. But what could be her reason? A maid of high birth, the daughter of a high priest, to escape thus from her palace, alone and without informing anyone of her intention! It may be there is some love affair at the bottom of this mystery."

As this thought occurred to him, the Pharaoh's face flushed red as if under the reflection of a fire; the blood had rushed from his heart to his face. The redness was followed by dreadful pallor; his eyebrows writhed like the uræus in his diadem, his mouth was contracted, he grated his teeth, and his face became so terrible that the terrified Timopht fell on his face upon the pavement as falls a dead man.

But the Pharaoh resumed his coolness, his face regained its majestic, weary, placid look, and seeing that Timopht did not rise, he kicked him disdainfully.

When Timopht, who already saw himself stretched on the funeral bed supported by jackal's feet in the Memnonia quarter, his side open, his stomach emptied, and himself ready to be plunged into a bath of pickle, — when Timopht raised himself, he dared not look up to the King, but remained crouched on his heels, a prey to the bitterest anguish.

"Come, Timopht!" said His Majesty, "rise up, run, and dispatch emissaries on all sides; have temples, palaces, houses, villas, gardens, yea, the meanest of huts searched, and find Tahoser. Send chariots along every road; have the Nile traversed in every direction by boats; go yourself and ask those whom you meet if they have not seen such and such a woman. Violate the tombs, if she has taken refuge in the abodes of death, far within some passage or hypogeum. Seek her out as Isis sought her husband Osiris torn away by Typhon, and, dead or alive, bring her back, — or by the uræus of my pschent, by the lotus of my scepter, you shall perish in hideous tortures."

Timopht went off with the speed of a deer to carry out the orders of the Pharaoh, who, somewhat calmer, took one of those poses of tranquil grandeur which the sculptors love to give to the colossi set up at the gates of the temples and palaces, and calm as beseems those whose sandals, covered with drawings of captives with bound elbows, rest upon the heads of nations, he waited.

A roar as of thunder sounded around the palace, and had the sky not been of unchangeable, lapis-lazuli blue it might have been thought that a storm had burst unexpectedly. The sound was caused by the swiftly revolving wheels of the chariots galloping off in every direction, and shaking the very ground. Soon the Pharaoh perceived from the top of the terrace the boats cleaving the stream under the impulse of the rowers, and his messengers scattering on the other bank through the country. The Libyan chain, with its rosy light, and its sapphire blue shadows, bounded the horizon and formed a background to the giant buildings of Rameses, Amenhôtep, and Amen Phtases; the pylons with their sloping angles, the walls with their spreading cornices, the colossi with their hands resting on their knees, stood out, gilded by the sunbeams, their size undiminished by distance.

But the Pharaoh looked not at these proud edifices. Amid the clumps of palms and the cultivated fields, houses and painted kiosks rose here and there, standing out against the brilliant colors of the vegetation.

Under one of these roofs, on one of these terraces, no doubt, Tahoser was hiding; and by some spell he wished he could raise them or make them transparent.

Hours followed on hours. The sun had sunk behind the mountains, casting its last rays on Thebes, and the messengers had not returned. The Pharaoh preserved his motionless attitude. Night fell on the city, cool, calm, blue; the stars came out and twinkled in the deep azure. On the corner of the terrace the Pharaoh, silent, impassible, stood out dark like a basalt statue fixed upon the entablature. Several times the birds of night swept around his head ere settling on it, but terrified by his deep, slow breathing, they fled with startled wings.

From the height where he sat, the King overlooked the city lying at his feet. Out of the mass of bluish shadow uprose the obelisks with their sharp pyramidions; the pylons, giant doors traversed by rays; high cornices; the colossi rising shoulder-high above the sea of buildings; the propylæa; the pillars, with capitals swelled out like huge granite flowers; the corners of temples and of palaces, brought out by a silvery touch of light. The sacred pools spread out shimmering like polished metal; the human-headed and the ram-headed sphinxes aligned along the avenues, stretched out their hind-quarters; and the flat roofs were multiplied infinitely, white under the moonlight, in masses cut here and there into great slices by the squares and the streets. Red points studded the darkness as if the stars had let sparks fall upon the earth. These were lamps still burning in the sleeping city. Still farther, between the less crowded buildings, faintly seen shafts of palm trees waved their fans of leaves; and beyond, the contours and the shapes were merged in a vaporous immensity, for even the eagle's glance could not have reached the limits of Thebes; and on the other side old Hopi was flowing majestically towards the sea.

Soaring in sight and thought over that vast city of which he was the absolute master, the Pharaoh reflected sadly on the limits set to human power, and his desire, like a raging vulture, gnawed at his heart. He said to himself: "All these houses contain beings who at the sight of me bow their faces into the dust, to whom my will is the will of the gods. When I pass upon my golden car or in my litter borne by the oëris, virgins feel their bosoms swell as their long, timid glance follows me; the priests burn incense to me in their censers, the people wave palms and scatter flowers; the whistling of one of my arrows makes the nations tremble; and the walls of pylons huge as precipitous mountains are scarce sufficient to record my victories; the quarries can scarce furnish granite enough for my colossal statues. Yet once, in my superb satiety, I form a wish, and that wish I cannot fulfill. Timopht does not reappear. No doubt he has failed. Oh, Tahoser, Tahoser! How great is the happiness you will have to bestow on me to make up for this long waiting!"

Meanwhile the messengers, Timopht at their head, were visiting the houses, examining the roads, inquiring after the priest's daughter, describing her to the travelers they met; but no one could answer them. The first messenger appeared on the terrace and announced to the Pharaoh that Tahoser could not be found. The Pharaoh stretched out his scepter, and the messenger fell dead, in spite of the proverbial hardness of the Egyptian skull. A second came up; he stumbled against the body of his comrade stretched on the slabs; he trembled, for he saw that the Pharaoh was angry.

"What of Tahoser?" said the Pharaoh, without changing his attitude.

"O Majesty! all trace of her is lost," replied the poor wretch, kneeling in the darkness before the black shadow, which was more like a statue of Osiris than a living king.

The granite arm was outstretched from the motionless torso, and the metal scepter fell like a thunderbolt. The second messenger rolled on the ground by the side of the first.

The third shared the same fate.

Timopht, in the course of his search, reached the house of Poëri, who, having returned from his nocturnal excursion, had been amazed that morning at not seeing the sham Hora. Harphre and the servants who, the night before, had supped with her, did not know what had become of her; her room had been found empty; she had been sought for in vain through the gardens, the cellars, the granaries, and the wash-ing-places.

Poëri replied, when questioned by Timopht, that it was true that a young girl had presented herself at his gate in the supplicating posture of misfortune, imploring hospitality on her knees; that he had received her kindly; had offered her food and shelter; but that she had left in a mysterious fashion for a reason which he could not fathom. In what direction had she gone? That he did not know. No doubt, having rested, she had continued on her way to some unknown place. She was beautiful, sad, wore a garment of common stuff, and appeared to be poor. Did the name of Hora which she had given stand for that of Tahoser? It was for Timopht to answer that question.

Provided with this information, Timopht returned to the palace, and keeping well out of the reach of the Pharaoh's scepter, he repeated what he had learned.

"What did she go to Poëri's for?" said the Pharaoh to himself. "If Hora is really Tahoser, she loves Poëri. And yet, no! for she would not have fled thus, after having been received under his roof. I shall find her again, even if I have to upset the whole of Egypt from the Cataracts to the Delta."

## XI

Ra'hel, who from the threshold of the hut was watching Poëri go away, thought she heard a faint sigh. She listened; some dogs were baying to the moon, an owl uttered its doleful hoot, and the crocodiles moaned between the reeds of the river, imitating the cry of a child in distress. The young Israelite was about to reenter the hut when a more distinct moan, which could not be attributed to the vague sounds of night, and which certainly came from a human breast, again struck her ear. Fearing some ambush, she drew cautiously near the place whence came the sound, and close to the wall of the hut she perceived in the blue transparent darkness the shape of a body fallen to the ground. The wet drapery outlined the limbs of the false Hora and betrayed her sex.

Ra'hel, seeing that she had to do with a fainting woman only, lost all fear and knelt by her, questioning the breathing of her lips and the beating of her heart; the one was just expiring on the pale lips, the other scarce beat under the cold breasts.

Feeling the water which had soaked the stranger's dress, Ra'hel thought at first that it was blood, and imagined that the woman must be the victim of a murder. In order to help her to better purpose, she called Thamar, her servant, and the two women carried Tahoser into the hut. They laid her upon the couch. Thamar held up a lamp, while Ra'hel, bending over the girl, looked for the wound; but no red streak showed upon the pallor of Tahoser, and her dress had no crimson stain.

They stripped off her wet garment, and cast over her a piece of striped wool, the gentle warmth of which soon restored her suspended circulation. Tahoser slowly opened her eyes and cast around her a terrified glance like that of a captured gazelle. It took her some time to regain control of her thoughts. She could not understand how she happened to be in that room, on the bed, where but a moment ago she had seen Poëri and the young Israelite seated side by side with clasped hands, speaking of love, while she, breathless, amazed, watched through the crack of the wall; but soon memory returned, and with it the feeling of her situation.

The light fell full on Ra'hel's face. Tahoser studied it silently, grieved to find her so perfectly beautiful. In vain, with all the fierceness of feminine jealousy, she tried to note defects in her; she felt herself not vanquished, but equaled; Ra'hel was the Hebrew ideal, as Tahoser was the Egyptian. Hard though it was to her loving heart, she was compelled to admit that Poëri's love was justified and well bestowed. The eyes with their full black eyelashes, the beautiful nose, the red mouth with its dazzling smile, the long, elegant oval face, the arms, full near the shoulders and ending in childish hands, the round, plump neck which, as it turned, formed folds more beautiful than necklaces of gems, — all this, set off by a quaint, exotic dress, was sure to please.

"I made a great mistake," said Tahoser to herself, "when I presented myself to Poëri in the humble attitude of a suppliant, trusting to my charms overpraised by flatterers. Fool that I was! I acted as a soldier who should go to war without breastplate or weapons. If I had appeared in all my splendor, covered with jewels and enamels, standing on my golden car followed by my numerous slaves, I might perhaps have touched his fancy, if not his heart."

"How do you feel now?" said Ra'hel in Egyptian to Tahoser; for by the outline of the face and the dressing of the hair, she had perceived that the maiden did not belong to the Israelitish race. The sound of her voice was sympathetic and sweet, and the foreign accent added greater grace to it.

Tahoser was touched in spite of herself, and replied, "I feel better. Your kind care will soon have restored me."

"Do not tire yourself with speaking," answered the Israelite, placing her hand on Tahoser's lips. "Try to sleep, to regain your strength. Thamar and I will watch over you."

Her agitation, the swim across the Nile, the long walk through the poor quarters of Thebes, had wearied out Petamounoph's daughter; her delicate frame was exhausted, and soon her long lashes closed, forming a dark semicircle upon her cheeks flushed with fever. Sleep came to her, but broken, restless, distorted by strange dreams, troubled by threatening hallucinations; nervous shivers made the sleeper start, and broken words, replying to the dream dialogue, were spoken by the half-opened lips.

Seated at the bed head, Ra'hel followed the changes in the features of Tahoser; troubled when she saw them contract and fill with grief, quieted again when the girl calmed down. Thamar, crouching beside her mistress, was also watching the priest's daughter, but her face expressed less kindliness. Coarse instincts showed in the wrinkles of her brow, pressed down by the broad band of the Hebrew headdress; her eyes, still bright in spite of her age, sparkled with curious questionings in their brown and wrinkled orbits; her bony nose, shining and curved like a vulture's beak, seemed to scent out secrets; and her lips, slightly moving, appeared to be framing interrogations.

She was very much concerned about this stranger picked up at the door of the hut. Whence came she? How did she happen to be there? What was her purpose? Who could she be? Such were the questions which Thamar asked herself, and to which, very regretfully, she could find no satisfactory replies. Besides, Thamar, like all old women, was prejudiced against beauty, and in this respect Tahoser proved very unpleasant to her. The faithful servant forgave beauty in her mistress only; for her good looks she considered as her property, and she was proud and jealous of them.

Seeing that Ra'hel kept silence, the old woman rose and sat down near her, and winking her eyes, the brown lids of which rose and fell like a bat's wing, she whispered in the Hebrew tongue, "Mistress, nothing good will come of this woman."

"Why do you think so, Thamar?" answered Ra'hel, in the same low tone and using the same language.

"It is strange," went on the suspicious Thamar, "that she should have fainted there, and not elsewhere."

"She fell at the spot where weakness came upon her."

The old woman shook her head doubtfully.

"Do you suppose," said Poëri's beloved, "that her faint was simulated? The dissector might have cut her side with his sharp stone, so like a dead body did she seem. Her dull eyes, her pale lips, her pallid cheeks, her limp limbs, her skin as cold as that of the dead, — these things cannot be counterfeited."

"No, doubtless," replied Thamar, "although there are women clever enough to feign all these symptoms, for some reason or another, so skillfully as to deceive the most clearsighted. I believe that the maiden had swooned, as a matter of fact."

"Then what are you suspicious of?"

"How did she happen to be there in the middle of the night; in this distant quarter inhabited only by the poor captives of our tribe whom the cruel Pharaoh employs in making brick, and to whom he refuses the straw necessary to burn the bricks? What motive brought that Egyptian woman to our wretched huts? Why was her garment soaking wet, as if she had just emerged from a pool or from the river?"

"I know no more than you do," replied Ra'hel.

"Suppose she were a spy of our masters'," said the old woman, whose fierce eyes were lighted up with hatred. "Great events are preparing, — who knows whether the alarm has not been given?"

"How could that young girl, ill as she is, hurt us? She is in our hands, weak, alone, ill. Besides, we can, at the least suspicious sign, keep her prisoner until the day of deliverance."

"In any case, she is not to be trusted. See how delicate and soft are her hands!"

And old Thamar raised one of the arms of the sleeping Tahoser.

"In what respect can the fineness of her skin endanger us?"

"Oh, imprudent youth!" said Thamar; "oh, mad youth! which cannot see anything, which walks through life trustfully, without believing in ambushes, in brambles under the grass, in hot coals under the ashes, and which would gladly caress a viper, believing it to be only a snake. Open your eyes!

That woman does not belong to the class of which she seems to be; her thumb has never been flattened on the thread of the spindle, and that little hand, softened by essences and pomades, has never worked. Her poverty is a disguise."

Thamar's words appeared to impress Ra'hel; she examined Tahoser more attentively. The lamp shed upon her its trembling rays, and the delicate form of the priest's daughter showed in the yellow light relaxed in sleep. The arm which Thamar had raised still rested upon the mantle of striped wool, showing whiter by contrast with the dark stuff; the wrist was circled with a bracelet of sandal wood, the commonplace adornment of the coquetry of poverty; but if the ornament was rude and roughly chased, the flesh it covered seemed to have been washed in the perfumed bath of riches. Then Ra'hel saw how beautiful was Tahoser, but the discovery excited no evil feeling in her heart; Tahoser's beauty softened, instead of irritating her as it did Thamar; she could not believe that such perfection concealed a vile and perfidious soul; and in this respect her youthful candor judged more correctly than the long experience of her maid.

Day at last dawned, and Tahoser's fever grew worse. She was delirious at times, and then would fall into a prolonged slumber.

"If she were to die here," said Thamar, "we should be accused of having killed her."

"She will not die," replied Ra'hel, putting a cup of cool water to the lips of the sick girl.

"If she does, I shall throw her body by night into the Nile," continued the obstinate Thamar, "and the crocodiles will undertake to make it disappear."

The day passed, the night came, and at the accustomed hour Poëri, having given the usual signal, appeared as he had done the night before on the threshold of the hut.

Ra'hel came to meet him, her finger on her lips, and signed to him to keep silence and to speak low, for Tahoser was sleeping. Poëri, whom Ra'hel led by the hand to the bed on which Tahoser rested, at once recognized the sham Hora, whose disappearance had preoccupied him a good deal, especially since the visit of Timopht, who was looking for her in his master's name.

Marked astonishment showed in his face as he rose, after
having bent over the bed to make quite certain that the young
girl who lay there was the one whom he had welcomed, for
he could not understand how she happened to be in this
place. His look of surprise smote Ra'hel to the heart. She
stood in front of Poëri to read the truth in his eyes, placed
her hands upon his shoulders, and fixing her glance upon
him, said, in a dry, sharp voice which contrasted with her
speech, usually as gentle as the cooing of a dove, —

"So you know her?"

Thamar grinned with satisfaction; she was proud of her
perspicacity, and almost glad to see her suspicions as regarded
the stranger partially justified.

"Yes," replied Poëri, quietly.

The bright eyes of the old woman sparkled with malicious
curiosity.

Ra'hel's face resumed its expression of trustfulness; she no
longer doubted her lover.

Poëri told her that a girl calling herself Hora had presented
herself at his home as a suppliant; that he had received her
as any guest should be received; that the next day she had
disappeared from among the maids, and that he could not
understand how she happened to be there. He also added that
the emissaries of the Pharaoh were everywhere looking for
Tahoser, the daughter of the high priest Petamounoph, who
had disappeared from her palace.

"You see that I was right, mistress," said Thamar, trium-
phantly. "Hora and Tahoser are one and the same person."

"That may be," replied Poëri, "but there are a number of
difficulties which my reason does not explain. First, why
should Tahoser, if it is she, don this disguise? Next, by what
miracle do I meet here the maiden whom I left last night on
the other bank of the Nile, and who certainly could not know
whither I was going?"

"No doubt she followed you," said Ra'hel.

"I am quite sure that at that time there was no other boat
on the river but mine."

"That is the reason her hair was so dripping-wet and her
garments soaked. She must have swum across the Nile."

"That may well be, — I thought for a moment that I had caught sight in the darkness of a human head above the waters."

"It was she, poor child!" said Ra'hel; "her fatigue and her fainting corroborate it, for after your departure I picked her up stretched senseless outside the hut."

"No doubt that is the way things occurred," said the young man. "I can see the acts, but I cannot understand the motive."

"Let me explain it," said Ra'hel, smiling, "although I am but a poor, ignorant woman, and you are compared, as regards your vast knowledge, to the priests of Egypt who study night and day within sanctuaries covered with mystic hieroglyphs, the hidden meaning of which they alone can penetrate. But sometimes men, who are so busy with astronomy, music, and numbers, do not guess what goes on in a maiden's heart. They can see a distant star in the heavens; they do not notice a love close to them. Hora — or rather, Tahoser, for it is she — took this disguise to penetrate into your house and to live near you; jealous, she glided in the shadow behind you; at the risk of being devoured by the crocodiles in the river she swam across the Nile. On arriving here she watched us through some crack in the wall, and was unable to bear the sight of our happiness. She loves you because you are very handsome, very strong, and very gentle. But I do not care, since you do not love her. Now do you understand?"

A faint blush colored Poëri's cheeks; he feared lest Ra'hel were angry and spoke thus to entrap him, but her clear, pure glance betrayed no hidden thought. She was not angry with Tahoser for loving the man whom she loved herself.

In her dreams Tahoser saw Poëri standing by her; ecstatic joy lighted up her features, and half raising herself, she seized the hand of the young man to bear it to her lips.

"Her lips are burning," said Poëri, withdrawing his hand.

"With love as much as with fever," replied Ra'hel, "but she is really ill. Suppose Thamar were to fetch Mosche. He is wiser than the wise men and the wizards of Pharaoh, every one of whose wonders he imitates. He knows the secret properties of plants, and makes drinks of them which would bring the dead to life. He shall cure Tahoser, for I am not cruel enough to wish her to lose her life."

Thamar went off grumbling, and soon returned, followed by a very tall old man, whose majestic aspect inspired reverence. A long white beard fell down over his breast, and on either side of his brow two huge protuberances caught and retained the light. They looked like two horns or two beams. Under his thick eyebrows his eyes shone like fire. He looked, in spite of his simple dress, like a prophet or a god.

Acquainted with the state of things by Poëri, he sat down by Tahoser's couch, and said, as he stretched his hand over her: "In the name of the Mighty One beside whom all other gods are idols and demons, — though you do not belong to the elect of the Lord, — maiden, be cured!"

## XII

*T*he tall old man withdrew solemnly, leaving, as it were, a trail of light behind him. Tahoser, surprised at feeling her sickness suddenly leave her, cast her eyes around the room, and soon, wrapping herself in the blanket with which the young Israelite had covered her, she put her feet to the ground and sat up on the edge of the bed. Fatigue and fever had completely left her; she was as fresh as after a long rest, and her beauty shone in all its purity. Pushing back with her little hands the plaited masses of her hair behind her ears, she showed her face lighted up with love, as if she desired Poëri to read it; but seeing that he remained motionless near Ra'hel without encouraging her by a sign or a glance, she rose slowly, drew near the young Israelite girl, and threw her arms around her neck. She remained thus, her head in Ra'hel's bosom, wetting it with her hot tears. Sometimes a sob she could not repress shook her convulsively upon her rival's breast.

The complete yielding up of herself, and her evident misery, touched Ra'hel. Tahoser confessed herself beaten, and implored her pity by mute supplication, appealing to her womanly generosity.

Ra'hel, much moved, kissed her and said, —

"Dry your tears and be not so sorrowful. You love Poëri? Well, love him, and I shall not be jealous. Yacoub, a patriarch of our race, had two wives; one was called Ra'hel as I am, and the other Leah. Yacoub preferred Ra'hel, and yet Leah, who was not beautiful like you, lived happily with him."

Tahoser knelt at Ra'hel's feet and kissed her hand. Ra'hel raised her and put her arm around her waist. They formed a charming group, these two women of different races, exhibiting, as they did, the characteristic beauty of each: Tahoser elegant, graceful, and slender, like a child that has grown too fast; Ra'hel dazzling, blooming, and superb in her precocious maturity.

"Tahoser," said Poëri, "for that is your name, I think, — Tahoser, daughter of the high priest Petamounoph?"

The young girl nodded assent.

"How is it that you, who live in Thebes in a rich palace, surrounded by slaves, and whom the handsomest among the Egyptians desire, — how is it you have chosen to love me, a son of a race reduced to slavery, a stranger who does not share your religious beliefs and who is separated from you by so great a distance?"

Ra'hel and Tahoser smiled, and the high priest's daughter replied, —

"That is the very reason."

"Although I enjoy the favor of the Pharaoh, although I am the steward of his domains and wear gilded horns in the festivals of agriculture, I cannot rise to you. In the eyes of the Egyptians I am but a slave, and you belong to the priestly caste, the highest and most venerated. If you love me — and I cannot doubt that you do — you must give up your rank."

"Have I not already become your servant? Hora kept nothing of Tahoser, not even the enameled collars and the transparent gauze calasiris; that is why you thought me ugly."

"You will have to give up your country and follow me to unknown regions, through the desert where burns the sun, where blows the fire-wind, where the moving sand tangles and effaces the paths, where no tree grows, where no well springs, through the lost valleys of death strewn with whitened bones that mark the way."

"I shall go," said Tahoser, quietly.

"That is not all," continued Poëri. "Your gods are not mine, — your gods of brass, basalt, and granite, fashioned by the hand of man, your monstrous idols with heads of eagle, monkey, ibis, cow, jackal, and lion, which assume the faces of beasts as if they were troubled by the human face on which rests the reflection of Jehovah. It is said, 'Thou shalt worship neither stone nor wood nor metal.' Within these temples cemented with the blood of oppressed races grin and crouch the hideous, foul demons which usurp the libations, the offerings, and the sacrifices. One only God, infinite, eternal, formless, colorless, fills the immensity of the heavens which you people with a multitude of phantoms. Our God has created us; you have created your gods."

Although Tahoser was deeply in love with Poëri, his words affected her strangely, and she drew back in terror. The daughter of the high priest had been brought up to venerate the gods whom the young Hebrew was boldly blaspheming; she had offered up on their altars bouquets of flowers, and she had burned perfumes before their impassible images; amazed and delighted, she had walked through their temples splendid with brilliant paintings. She had seen her father performing the mysterious rites; she had followed the procession of priests who bore the symbolic bari through the enormous pylons and the endless sphinx avenues; she had admired tremblingly the psychostasis where the trembling soul appears before Osiris armed with the whip and the pedum, and she had noted with a dreamy glance the frescoes representing the emblematic figures traveling towards the regions of the West. She could not thus yield up all her beliefs. She was silent for a few moments, hesitating between religion and love. Love won the day, and she said:

"You shall tell me of your God; I will try to understand him."

"It is well," said Poëri; "you shall be my wife. Meanwhile remain here, for the Pharaoh, no doubt in love with you, is having you sought everywhere by his emissaries. He will never discover you under this humble roof, and in a few days we shall be out of his power. But the night is waning and I must depart."

Poëri went off, and the two young women, lying side by side on the soft bed, soon fell asleep, holding each other's hands like two sisters.

Thamar, who during the foregoing scene had remained crouched in her corner of the room, looking like a bat hanging from a corner by its talons, and had been muttering broken words and frowning, now unfolded her bony limbs, rose to her feet, and bending over the bed, listened to the breathing of the two sleepers. When the regularity of their breathing convinced her that they were sound asleep, she went towards the door, walking with infinite precaution. Once outside, she sprang with swift steps in the direction of the Nile, shaking off the dogs who hung on with their teeth at the edge of her tunic, or dragging them through the dust until they let go; or she glared at them with such fierce eyes that they drew back with frightened yelps and let her pass by.

She had soon passed the dangerous and deserted places inhabited at night by the members of the thieves' association, and entered the wealthy quarter of Thebes. Three or four streets bordered with tall buildings, the shadows of which fell in great angles, led her to the outer wall of the palace, which was the object of her trip. The difficulty was to enter, — no easy matter at that time of the night for an old Hebrew servant with dusty feet and shabby garments.

She went to the main pylon, before which watched, stretched at length, fifty ram-headed sphinxes, arranged in two lines like monsters ready to crush between their granite jaws the imprudent ones who should attempt to force a passage. The sentinels stopped her, struck her roughly with the shafts of their javelins, and then asked her what she wished.

"I want to see the Pharaoh," replied the old woman, rubbing her back.

"That's right, — very nice! Waken for this witch the Pharaoh, favorite of Phré, beloved of Ammon Ra, the destroyer of nations!" said the soldiers, laughing loudly.

Thamar repeated obstinately, "I want to see the Pharaoh at once."

"A very good time you have chosen for it! The Pharaoh slew but a short time ago three messengers with a blow of his scepter. He sits on his terrace, motionless and sinister like Typhon, the god of evil," said a soldier who condescended to give this explanation.

Ra'hel's maid endeavored to force her way through; the javelins rattled on her head like hammers on an anvil. She began to yell like a bird plucked alive.

An officer came out on hearing the tumult; the soldiers stopped beating Thamar.

"What does this woman want?" said the officer, "and why are you beating her in this way?"

"I want to see the Pharaoh," cried Thamar, dragging herself to the knees of the officer.

"Out of the question," replied the latter; "it is out of the question, — even if, instead of being a low wretch, you were one of the greatest personages in the kingdom."

"I know where is Tahoser," whispered the old woman in his ear, laying stress on each syllable.

On hearing this, the officer took Thamar by the hand, led her through the first pylon and through the avenue of pillars and the hypostyle hall into a second court, where rose the granite sanctuary, with its two outer columns with lotus capitals. There, calling Timopht, he handed Thamar over to him.

Timopht led the servant to the terrace where sat the Pharaoh, gloomy and silent.

"Keep well out of the reach of his scepter," was the advice Timopht gave to the Israelite.

As soon as she perceived the King through the darkness, Thamar threw herself with her face to the stone flags, by the side of the bodies which had not yet been removed, and then sitting up, she said in a firm voice, "O Pharaoh, do not slay me, I bring you good news."

"Speak without fear," replied the King, whose fury had passed away.

"Tahoser, whom your messengers have sought in the four corners of the world, — I know where she is."

At the name of Tahoser, Pharaoh rose as if moved by a spring and stepped towards Thamar, who was still kneeling.

"If you speak the truth, you may take from my granite halls as much as you can lift of gold and precious stones."

"I will put her in your hands, you may be sure," said the old woman, with a strident laugh.

What was the motive which had led Thamar to inform the Pharaoh of the retreat where the priest's daughter was in hiding?

She wished to prevent a union which she disliked. She entertained towards the race of Egypt, a blind, fierce, unreasoning, almost bestial hatred, and the thought of breaking Tahoser's heart delighted her. Once in the hands of the Pharaoh, Ra'hel's rival would be unable to escape; the granite walls of the palace would keep their prey.

"Where is she?" said Pharaoh; "tell me the spot. I want to see her at once."

"Your Majesty, I alone can guide you. I know the windings of those loathsome quarters, where the humblest of your servants would disdain to set foot. Tahoser is there, in a clay and straw hut which nothing marks from the huts which surround it, amid the heaps of bricks which the Hebrews make for you outside the regular dwellings of the city."

"Very well, I will trust you. Timopht, have a chariot brought around."

Timopht disappeared. Soon the wheels were heard rolling over the stones of the court, and the horses stamping and pawing as the equerries fastened them to the yoke.

The Pharaoh came down, followed by Thamar. He sprang up on the chariot, took the reins, and seeing that Thamar hesitated, —

"Come, get up," he said.

He clucked his tongue, and the horses started. The awakened echoes gave back the sound of the wheels, which sounded like low thunder through the vast halls, in the midst of the night silence. The hideous old woman, clinging with her bony fingers to the rim of the chariot by the side of the godlike Pharaoh, presented a strange sight, which fortunately was seen by none but the stars twinkling in the deep blue heavens. She resembled one of the evil genii of mysterious face which accompany the guilty souls to Hades.

"Is this the way?" said the Pharaoh to the woman at the forks of a street.

"Yes," replied Thamar, stretching her withered hand in the right direction.

The horses, urged on by the whip, sprang forward, and the chariot leaped upon the stones with a noise of brass.

Meanwhile Tahoser slept by the side of Ra'hel. A strange dream filled her sleep. She seemed to be in a temple of immense size. Huge columns of prodigious height upbore the blue ceiling studded with stars like the heavens; innumerable lines of hieroglyphs ascended and descended along the walls between the panels of symbolic frescoes painted in bright colors. All the gods of Egypt had met in this universal sanctuary, not as brass, basalt, or porphyry effigies, but as living shapes. In the first rank were seated the gods Knef, Buto, Phtah, Pan-Mendes, Hathor, Phré, Isis; then came the twelve celestial gods, — six male gods: Rempha, Pi-Zeous, Ertosi, Pi-Hermes, Imuthi; and six female deities: the Moon, Ether, Fire, Air, Water, Earth. Behind these swarmed vaguely and indistinctly three hundred and sixty-five Decans, the familiar dæmons of each day. Next appeared the terrestrial deities: the second Osiris, Haroeri, Typhon, the second Isis, Nephthys, the dog-headed Anubis, Thoth, Busiris, Bubastis, the great Serapis. Beyond, in the shade, were faintly seen idols in form of animals, — oxen, crocodiles, ibises, hippopotami. In the center of the temple, in his open mummy-case, lay the high priest Petamounoph, who, the bandages having been unwound from his face, gazed with an ironical air at that strange and mysterious assembly. He was dead, not living, and spoke, as it often happens in dreams; and he said to his daughter, "Question them and ask them if they are gods."

And Tahoser proceeded to put to each one that question, and each and all replied: "We are only numbers, laws, forces, attributes, effluvia, and thoughts of God, but not one of us is the true God."

Then Poëri appeared on the threshold of the temple, and took Tahoser by the hand and led her to a light so brilliant that in comparison with it the sun would have seemed black, and in the center of which blazed in a triangle words unknown to her.

Meanwhile Pharaoh's chariot flew over all obstacles, and the axles of the wheels rayed the walls in the narrow lanes.

"Pull in your horses," said Thamar to the Pharaoh; "the noise of the wheels in this solitude and silence might startle the fugitive, and she would again escape you."

The Pharaoh thought this advice sound, and in spite of his impatience made his horses slacken their impetuous pace.

"There is the place," said Thamar; "I left the door open. Go in. I shall look after the horses."

The king descended from the chariot, and bowing his head, entered the hut. The lamp was still burning, and shed its dying beams on the two sleeping girls. The Pharaoh caught up Tahoser in his strong arms and walked towards the door of the hut.

When the priest's daughter awoke, and saw flaming near her face the shining face of the Pharaoh, she thought at first that it was one of the fancies of her dream transformed; but the air of night which struck her face soon restored her to the sense of reality. Mad with terror, she tried to scream, to call for help; the cry remained in her throat, — and then, who would have helped her against the Pharaoh?

With one bound the King sprang on to his chariot, threw the reins around his back, and pressing to his breast the half-dead Tahoser, sent his coursers at their top speed towards the Northern Palace.

Thamar glided like a serpent into the hut, crouched down in her accustomed place, and gazed with a look almost as tender as a mother's on her dear Ra'hel, who was still sound asleep.


## XIII


*T*he draft of cold air, due to the speed of the chariot, soon made Tahoser recover from her faint. Pressed and crushed against the breast of the Pharaoh, by his two stony arms, her heart had scarce room to beat, and the hard enameled collars were making their mark on her heaving bosom. The horses, whose reins the King slackened by bending towards the front of the car, rushed furiously forward, the wheels went round like whirlwinds, the brazen plates justled, the heated axles smoked. Tahoser, terrified, saw vaguely, as in a dream, flash to the right and left vast masses of buildings, clumps of trees, palaces, temples, pylons, obelisks, colossi, which the night made more fantastic and terrible. What were the thoughts that filled her mind during that mad rush? She thought as little as thinks a dove, fluttering in the talons of a hawk which is carrying it away to its aerie. Mute terror stupefied her, made her blood run cold and dulled her feelings. Her limbs hung limp; her will was relaxed like her muscles, and, had she not been held firmly in the arms of the Pharaoh, she would have slipped and fallen in a heap on the bottom of the chariot like a piece of stuff which is let drop. Twice she thought she felt upon her cheek a burning breath and two lips of fire; she did not attempt to turn away her head, terror had killed modesty in her. When the chariot struck violently against a stone, a dim instinct of self-preservation made her cling with her hands to the shoulder of the King and press closer to him; then she let herself go again and leaned with her whole weight, light though it was, upon those arms which held her.

The chariot entered the avenue of sphinxes, at the end of which rose a giant pylon crowned with a cornice on which the symbolic globe displayed its wings; the lessening darkness allowed the priest's daughter to recognize the King's palace. Then despair filled her heart; she struggled, she strove to free herself from the embrace which held her close; she pressed her frail hands against the stony breast of the Pharaoh, stiffened out her arms, throwing herself back over the edge of the chariot. Her efforts were useless, her struggles were vain. Her ravisher brought her back to his breast with an irresistible, slow pressure, as if he would have driven her into it. She tried to scream; her lips were closed with a kiss.

Meanwhile the horses in three or four strides reached the pylon, under which they passed at full gallop, glad to return to the stable, and the chariot rolled into the vast court. The servants hastened up and sprang to the heads of the horses, whose bits were white with foam.

Tahoser cast a terrified glance around her. High brick walls formed a vast square enclosure in which rose on the east a palace, on the west a temple, between two great pools, the piscinæ of the sacred crocodiles. The first rays of the sun, the orb of which was already rising behind the Arabian mountains, flushed with rosy light the top of the buildings, the lower portions of which were still plunged in bluish shadows.

There was no hope of flight. The buildings, though in no wise gloomy, had a look of irresistible strength, of absolute will, of eternal persistence: a world catastrophe alone could have opened an issue through these thick walls, through these piles of hard sandstone. To overthrow the pylons built of fragments of mountains, the earth itself would have had to quake; even a conflagration could only have licked with its fiery tongues those indestructible blocks.

Poor Tahoser did not have at her command such violent means, and she was compelled to allow herself to be carried like a child by the Pharaoh, who had sprung from his chariot.

Four high columns with palm-leaf capitals formed the propylæum of the palace into which the king entered, still pressing to his breast the daughter of Petamounoph. When he had passed through the door, he gently placed his burden on the ground, and seeing Tahoser stagger, he said to her: "Be reassured. You rule the Pharaoh, and the Pharaoh rules the world."

These were the first words he had spoken to her.

If love followed the dictates of reason, Tahoser would certainly have preferred the Pharaoh to Poëri. The King was endowed with supreme beauty. His great, clean, regular features seemed to be chiseled, and not the slightest imperfection could be detected in them. The habit of command had given to his glance that penetrating gleam which makes divinities and kings so easily recognizable. His lips, one word from which would have changed the face of the world and the fate of nations, were of a purple red, like fresh blood upon the blade of a sword, and when he smiled, they possessed that grace of terrible things which nothing can resist. His tall, well proportioned, majestic figure presented the nobility of form admired in the temple statues; and when he appeared solemn and radiant, covered with gold, enamels, and gems, in the midst of the bluish vapor of the censers, he did not seem to belong to that frail race which from generation to generation falls like leaves, and is stretched, sticky with bitumen, in the dark depths of the mummy pits.

What was poor Poëri by the side of this demigod? Nevertheless, Tahoser loved him.

The wise have long since given up attempting to explain the heart of woman. They are masters of astronomy, astrology, and arithmetic; they know the origin of the world, and can tell where were the planets at the very moment of creation; they are sure that the moon was then in the constellation of Cancer, the sun in that of the Lion, Mercury in that of the Virgin, Venus in the Balance, Mars in the Scorpion, Jupiter in Sagittarius, Saturn in Capricorn; they trace on papyrus or granite the direction of the celestial ocean, which goes from the east to the west; they have summed up the number of stars strewn over the blue robe of the Goddess Neith, and make the sun travel in the lower or the superior hemisphere with the twelve diurnal and the twelve nocturnal baris under the conduct of the hawk-headed pilot and of Neb Wa, the Lady of the Bark; they know that in the second half of the month of Tobi, Orion influences the left ear, and Sirius the heart; but they are absolutely ignorant why a woman prefers one man to another, a wretched Israelite to an illustrious Pharaoh.

After having traversed several halls with Tahoser, whom he led by the hand, the King sat down on a seat in the shape of a throne in a superbly decorated room.

Golden stars gleamed in the blue ceiling, and against the pillars which supported the cornice were placed the statues of kings wearing the pschent, their legs merging into the block of stone and their arms crossed on their chest, looking into the room with frightful intensity out of their black-lined eyes. Between every two pillars burned a lamp placed upon a pedestal, and on the base of the walls was represented a sort of ethnographic procession: the nations of the four quarters of the world were represented there with their particular faces and their particular dress.

At the head of the series, guided by Horus the shepherd of the nations, walked the man of men, the Egyptian, the

Rot'en'no with a gentle face, slightly aquiline nose, plaited hair, and his dark red skin brought out by the whiteness of the loin-cloth; next came the Negro or Nahasi, with his black skin, thick lips, protruding cheekbones and woolly hair; then the Asiatic or Namou, with yellow flesh-color, strongly aquiline nose, thick black beard cut to a point, wearing a striped skirt fringed with tufts; then the European or Tamhou, the least civilized of all, differing from the others by his white complexion, his red beard and hair, his blue eyes, an undressed ox-skin cast over his shoulder, and his arms and legs tattooed. The other panels were filled with various subjects, scenes of war and triumph and hieroglyphic inscriptions.

In the center of the room, on a table supported by prisoners bound by the elbows, so skillfully carved that they seemed to live and suffer, bloomed a vast bouquet of flowers whose sweet scent perfumed the atmosphere.

So in this vast hall, surrounded by the effigies of his ancestors, all things spoke and sang of the glory of the Pharaoh. The nations of the world walked behind Egypt and acknowledged her supremacy, and he governed Egypt. Yet the daughter of Petamounoph, far from being dazzled by this splendor, thought of the rustic villa, of Poëri, and especially of the mean hut of mud and straw in the Hebrew quarter, where she had left Ra'hel, — Ra'hel, from henceforward the happy and only spouse of the young Hebrew.

The Pharaoh held the tips of the fingers of Tahoser, who stood before him, and he fixed upon her his hawk eyes, the eyelids of which never moved. The young girl had no other garment than the drapery substituted by Ra'hel for the dress which had been soaked during the swim across the Nile, but her beauty was in no wise impaired. She remained thus, half nude, holding with one hand the coarse stuff which slipped, and the whole upper portion of her beautiful body appeared in its golden fairness. When she was adorned with her jewels, one was tempted to regret that any part of her form should be concealed by her necklaces, her bracelets, and her belts of gold or of gems; but on seeing her thus devoid of all ornament, admiration was satisfied, or rather exalted. Certainly many very beautiful women had entered the Pharaoh's harem, but not one of them comparable to Tahoser; and the eyes of the King flashed such burning glances that, unable to bear their brilliancy, she was obliged to cast down her eyes.

In her heart, Tahoser was proud of having excited love in the Pharaoh; for who is the woman, however perfect she may be, who has not some vanity. Yet she would have preferred to follow the young Hebrew into the desert. The King terrified her, she felt herself dazzled by the splendor of his face, and her limbs gave way under her.

The Pharaoh noticed her emotion, and made her sit down at his feet on a red cushion adorned with tufts.

"Oh, Tahoser," he said, kissing her hair, "I love you. When I saw you from the top of my triumphal palanquin, borne higher than the heads of men by the generals, an unknown feeling entered into my soul. I, whose every desire is fore-stalled, desired something; I understood that I was not every-thing. Until then I had lived solitary in my almightiness, in the depths of my vast palaces, surrounded by mere shadows which called themselves women, and who had no more effect upon me than the painted figures in the frescoes. I heard in the distance, muttering and complaining low, the nations upon whose heads I wipe my sandals or which I lift by their hair, as I am represented doing on the symbolical *bassi-relievi* of the palaces, and in my cold breast, as strong as that of a basalt god, I never heard the beat of my own heart. It seemed to me that there was nowhere on earth a being like myself, a being who could move me. In vain I brought back from my expeditions into foreign lands choice virgins and women famous for their beauty in their own country; I cast them aside like flowers, after having breathed their scent for a moment. None inspired me with a desire to see her again. When they were present, I scarce glanced at them; when they were absent, I immediately forgot them. Twea, Taïa, Amense, Hont-Reché, whom I have kept to avoid the disgust of having to find others who the next day would have been as indiffer-ent as themselves, have never been, when in my arms, aught but vain phantoms, perfumed and graceful forms, beings of another race with whom my nature could not mingle any-more than the leopard can mate with the gazelle, the dweller in the air with the dweller in the waters. I had come to think that, placed by the gods apart from and above all mortals, I was never to share either their pains or their joys. Fearful weariness, like that which no doubt tires the mummies, who, wrapped up in their bands, wait in their caves in the depths of the hypogea until the soul shall have finished the cycle of migrations, — a fearful weariness had fallen upon me on my throne; for I often remained with my hands on my knees like a granite colossus, thinking of the impossible, the infinite, the eternal. How many a time have I thought of raising the veil of Isis, at the risk of falling blasted at the feet of the goddess. Perhaps, I said to myself, that mysterious face is the one I have been dreaming of, the one which is to inspire me with love. If earth refuses me happiness, I shall climb to heaven. But I saw you; I felt a strange, unaccustomed sensation; I understood that there existed outside myself a being necessary, imperious, and fatal to me, whom I could not live without, and who possessed the power of making me unhappy. I was a king, almost a god, and you, O Tahoser, have made of me a man."

Never, perhaps, had the Pharaoh uttered so long a speech; usually a word, a gesture, a motion of the eye sufficed to manifest his will, which was immediately divined by a thousand attentive, restless eyes; performance followed his thought, as the lightning follows the thunder-clap. But with desire he seemed to have given up his granitic majesty; he spoke and explained himself like a mortal.

Tahoser was a prey to singular emotion. However much she felt the honor of having inspired love in the man preferred of Phré, in the favored of Ammon Ra, the destroyer of nations, in the terrifying, solemn and superb being upon whom she scarce dared to gaze, she felt no sympathy for him, and the idea of belonging to him filled her with terror and repulsion. To the Pharaoh who had carried off her body she could not give her soul, which had remained with Poëri and Ra'hel; and as the King appeared to await a reply, she said, —

"How is it, O King, that amid all the maids of Egypt your glance should have fallen on me, — on me whom so many others surpass in beauty, in talent, in gifts of all sorts? How is it that in the midst of clumps of white, blue, and rose lotus, with open corollas, with delicate scent, you have chosen the modest blade of grass which nothing marks?"

"I know not, but I know that you alone exist in this world for me, and that I shall make kings' daughters your servants."

"But suppose I do not love you?" said Tahoser, timidly.

"What care I, if I love you," replied the Pharaoh. "Have not the most beautiful women in the world thrown themselves down upon my threshold weeping and moaning, tearing their cheeks, beating their breasts, plucking out their hair, and have they not died imploring a glance of love which never fell upon them? Never has passion in anyone made my heart of brass beat within my stony breast. Resist me, hate if you will, — you will only be more charming; for the first time an obstacle will have come in the way of my will, and I shall know how to overcome it."

"But suppose I love another?" continued Tahoser, more boldly.

At this suggestion the eyebrows of the Pharaoh were bent; he violently bit his lower lip, in which his teeth left white marks, and he pressed to the point of hurting her the fingers of the maid which he still held. Then he cooled down again, and said in a low, deep voice, —

"When you shall have lived in this palace, in the midst of these splendors, surrounded by the atmosphere of my love, you will forget everything as does he who eats nepenthe. Your past life will appear to you like a dream, your former feelings will vanish as incense upon the coals of the censer. The woman who is loved by the King no longer remembers men. Go, come; accustom yourself to Pharaonic magnificence; help yourself as you please to my treasures; make gold flow, heap up gems; order, make, unmake, raise, destroy; be my mistress, my wife, my queen. I give you Egypt with its priests, its armies, its toilers, its numberless population, its palaces, its temples and cities. Crumple it up as you would crumple up gauze, — I will win other kingdoms for you, larger, fairer, and richer. If the world is not sufficient, I will conquer planets for you, I will dethrone the gods. You are she whom I love; Tahoser, the daughter of Petamounoph is no more."

## XIV

*W*hen Ra'hel awoke, she was amazed not to find Tahoser by her side, and cast her glance around the room, thinking the Egyptian had already risen. Crouching in a corner, her arms crossed on her knees, her head upon her arms, which formed a bony pillow, Thamar slept, — or rather, pretended to sleep; for through the long locks of her disordered hair which fell to the ground, might have been seen her eyes as yellow as those of an owl, gleaming with malicious joy and satisfied wickedness.

"Thamar," cried Ra'hel, "what has become of Tahoser?"

The old woman, as if startled into wakefulness by the voice of her mistress, slowly uncoiled her spiderlike limbs, rose to her feet, rubbed several times her brown eyelids with the back of her left hand, yellower than that of a mummy, and said with a well assumed air of astonishment: "Is she not there?"

"No," replied Ra'hel; "and did I not yet see her place hollowed out on the bed by the side of my own, and hanging on that peg the gown which she threw off, I could believe that the strange events of the past night were but an illusion and a dream."

Though she was perfectly well aware of the manner of Tahoser's disappearance, Thamar raised a piece of the drapery stretched in the corner of the room, as if the Egyptian might have been concealed behind it. She opened the door of the hut and standing on the threshold minutely explored the neighborhood with her glance; then turning towards the interior, she signed negatively to her mistress.

"It is strange," said Ra'hel, thoughtfully.

"Mistress," said the old woman, drawing near the Israelite, with a gentle, petting tone, "you know that I disliked the foreign woman."

"You dislike everyone, Thamar," replied Ra'hel, smiling.

"Except you, mistress," answered the old woman, placing to her lips one of the young woman's hands.

"I know it. You are devoted to me."

"I never had any children, and sometimes I fancy that I am your mother."

"Good Thamar," said Ra'hel, moved.

"Was I wrong," continued Thamar, "to consider her appearance so strange? Her disappearance explains it. She said she was Tahoser, the daughter of Petamounoph. She was nothing but a fiend which took that form to seduce and tempt a child of Israel. Did you see how troubled she was when Poëri spoke against the idols of wood, stone, and metal, and how difficult it was for her to say, 'I will try to believe in your God'? It seemed as though the words burned her lips like hot coals."

"The tears which fell upon my breast were genuine tears, — a woman's tears," said Ra'hel.

"Crocodiles weep when they want, and hyenas laugh to attract their prey," continued the old woman. "The evil spirits which prowl at night in the stones and ruins know many a trick and play every part."

"So, according to you, poor Tahoser was nothing but a phantom raised up by hell?"

"Unquestionably," replied Thamar. "Is it likely that the daughter of the priest Petamounoph would have fallen in love with Poëri and preferred him to the Pharaoh, who, it is said, loves her?"

Ra'hel, who did not admit that anyone in the world was superior to Poëri, did not think this unlikely.

"If she loved him as much as she said she did, why did she run off when, with your consent, he accepted her as his second wife? It was the condition that she must renounce the false gods and adore Jehovah which put to flight that devil in disguise."

"In any case, that devil had a very sweet voice and very tender eyes."

At bottom Ra'hel was perhaps not greatly dissatisfied with the disappearance of Tahoser; she thus kept wholly to herself the heart which she had been willing to share, and yet she had the merit of the sacrifice she had made.

Under pretext of going to the market, Thamar went out and started for the King's palace, her cupidity not having allowed her to forget his promise. She had provided herself with a great bag of coarse cloth which she proposed to fill with gold.

When she appeared at the palace gate the soldiers did not beat her as they had done the first day. She enjoyed the king's favor, and the officer of the guard made her enter at once. Timopht brought her to the Pharaoh.

When he perceived the vile old hag crawling towards his throne like a crushed insect, the King remembered his promise and gave orders to open one of the granite chambers of the treasury, and to allow her to take as much gold as she could carry away. Timopht, whom Pharaoh trusted, and who knew the secret of the lock, opened the stone gate.

The vast mass of gold sparkled in the sunbeams, but the brilliancy of the metal was no brighter than the glance of the old woman. Her eyes turned yellow and flashed strangely. After a few moments of dazzled contemplation, she pulled up the sleeves of her patched tunic and bared her withered arms, on which the muscles stood out like cords, and which were deeply wrinkled above the elbow; then she opened and closed her curved fingers, like the talons of a griffin, and sprang at the mass of golden bars with fierce and bestial avidity. She plunged her arms amid the ingots, moved them, stirred them round, rolled them over, threw them up; her lips trembled, her nostrils swelled, and down her spine ran convulsive tremors. Intoxicated, mad, shaken by trepidation and spasmodic laughter, she cast handfuls of gold into her bag, saying, "More! more! more!" so that soon it was full up to the mouth.

Timopht, amused at the sight, let her have her way, not dreaming that such a skinny specter could move so enormous a weight. But Thamar bound the mouth of her sack with a cord, and to the great surprise of the Egyptian, lifted it on her back. Avarice lent to that broken-down frame unexpected strength of muscles; all the nerves and fibers of the arms, the neck, the shoulders, strained to breaking, bore up under a mass of metal which would have made the most robust Nahasi porter bow down. Her brows bent, like those of an ox when the plowshare strikes a stone, Thamar staggered out of the palace, knocking up against the walls, walking almost on all-fours, for every now and then she put her hands out to save herself from being crushed under her burden. But at last she got out, and the load of gold was her legitimate property. Breathless, exhausted, covered with sweat, her back bruised and her fingers cut, she sat down at the palace gate upon her beloved sack, and never did any seat appear to her so soft. After a short time, she perceived a couple of Israelites, passing by with a litter on which they had been bearing a burden. She called them, and promising them a handsome reward, induced them to take up the sack and to follow her. The Israelites, preceded by Thamar, went down the streets of Thebes, reached the waste places studded with mud huts and placed the sack in one of them. Thamar paid them grumblingly the promised reward.

Meanwhile Tahoser had been installed in a splendid apartment, a regal apartment as beautiful as that of the Pharaoh. Elegant pillars with lotus capitals upbore the starry roof, framed in by a cornice of blue palm-branches painted upon a golden background. Panels of a tender lilac-color with green lines ending in flower buds showed symmetrically on the walls; fine matting covered the stone slabs of the flooring; sofas, inlaid with plates of metal alternating with enamels, and covered with black stuffs adorned with red circles, arm-chairs with lions' feet, with cushions that fell over the back, stools formed of swans' necks interlaced, piles of purple leather cushions filled with thistle-down, seats which could hold two persons, tables of costly woods supported by statues of Asiatic captives, — formed the furniture of the room.

On richly carved pedestals rested tall porcelain vases and great golden bowls, the workmanship of which was even more precious than the material. One of them with a slender base, was supported by two horses' heads with fringed hoods and harness. The handles were formed of two lotus stalks gracefully falling over two rose ornaments; on the cover were ibises with erect ears and sharp horns, and on the body of the vase were represented gazelles flying from the dogs amid stalks of papyrus. Another, no less curious, had for cover a monstrous Typhon head, adorned with palms and grimacing between two vipers. The sides were ornamented with leaves and denticulated bands.

One of the bowls, supported by two figures wearing miters and dressed in robes with broad borders, with one hand upbearing the handle and with the other the foot, amazed by its huge size and the perfection and finish of the ornamentation. The other, smaller and more perfect in shape perhaps, spread out gracefully; the slender and supple bodies of jackals whose paws rested upon the edge as if the animals sought to drink, formed the handles. Metal mirrors, framed with deformed faces, as though to give the beauty who looked into them the pleasure of contrast, coffers of cedar or sycamore wood painted and ornamented, caskets of enameled ware, flagons of alabaster, onyx, and glass, boxes of perfumes, — all these testified to the magnificence that the Pharaoh lavished upon Tahoser. The precious objects contained in that room were well worth a kingdom's ransom.

Seated upon an ivory seat, Tahoser looked at the stuffs and gems shown her by nude maidens, who scattered around the wealth contained in the coffers. Tahoser had just emerged from the bath, and the aromatic oils with which she had been rubbed, still further softened her delicate, satinlike skin; her flesh was almost translucent. She was of superhuman beauty, and when she gazed upon the burnished metal mirror, with her eyes brightened with antimony, she could not help smiling upon her reflection. A full gauze robe enveloped her fair form without veiling it. For sole ornament she wore a necklace composed of lapis-lazuli hearts surmounted by crosses, hanging from a string of gold and pearls.

The Pharaoh appeared on the threshold of the hall. A golden asp bound his thick hair, and a calasiris, the folds of which, brought forward, formed a point, enclosed his body from the belt to the knees; a single necklace encircled his unconquered, muscular neck.

On perceiving the King, Tahoser rose from her seat to prostrate herself, but the Pharaoh came to her, raised her up, and made her sit down.

"Do not thus humble yourself, Tahoser," he said in a gentle voice. "I will you to be my equal. I am weary of being alone in the universe. Although I am almighty and possess you, I shall wait until you love me as if I were but a man. Put away all fear; be a woman with a woman's will, sympathies, antipathies, and caprices. I have never seen one. But if your heart at last speaks in my favor, hold out to me, when I enter your room, in order that I may know it, the lotus flower out of your hair."

Though he strove to prevent it, Tahoser threw herself at the knees of the Pharaoh and let fall a tear upon his bare feet.

"Why is my soul Poëri's?" she said to herself as she resumed her place upon the ivory seat.

Timopht, putting one hand on the ground and the other on his head, entered the room.

"O King," he said, "a mysterious personage seeks to speak to you. His grey beard falls down to his waist, shining horns emerge from his bare brow, and his eyes shine like fire. An unknown power precedes him, for all the guards fall back and all the gates open before him. What he says must be done, and I have come to you in the midst of your pleasures, even were death to be the punishment of my audacity."

"What is his name?" said the King.

"Mosche," replied Timopht.

## XV

*T*he King passed into another hall to receive Mosche, and sat down on a throne, the arms of which were formed of lions, hung a broad pectoral ornament on his breast, and assumed a pose of supreme indifference.

Mosche appeared, accompanied by another Hebrew, called Aharon. August though the Pharaoh was, as he sat on his golden throne, surrounded by his officers and his fan-bearers, within that high hall with its huge columns, against that background of paintings which depicted the deeds of his ancestors or his own, Mosche was no less imposing. In him the majesty of age equaled the majesty of sovereignty. Although he was seventy years old, he seemed endowed with manly vigor, and nothing in him showed decadence into senility. The wrinkles on his brow and his cheeks, like the marks of the chisel on the granite, made him venerable without telling his age. His brown and wrinkled neck was joined to his powerful shoulders by gaunt but still powerful muscles, and a network of sinewy veins showed upon his hands, which did not tremble as old men's hands generally do. A soul more energetic than a human soul vivified his body, and on his face shone in the shadow a strange light. It seemed like the reflection of an invisible sun.

Without prostrating himself, as was the custom when men approached the King, Mosche drew near the throne of the Pharaoh and said to him: "Thus saith the Lord God of Israel: 'Let my people go, that they may hold a feast unto me in the wilderness.'"

The Pharaoh replied, "Who is the Lord, that I should obey his voice to let Israel go? I know not the Lord, neither will I let Israel go."

Without being intimidated by the King's words, the tall old man replied unhesitatingly, for the stuttering which had formerly affected him had disappeared, —

"The God of the Hebrews hath met with us. Let us go, we pray thee, three days' journey into the desert, and sacrifice unto the Lord our God; lest he fall upon us with pestilence, or with the sword."

Aharon confirmed by a nod the demand of Mosche.

"Wherefore do ye, Mosche and Aharon, let the people from their works?" replied the Pharaoh. "Happily for you I am today in a clement humor, for I might have had you beaten with rods, had your tongues and ears cut off, or thrown you living to the crocodiles. Know, for I tell you so, there is no other god than Ammon Ra, the supreme and primeval being, at once male and female; who is his own father and his own mother, whose husband he is also; from whom come all the other gods which unite heaven to earth and which are but forms of those two obscure principles. The wise know it, and the priests, who have long studied mysteries in the colleges and in the temples consecrated to his diverse representations. Do not, therefore, allege another god of your own invention to move the Hebrews to revolt, and to prevent them from doing their appointed work. Your pretext of sacrifice is plain,

— you wish to flee. Withdraw from before me, and continue to mold clay for my royal and priestly buildings, for my pyramids, my palaces, and my walls. Go! I have spoken."

Mosche, seeing that he could not move the Pharaoh's heart, and that if he insisted he would excite his wrath, withdrew in silence, followed by Aharon in dismay.

"I have obeyed the Lord God," said Mosche to his companion when they had crossed the pylon, "but the Pharaoh remains as insensible as if I had been speaking to those granite figures seated upon thrones at the palace gates, or to those idols with heads of dogs, monkeys, or hawks to which the priests burn incense within the depths of the sanctuaries. What shall we reply to the people when they question us on the result of our mission?"

The Pharaoh, fearing lest the Hebrews should bethink themselves of throwing off their yoke in accordance with the suggestions of Mosche, made them work more severely than before, and refused them straw to make their bricks. Thenceforth the children of Israel spread throughout Egypt, plucking the stubble and cursing their tyrants; for they were very unhappy, and they said that the advice of Mosche had increased their misery.

One day Mosche and Aharon reappeared in the palace, and once again called upon the King to let the Hebrews go to sacrifice unto the Lord in the wilderness.

"What proof have I," replied the Pharaoh, "that it is the Lord who sends you to me to tell me these things, and that you are not, as I fancy, vile impostors?"

Aharon threw down his wand before the King, and the wood began to twist, to curl, to grow scales, to move its head and tail, to rise up, and to utter horrible hissings: the wand had been changed into a serpent. Its rings grated over the flags, it swelled its hood, it whipped out its forked tongue, and rolling its red eyes, seemed to select the victim which it was about to bite.

The officers and servants ranged around the throne remained motionless and mute with terror at the sight of this prodigy; the bravest half drew their swords.

But the Pharaoh was in no wise moved. A disdainful smile flitted over his lips, and he said, —

"Is that all you can do? The miracle is slight, and the prodigy poor. Send for my wise men, my sorcerers and my magicians."

They came. They were men of venerable and mystic appearance, with shaven heads, wearing sandals of byblos, dressed in long linen robes, holding in their hands wands on which were engraved hieroglyphs. They were yellow and dried up like mummies by night watches, study, and austerity; the fatigue entailed by successive initiations could be read upon their faces, in which their eyes alone seemed to retain life.

They drew up in a line before the throne of the Pharaoh without paying the least attention to the serpent, which wriggled, crawled, and hissed.

"Can you," said the King, "change your wands into reptiles as Aharon has done?"

"O King, is it for such child's play," said the oldest of the band, "that you have sent for us from the recesses of the secret chambers where under the starry ceilings, by the light of the lamps, we are meditating, bending over undecipherable papyri, kneeling before the hieroglyphic stelæ with their mysterious, deep meanings, forcing the secrets of nature, calculating the power of numbers, bearing our trembling hand to the border of the veil of the great Isis? Let us go back, for life is short, and the wise man has scarce time to tell to another the word which he has learned. Let us go back to our laboratories. The merest juggler, the first charmer of serpents who plays the flute on the public squares, will suffice to satisfy you."

"Ennana, do what I wish," said the Pharaoh to the chief of the wise men and the magicians.

Old Ennana turned towards the band of sages, who remained standing motionless, their minds already lost again in deep meditations.

"Cast down every man your rod as you whisper the magic word."

The rods fell together with a sharp sound upon the stone slabs, and the wise men resumed their perpendicular attitude like the statues placed against the pillars of the tombs. They did not even deign to look at their feet to see if the miracle were being wrought, so sure were they of the power of their formula.

And then was seen a strange and horrible sight. The rods twisted like branches of green wood in the fire, the ends flattened out into the shape of heads, thinned out into the shape of tails. Some remained smooth, others became scaly, according to the kind of serpent. All these swarmed and crawled and hissed, interlaced and knotted into hideous knots. There were vipers bearing the mark of the spearhead upon their low brows, horned snakes with menacing protuberances, greenish, viscous hydras, asps with movable fangs, yellow trigonocephalæ, orvets or blind serpents, crotalidæ with short heads, black skins, and rattles on their tails, amphisbena, which can glide forward or backward, boas opening mouths wide enough to swallow an ox, serpents with eyes surrounded with discs like those of owls; — the pavement of the hall was covered with them.

Tahoser, who shared the throne of the Pharaoh, raised her beautiful bare feet and pulled them back under her, pale with terror.

"Well," said the Pharaoh to Mosche, "you see that the skill of my magicians equals, and even surpasses yours; their rods have turned into serpents like that of Aharon. Invent another prodigy if you seek to convince me."

Mosche stretched forth his hand, and Aharon's serpent glided towards the twenty-four reptiles. The struggle was not long; it soon had swallowed the hideous things, real or seeming creations of the wise men of Egypt. Then it resumed its former wand shape.

This result seemed to amaze Ennana. He bent his head, thought for a moment, and said, like a man who perceives something: "I shall find the word and the sign. I have interpreted wrongly the fourth hieroglyph of the fifth perpendicular line in which is the spell of serpents. O King, do you still need us?" said the chief of the wise men aloud. "I long to resume the reading of Hermes Trismegistus, which contains more important secrets than these sleight-of-hand tricks."

The Pharaoh signed to the old man that he might withdraw, and the silent procession returned to the depths of the palace.

The King reentered the harem with Tahoser. The priest's daughter, terrified and still trembling at these prodigies, knelt down before him and said: "O Pharaoh, do you not fear to anger by your resistance the unknown god who has ordered these Israelites to go a three days' journey into the desert to sacrifice unto him? Let Mosche and his Hebrews depart to fulfill their rites, for perhaps the Lord, as they call him, will afflict the land of Egypt and bring death upon us."

"What! does that reptile jugglery frighten you?" replied the Pharaoh. "Did you not see that my wise men produced serpents with their wands?"

"Yes, but Aharon's devoured them, and that is an ill omen."

"What matters it? Am I not the favorite of Phré, the preferred of Ammon Ra? Have I not under my sandals the effigies of conquered nations? With one breath I shall sweep away when I please the whole of that Hebrew race, and I shall see if their god can protect them."

"Beware, Pharaoh," said Tahoser, who remembered Poëri's words about the power of Jehovah. "Do not allow pride to harden your heart. Mosche and Aharon terrify me; they must be supported by a more powerful god, for they braved your wrath."

"If their god is so powerful," said the Pharaoh, answering the fear expressed by Tahoser, "would he leave them thus captives, humiliated and bowing like beasts of burden under the harvest labor? Let us forget these vain prodigies and live in peace. Think rather of the love I bear you, and remember that the Pharaoh is more powerful than the Lord, the fanciful god of the Hebrews."

"Yes, you are the destroyer of the nations and the ruler of thrones, and men are before you like grains of sand blown by the southern wind. I know it," replied Tahoser.

"And yet I cannot make you love me," said the Pharaoh, with a smile.

"The ibex fears the lion, the dove dreads the hawk, the eye shrinks from the sun, and I can see you yet only through terror and blazing light. It takes human weakness a long time to become familiar with royal majesty; a god always terrifies a mortal."

"You fill me with regret, Tahoser, that I am not the first-comer, an officer, a nomarch, a priest, a laborer, or even less. But since I cannot make the King into a man, I can make a queen out of the woman and bind the golden uræus upon your lovely brow. The Queen will no longer dread the King."

"Even when you make me sit by you on your throne, my thoughts remain kneeling at your feet. But you are so good in spite of your superhuman beauty, your power so boundless and your splendor so dazzling, that perhaps my heart will grow bold and will dare to beat against yours."

Thus talked the Pharaoh and Tahoser. The priest's daughter could not forget Poëri, and sought to gain time by flattering the passion of the King. To escape from the palace, to find the young Hebrew again, was impossible. Besides, Poëri had accepted her love rather than shared it. Ra'hel, in spite of her generosity, was a dangerous rival; and then, the love of the Pharaoh touched the priest's daughter, — she desired to love him, and perhaps she was not so far from doing so as she believed.

## XVI

*A* few days later the Pharaoh was driving along the Nile, standing on his chariot and followed by his court. He had gone forth to observe the height of the flood, when in the center of the road appeared, like two phantoms, Aharon and Mosche. The king drew in his horses, the foam of whose mouths was already flecking the breast of the tall, motionless old man.

Mosche, with slow and solemn voice repeated his adjuration.

"Prove to me by some wonder the power of your god," answered the King, "and I will grant your request."

Turning towards Aharon, who was a few steps behind him, Mosche said, "Take thy rod, and stretch out thine hand upon the waters of Egypt, upon their streams, upon their rivers, and upon their ponds, and upon all their pools of water, that they may become blood; and that there may be blood throughout all the land of Egypt, both in vessels of wood and in vessels of stone."

Aharon lifted up his rod and smote the waters that were in the river. The train of the Pharaoh awaited the result anxiously. The King, who had a heart of brass within a breast of granite, smiled disdainfully, trusting in the skill of his wise men to confound the foreign magicians. As soon as the river had been smitten by the rod of the Hebrew, — the rod which had been a serpent, — the waters began to turn muddy and to boil; their mud color was gradually changed; reddish tones began to mingle with it; then the whole mass assumed a somber purple color, and the Nile seemed a river of blood with scarlet waves that edged the banks with rosy foam. It seemed to reflect a vast conflagration or a sky rayed by lightning, but the atmosphere was calm, Thebes was not burning, and the unchanging azure spread over the red stream, marked here and there by the white bellies of dead fishes. The long crocodiles, using their crooked paws, emerged from the river on to the bank, and the heavy hippopotami, like blocks of rose granite covered with leprous, black moss, fled through the reeds, or raised above the stream their mighty heads, unable to breathe in that water of blood. The canals, the fishponds, and the pools had all turned the same color, and the vessels full of water were red like the basins in which the blood of victims is collected.

The Pharaoh was not astonished at the wonder, and said to the Hebrews, —

"This miracle might terrify a credulous and ignorant people, but it has nothing surprising for me. Let Ennana and the wise men come. They will repeat this enchantment."

The wise men came, led by their chief. Ennana cast a glance on the river and its purple waves, and saw at once what was the matter.

"Restore things to their primitive condition," he said to Mosche's companion; "I will repeat your wonder."

Aharon again smote the stream, which at once resumed its natural color. Ennana nodded briefly, like an impartial expert who does justice to the skill of a colleague; he considered the enchantment was well wrought for one who had not had, like himself, the opportunity of studying wisdom in the mysterious chambers of the labyrinth, where a very few of the initiated can alone enter, so trying are the tests which have to be undergone.

"It is my turn now," he said; and he stretched out over the Nile his rod engraved with hieroglyphic signs, muttering a few words of a tongue so old that it had probably ceased to be understood even in the days of Mene, the first king of Egypt, — a language spoken by sphinxes, with syllables of granite.

A vast red flood stretched suddenly from one bank to the other, and the Nile again rolled ensanguined waves to the sea. The twenty-four magicians saluted the king as if they were about to withdraw.

"Remain," said the Pharaoh.

They resumed their impassible countenances.

"Have you no other proof of your mission than that? My wise men, you see, imitate your wonders very well."

Without appearing discouraged by the ironical words of the King, Mosche replied: "In seven days' time, if you have not made up your mind to let Israel go into the desert to sacrifice to the Lord according to their rites, I shall return and perform another wonder before you."

At the end of seven days Mosche reappeared. He spoke to his servant Aharon the words of the Lord: —

"Stretch out thine hand with thy rod over the streams, over the rivers, and over the ponds, and cause the frogs to come up upon the land of Egypt."

As soon as Aharon had done as he was bidden, millions of frogs emerged from the canals, the rivers, and the marshes; they covered the fields and the roads, they hopped upon the steps of the temples and the palaces, they invaded the sanctuaries and the most secret chambers; legions of other frogs followed those which had first appeared; they were found in the houses, in the kneading-troughs, in the ovens, in the coffers; no one could step anywhere without crushing some. As if moved by springs, they jumped between peoples' legs, to the right and the left, forward and backward; as far as the eye could reach, they were seen rippling, hopping, jumping past one another, for they already lacked room, and their numbers grew, their ranks became denser, they formed heaps here and there; innumerable green backs turned the country-side into a sort of animated green meadow, on which their yellow eyes shone like flowers. The animals, — horses, asses, goats, — terrified and startled, fled across the fields, but everywhere came upon the loathsome swarms.

The Pharaoh, who from the threshold of his palace beheld this rising tide of frogs with weariness and disgust, crushed as many as he could with the end of his scepter and pushed back the others with his curved sandals, but his labor was lost; more frogs came no one knew whence, and took the places of the dead, swarming more than they did, croaking more than they did, more loathsome, more uncomfortable, bolder, showing the vertebræ on their backs, staring at him with their big, round eyes, spreading out their webbed feet, wrinkling the white skin of their throats. The vile animals seemed endowed with intelligence, and they formed denser shoals around the King than anywhere else.

The swarming flood grew and still grew: on the knees of the colossi, on the cornices of the palaces, on the backs of the sphinxes, on the entablatures of the temples, on the shoulders of the gods, on the pyramidions of the obelisks, the hideous reptiles, with swollen backs and indrawn feet, had taken up their places. The ibises, which at first had rejoiced at this unexpected treat, and had lanced them with their long beaks, now alarmed by this mighty invasion fled to the upper regions of the sky, snapping their long bills.

Aharon and Mosche triumphed. Ennana, having been summoned, was sunk in thought; his finger, placed upon his bald brow, his eyes half-closed, he seemed to be seeking within his memory for a forgotten magic formula.

The Pharaoh, somewhat uneasy, turned towards him. "Well, Ennana, have you lost your mind by dint of thought? Is this wonder beyond the reach of your wisdom?"

"In no wise, O King; but when a man is engaged in measuring the infinite and calculating eternity and in spelling out the incomprehensible, it may happen that he does not at once recall the odd word which rules reptiles, makes them live or destroys them. Watch! all this vermin is about to vanish."

The old magician waved his wand and whispered a few words; in an instant the fields, the squares, the roads, the quays along the stream, the streets in the city, the courts of the palaces, the rooms of the houses, were cleansed of their croaking guests, and restored to their primitive condition.

The King smiled, proud of the power of his magician.

"It is not enough to have broken the spell of Aharon," said Ennana; "I shall repeat it."

Ennana waved his wand in the opposite direction and muttered the contrary formula. Immediately the frogs reappeared in greater numbers than before, leaping and croaking. In a twinkling the whole land was covered with them, and then Aharon stretched out his rod, and the Egyptian magician was unable to dispel the invasion called up by his enchantment. In vain he spoke the mysterious words, the incantation had lost its power. The bands of wise men withdrew, pursued by the loathsome scourge, and the brows of the Pharaoh were bent with anger, but he hardened his heart and would not grant the prayer of Mosche; his pride strove to struggle and to fight against the unknown God of Israel.

However, unable to get rid of the terrible reptiles, Pharaoh promised Mosche, if he would intercede for him with his God, to grant the Hebrews permission to go into the desert to sacrifice.

The frogs died or returned to the waters, but the Pharaoh hardened his heart, and in spite of the gentle remonstrances of Tahoser, he did not keep his promise.

Then was let loose upon Egypt a multitude of scourges and plagues. A fierce warfare was waged between the wise men and the two Hebrews whose wonders they reproduced. Mosche changed all the dust in Egypt into lice; Ennana did the same. Mosche took two handfuls of ashes of the furnace and sprinkled them toward the heaven in the sight of the Pharaoh, and immediately they became a boil breaking forth with blains upon man and upon beast among the Egyptians, but not upon the Hebrews.

"Imitate that wonder!" cried the Pharaoh, beside himself with anger, and as red as if he were standing in front of a fiery furnace, as he addressed himself to the chief of the wise men.

"It would be useless," replied the old man, in a tone of discouragement. "The finger of the Unknown is in all this; our vain formulæ cannot prevail against that mysterious power. Submit, and let us return to our sanctuaries to study this new god, this Lord, who is more powerful than Ammon Ra, Osiris, and Typhon. The learning of Egypt has been overcome, the riddle of the sphinx cannot be answered, and the vast mystery of the great Pyramid covers nothingness only."

As the Pharaoh still refused to let the Hebrews go, all the cattle of the Egyptians were smitten with death; the Israelites lost not a single head.

A wind from the south arose and blew all night long, and in the morning when day dawned, a vast red cloud concealed the whole of the heavens. Through the dun-colored fog the sun shone red like a buckler in the forge, and seemed to have lost its beams. The cloud was different from other clouds, it was a living cloud; the noise of its wings was heard; it alighted on the earth, not in the shape of great drops of rain, but in shoals of rose, yellow, and green grasshoppers, more numerous than the grains of sand in the Libyan desert. They followed each other in swarms like the straw blown about by the storm; the air was darkened; they filled up the ditches, the ravines, the streams; they put out by their mere mass the fires lighted to destroy them; they struck against obstacles and then heaped up and overcame them. If a man opened his mouth, he breathed one in; they found their way into the folds of the clothing, into the hair, into the nostrils; their dense columns made chariots turn back; they overthrew the solitary passer-by and soon covered him. Their formidable army, springing and flying, marched over Egypt from the Cataracts to the Delta, over an immense breadth of country, destroying the grass, reducing the trees to the condition of skeletons, devouring plants to the roots, leaving behind but a bare earth trodden down like a threshing-floor.

At the request of the Pharaoh Mosche made the scourge cease. An extremely violent west wind carried all the grasshoppers into the Sea of Weeds; but the Pharaoh's obstinate heart, harder than brass, porphyry, or basalt, would not relent.

Hail, a scourge unknown to Egypt, fell from Heaven amid blinding lightning and deafening thunder, in enormous stones, cutting, bruising, breaking everything, mowing down the grain as if with a scythe. Then black, opaque, horrifying darkness, in which lights were extinguished as in the depths of the airless passages, spread its heavy clouds over the land of Egypt, so fair, so luminous, so golden under its azure sky, where the night is clearer than the daytime in other climes. The terrified people, believing themselves already shrouded in the impenetrable darkness of the sepulcher, groped their way or sat down by the propylæa, uttering plaintive cries and tearing their clothes.

One night, a night of terror and of horror, a specter flew across the whole of Egypt, entering every house the door of which was not marked with red, and the first-born of the males died, the son of the Pharaoh as well as the son of the meanest hind; yet the King, notwithstanding all these dread signs, would not yield.

He remained within the recesses of his palace, fierce, silent, gazing at the body of his son stretched out upon the funeral couch with the jackals' feet, and heedless of the tears of Tahoser which wetted his hand.

Mosche stood upon the threshold of the room without anyone having introduced him, for all the servants had fled hither and thither; and he repeated his demand with imperturbable serenity.

"Go," said Pharaoh at last, "and sacrifice unto your God as you please."

Tahoser threw herself on the King's neck, and said to him, "Now I love you, for you are a man, and not a god of granite."

## XVII

*T*he Pharaoh did not answer Tahoser; he gazed with a somber eye upon the body of his first-born son; his untamed pride rebelled, even as he yielded. In his heart he did not believe in the Lord, and he explained away the scourges which had smitten Egypt by attributing them to the magic power of Mosche and Aharon, which was greater than that of his magicians. The thought of yielding exasperated his violent, fierce soul.

But even had he wished to retain the Israelites, his terrified people would not have allowed it. The Egyptians, dreading to die, would all have driven out the foreigners who were the cause of their ills and suffering. They kept away from them with superstitious terror, and when the great Hebrew passed, followed by Aharon, the bravest fled, fearing some new prodigy, and they said, "Is not the rod of his companion about to turn into a serpent again and coil itself around us?"

Had Tahoser then forgotten Poëri when she threw her arms around the Pharaoh's neck? In no wise; but she felt, springing up within the King's obstinate soul, projects of vengeance and of extermination; she feared massacres in which would have fallen the young Hebrew and the gentle Ra'hel, — a general destruction, which this time would have changed the waters of the Nile into real blood; and she strove to turn away the King's wrath by her caresses and gentle words.

The funeral procession came for the body of the young prince, to carry it to the Memnonia quarter, where it was to undergo the preparation for embalming, which lasts seventy days. The Pharaoh saw the body depart with a gloomy look, and he said, as if filled with a melancholy presentiment, —

"Now have I no longer a son, O Tahoser. If I die, you will be Queen of Egypt."

"Why speak of death?" said the priest's daughter; "years will follow years without leaving a trace of their passage upon your robust body, and generations will fall around you like the leaves around a tree which remains standing."

"Have I not been vanquished, — I who am invincible?" replied the Pharaoh. "Of what use are the *bassi-relievi* of the temples and the palaces which represent me armed with a scourge and a scepter, driving my war chariot over bodies, and dragging by their hair subject nations, if I am obliged to yield to the spells of a foreign magician, — if the gods to whom I have raised so many vast temples, built for eternity, do not defend me against the unknown god of that low race? The prestige of my power is forever gone; my wise men, reduced to silence, abandon me; my people murmur against me. I am only a mighty simulacrum. I willed, and I could not perform. You were right when you said just now, Tahoser, that I am a man. I have come down to the level of men. But since you love me now, I shall try to forget; I shall wed you when the funeral ceremonies are over."

Fearing lest the Pharaoh should recall his word, the Hebrews were getting ready for departure, and soon their cohorts started, led by a cloud of smoke during the day and a pillar of fire by night. They took their way through the sandy wastes that lie between the Nile and the Sea of Weeds, avoiding the tribes which might have opposed their passage. One after another, the Hebrew tribes defiled in front of the copper statue made by the magicians, which possessed the property of stopping escaping slaves, but this time the spell, which had been invincible for centuries, failed to work; the Lord had destroyed it. The vast multitude advanced slowly, covering the land with its flocks, its beasts of burden laden with the riches borrowed from the Egyptians, dragging the enormous baggage of a nation which is suddenly migrating. The human eye could see neither the head nor the tail of the column, which disappeared on either horizon in a cloud of dust. If anyone had sat down by the roadside to see pass the whole procession, he would have seen the sun rise and set more than once. Men came and came and came always. The sacrifice to the Lord was a vain pretext; Israel was leaving the land of Egypt forever, and the mummy of Yusouf, in its painted and gilded case, was carried along on the shoulders of bearers who were relieved at regular intervals.

So the Pharaoh became very wroth indeed, and resolved to pursue the fleeing Hebrews. He ordered six hundred war chariots to be prepared, called together his commanders, bound around his body his broad crocodile-leather belt, filled the two quivers in his car with arrows and javelins, drew on his wrist his brazen bracelet which deadens the vibration of the cord, and started, followed by a nation of soldiers. Furious and formidable, he urged his horses to their topmost speed, and behind him the six hundred chariots sounded with the noise of brass like earthly thunder. The foot-soldiers hastened on, but they were unable to keep up with his impetuous speed.

Often the Pharaoh was obliged to stop and await the rest of his army. During these halts he struck with his fist the edge of his chariot, stamped with impatience, and ground his teeth. He bent towards the horizon, seeking to perceive, behind the sand whirled by the wind, the fleeing tribes of the Hebrews, and raged at the thought that every hour increased the interval which separated them. Had not his officers held him back, he would have driven straight before him at the risk of finding himself single-handed against a whole people.

They were no longer traversing the green valley of Egypt, but plains varied with many changing hills and barred with undulations like the surface of the sea; the framework of the land was visible through the thin soil. Jagged rocks, broken into all sorts of shapes, as if giant animals had trampled them under foot when the earth was still in a condition of mud, on the day when it emerged from chaos, broke the stretches here and there, and relieved from time to time by their abrupt breaks the flat horizon-line which merged into that of the sky in a zone of reddish mist. At vast distances grew palm trees, outspreading their dusty leaves near some spring, frequently dried up, and in the mud of which the thirsty horses plunged their bloodshot nostrils.

But the Pharaoh, insensible to the rain of fire which fell from the white-hot heavens, at once gave the signal for departure, and horsemen and footmen started again on the march. Bodies of oxen or beasts of burden lying on either side, with spirals of vultures sweeping around above them, marked the passage of the Hebrews, and prevented the angry King from losing their track.

A swift army, practiced to marching, goes faster than a migrating people which drags with it women, children, old men, baggage, and tents; so the distance was rapidly diminishing between the Egyptian troops and the Israelite tribes.

It was near Pi-ha'hiroth that the Egyptians came up with the Hebrews. The tribes were camped on the shore, but when the people saw shining in the sun the golden chariot of the Pharaoh, followed by his war chariots and his army, they uttered a mighty shout of terror, and began to curse Mosche, who had led them to destruction.

In point of fact their situation was desperate: in front of the Hebrews was the line of battle, behind them the deep sea. The women rolled on the ground, tearing their clothes, pulling at their hair, beating their breasts.

"Why did you not leave us in Egypt? Slavery is better than death, and you have led us into the desert to die. Were you afraid that we should not have sepulchers enough?"

Thus yelled the multitudes, furious with Mosche, who remained impassible. The bolder took up their arms and prepared to defend themselves, but the confusion was frightful, and the war chariots, when they charged through that compact mass, would certainly make an awful slaughter.

Mosche stretched out his hand over the sea, after having called upon the name of the Lord, and then took place a wonder which no magician could have repeated; there arose an east wind of startling violence which blew through the waters of the Sea of Weeds like the share of a giant plow, throwing to right and left briny mountains crowned with crests of foam. Divided by the impetuosity of that irresistible wind, which would have swept away the pyramids like grains of dust, the waters rose like liquid walls and left free between them a broad way which could be traversed dry shod. Through their translucency, as behind thick glass, were seen marine monsters twisting and squirming, terrified at being surprised by daylight in the mysterious depths of the abyss.

The Hebrew tribes rushed through this miraculous issue, forming a human torrent that flowed between two steep banks of green waters. An innumerable race marked with two millions of black dots the livid bottom of the gulf, and impressed its feet upon mud which the belly of the leviathans alone had rayed; and the terrible wind still blew, passing over the heads of the Hebrews, whom it would have thrown to the ground like grain, and keeping back by its breath the heap of roaring waters.

It was the breath of the Lord which was dividing the sea.

Terrified at the wonder, the Egyptians hesitated to pursue the Hebrews, but the Pharaoh, with that high courage which nothing could daunt, urged on his horses, which reared and plunged, lashing them in turn with his terrible thonged whip, his eyes bloodshot, foaming at the lips, and roaring like a lion whose prey is escaping. He at last compelled them to enter that strangely opened road. The six hundred cars followed. The Israelites of the rear guard, among whom were Poëri, Ra'hel, and Thamar, believed themselves lost when they saw the enemy taking the same road that they had traversed. But when the Egyptians were fairly within the gulf, Mosche made a sign, the wheels of the cars fell off, and there was a horrible confusion of horses and warriors falling against each other. Then the mountains of water, miraculously sustained, suddenly fell, and the sea closed in, whirling in its foam men and animals and chariots like straw caught by the eddies in the current of a river.

Alone the Pharaoh, standing within his chariot, which had come to the surface, shot, drunk with pride and anger, the last arrows of his quiver against the Hebrews, who were now reaching the other shore. Having exhausted his arrows, he took up his javelin, and although already nearly half engulfed, with his arm alone above the water, he hurled it, a powerless weapon, against the unknown God whom he still braved from the depths of the abyss. A mighty billow, which rolled two or three times over the edge of the sea, engulfed the last remains.

Nothing was left of the glory and of the army of the Pharaoh.

On the other bank Miriam, the sister of Aharon, exulted and sang as she played on the timbrel, and all the women of Israel beat time upon onager-skins. Two millions of voices were singing the hymn of deliverance.

## XVIII

*T*ahoser in vain awaited Pharaoh, and then reigned over Egypt. Then she also died after a short time. She was placed

in the magnificent tomb which had been prepared for the
king, whose body was never found; and her story, written
upon papyrus, with the headings of the pages in red characters, by Kakevou, a scribe of the double chamber of light and
keeper of the books, was placed by her side under the network
of bands.

Was it the Pharaoh or Poëri she regretted? Kakevou the
scribe does not tell us, and Dr. Rumphius, who translated the
hieroglyphs of the Egyptian grammat, did not venture to
settle the question.

As for Lord Evandale, he never married, although he was
the last of his race. His young countrywomen cannot understand his coldness towards their sex. But it would never occur
to them that Lord Evandale is retrospectively in love with
Tahoser, the daughter of the high priest Petamounoph, who
died three thousand five hundred years ago. Yet there are
English crazes which have less sound reason for their existence than this one.

# Egypt

# The Unwrapping of a Mummy

*D*uring the Exhibition of 1857, I was invited to be present at the opening of one of the mummy cases in the collection of Egyptian antiquities, and at the unwrapping of the mummy it contained. My curiosity was indeed lively. My readers will easily understand the reason: the scene at which I was to be present I had imagined and described beforehand in the "Romance of a Mummy." I do not say this to draw attention to my book, but to explain the peculiar interest I took in this archæological and funereal meeting.

When I entered the room, the mummy, already taken from the case, was laid on a table, its human shape showing indistinctly through the thickness of the wrappings. On the faces of the coffin was painted the Judgment of the Soul, the scene which is usually represented in such cases. The soul of the dead woman, led by two funeral genii, the one hostile, the other favorable, was bowing before Osiris, the great judge of the dead, seated on his throne, wearing the pschent, the conventional beard on the chin, and a whip in his hand. Farther on, the dead woman's actions, good or bad, represented by a pot of flowers and a rough piece of stone, were being weighed in scales. A long line of judges, with heads of lions, hawks, or jackals, were awaiting in hieratic attitudes the result of the weighing before delivering judgment. Below this painting were inscribed the prayers of the funeral ritual and the confession of the dead, who did not own to her faults, but stated, on the contrary, those she had not committed, —

"I have not been guilty of murder, or of theft, or of adultery," etc. Another inscription contained the genealogy of the woman, both on the father's and on the mother's side. I do not transcribe here the series of strange names, the last of which is that of Nes Khons, the lady enclosed in the case, where she believed herself sure of rest while awaiting the day on which her soul would, after many trials, be reunited to its well-preserved body, and enjoy supreme felicity with its own flesh and blood; a broken hope, for death is as disappointing as life.

The work of unrolling the bandages began; the outer envelope, of stout linen, was ripped open with scissors. A faint, delicate odor of balsam, incense, and other aromatic drugs spread through the room like the odor of an apothecary's shop. The end of the bandage was then sought for, and when found, the mummy was placed upright to allow the operator to move freely around her and to roll up the endless band, turned to the yellow color of écru linen by the palm wine and other preserving liquids.

Strange indeed was the appearance of the tall rag-doll, the armature of which was a dead body, moving so stiffly and awkwardly with a sort of horrible parody of life, under the hands that were stripping it, while the bandages rose in heaps around it. Sometimes the bandages held in place pieces of stuff like fringed serviettes intended to fill hollows or to support the shape.

Pieces of linen, cut open in the middle, had been passed over the head and, fitted to the shoulders, fell down over the chest. All these obstacles having been removed, there appeared a sort of veil like coarse India muslin, of a pinkish color, the soft tone of which would have delighted a painter. It appears to me that the dye must have been anatto, unless the muslin, originally red, turned rose-color through the action of the balsam and of time. Under the veil there was another series of bandages, of finer linen, which bound the body more closely with their innumerable folds. Our curiosity was becoming feverish, and the mummy was being turned somewhat quickly. A Hoffmann or an Edgar Poe could have found here a subject for one of his weird tales. It so happened that a sudden storm was lashing the windows with heavy drops of rain that rattled like hail; pale lightnings illumined on the shelves of the cupboards the old yellowed skulls and the grimacing death's-heads of the Anthropological Museum; while the low rolling of the thunder formed an accompaniment to the waltz of Nes Khons, the daughter of Horus and Rouaa, as she pirouetted in the impatient hands of those who were unwrapping her.

The mummy was visibly growing smaller in size, and its slender form showed more and more plainly under its diminishing wrappings. A vast quantity of linen filled the room, and we could not help wondering how a box which was scarcely larger than an ordinary coffin had managed to hold it all. The neck was the first portion of the body to issue from the bandages; it was covered with a fairly thick layer of naphtha which had to be chiseled away. Suddenly, through the black remains of the natron, there flashed on the upper part of the breast a bright gleam of gold, and soon there was laid bare a thin sheet of metal, cut out into the shape of the sacred hawk, its wings outspread, its tail fanlike like that of eagles in heraldry. Upon this bit of gold — a funeral jewel not rich enough to tempt body-snatchers — had been written with a reed and ink a prayer to the gods, protectors of the tombs, asking that the heart and the visceræ of the dead should not be removed far from her body. A beautiful microscopic hawk, which would have made a lovely watch-charm, was attached by a thread to a necklace of small plates of blue glass, to which was hung also a sort of amulet in the shape of a flail, made of turquoise-blue enamel. Some of the plates had become semi-opaque, no doubt owing to the heat of the boiling bitumen which had been poured over them, and then had slowly cooled.

So far, of course, nothing unusual had been found; in mummy cases there are often discovered numbers of these small trifles, and every curiosity shop is full of similar blue ware-ware figures; but we now came upon an unexpected and touchingly graceful detail. Under each armpit of the dead woman had been placed a flower, absolutely colorless, like plants which have been long pressed between the leaves of a herbarium, but perfectly preserved, and to which a botanist could readily have assigned a name. Were they blooms of the lotus or the persea? No one of us could say. This find made me thoughtful. Who was it that had put these poor flowers there, like a supreme farewell, at the moment when the beloved body was about to disappear under the first rolls of bandages? Flowers that are three thousand years old, so frail and yet so eternal, make a strange impression upon one.

There was also found amid the bandages a small fruit-berry, the species of which it is difficult to determine. Perhaps it was a berry of the nepenthe, which brought oblivion. On a bit of stuff, carefully detached, was written within a cartouche the name of an unknown king belonging to a dynasty no less forgotten. This mummy fills up a vacant place in history and tells of a new Pharaoh.

The face was still hidden under its mask of linen and bitumen, which could not be easily detached, for it had been firmly fixed by an indefinite number of centuries. Under the pressure of the chisel a portion gave way, and two white eyes with great black pupils shone with fictitious life between brown eyelids. They were enameled eyes, such as it was customary to insert in carefully prepared mummies. The clear, fixed glance, gazing out of the dead face, produced a terrifying effect; the body seemed to behold with disdainful surprise the living beings that moved around it. The eyebrows showed quite plainly upon the orbit, hollowed by the sinking of the flesh. The nose, I must confess, — and in this respect Nes Khons was less pretty than Tahoser, — had been turned down to conceal the incision through which the brain had been drawn from the skull, and a leaf of gold had been placed on the mouth as the seal of eternal silence. The hair, exceedingly fine, silky, and soft, dressed in light curls, did not fall below the tops of the ears, and was of that auburn tint so much prized by Venetian women. It looked like a child's hair dyed with henna, as one sees it in Algeria. I do not think that this color was the natural one; Nes Khons must have been dark like other Egyptians, and the brown tone was doubtless produced by the essences and perfumes of the embalmer.

Little by little the body began to show in its sad nudity. The reddish skin of the torso, as the air came in contact with it, assumed a bluish bloom, and there was visible on the side the cut through which had been drawn the entrails, and from which escaped, like the sawdust of a ripped-up doll, the sawdust of aromatic wood mixed with resin in grains that looked like colophony. The arms were stretched out, and the bony hands with their gilded nails imitated with sepulchral modesty the gesture of the Venus of Medici. The feet, slightly contracted by the drying up of the flesh and the muscles, seemed to have been shapely and small, and the nails were gilded like those of the hand.

What was she, after all, this Nes Khons, daughter of Horus and Rouaa, called Lady in her epitaph? Young or old, beautiful or ugly? It would be difficult to say. She is now not much more than a skin covering bones, and it is impossible to discover in the dry, sharp lines the graceful contours of Egyptian women, such as we see them depicted in temples, palaces, and tombs. But is it not a surprising thing, one that seems to belong to the realm of dreams, to see on a table, in still appreciable shape, a being which walked in the sunshine, which lived and loved five hundred years before Moses, two thousand years before Jesus Christ? For that is the age of the mummy which the caprice of fate drew from its cartonnage in the midst of the Universal Exposition, amid all the machinery of our modern civilization.

# From Alexandria to Cairo

*T*he railway to Cairo runs first along a narrow strip of sand which separates the Baheirehma'adieh, or Lake of Aboukir, from Lake Mareotis, now filled with salt water. As you go towards Cairo, Lake Mareotis is on your right and the Lake of Aboukir on your left. The former stretches out like a sea between shores so low that they disappear, and thus make it impossible to estimate the size of the lake, which melts away into the sky on the horizon.

The sunlight fell perpendicularly upon its smooth waters, and made them flash and sparkle until the eye was weary; in other places, the grey waters lay stagnant amid the grey sands, or else were of the dead white of tin. It would have been easy to believe one's self in the Holland Polders, traveling along one of the sleepy inland seas. The heavens were as colorless as Van der Velde's skies, and the travelers, who, trusting to painters, had dreamed of a blaze of color, gazed with amazement upon the vast extent of absolutely flat, greyish toned land, which in no wise recalled Egypt, at least such as one imagines it to be. On the side opposite Lake Mareotis rose, in the midst of luxuriant gardens, the country homes of the rich merchants of the city, of the government officials and of the consuls, painted in bright colors, sky-blue, rose or yellow, picked out with white, and here and there the great sails of boats, bound to Foueh or to Rosetta through the Mahmoudieh Canal, showed above the vegetation and seemed to be traveling on dry land. This curious effect, which always causes surprise, is often met with in the neighborhood of Leyden, Dordrecht, and Haarlem, and in swampy countries where the water lies level with the ground, and sometimes even, kept in by dikes, is higher than the level of the country by several yards.

Where the salt water ends, the aspect of the country changes, not gradually, but suddenly; on the one hand absolute barrenness, on the other exuberant vegetation; and wherever irrigation brings a drop of water, plants spring up, and the sterile dust becomes fertile soil. The contrast is most striking. We had passed Lake Mareotis, and on either side of the railroad stretched fields of *doora* or maize, of cotton plants in various stages of growth, some opening their pretty yellow flowers, others shedding the white silk from their pods. Gutters full of muddy water rayed the black ground with lines that shone here and there in the light. These were fed by broader canals connected with the Nile. Small dikes of earth, easily opened with a blow of a pickaxe, dammed up the waters until watering-time. The rough wheels of the sakiehs, turned by buffaloes, oxen, camels, or asses, raised the water to higher levels. Sometimes, even, two robust fellahs, perfectly naked, tawny and shining like Florentine bronzes, standing on the edge of a canal and balancing like a swing a basket of waterproof esparto suspended from two ropes of which they held the ends, skimmed the surface of the water and dashed it into the neighboring field with amazing dexterity. Fellahs in short blue tunics were plowing, holding the handle of a primitive plow drawn by a camel and a humpbacked Sudanese ox; others gathered cotton and maize; others dug ditches; others again dragged branches of trees by way of a harrow over the furrows which the inundation had scarce left. Everywhere was seen an activity not much in accord with the traditional Oriental idleness.

The first fellahin villages seen on the right and left of the road impress one curiously. They are collections of huts of unbaked brick cemented with mud, with flat roofs occasionally topped with a sort of whitewashed turret for pigeons, the sloping walls of which faintly recall the outline of a truncated Egyptian pylon. A door as low as that of a tomb, and two or three holes pierced in the wall are the only openings in these huts, which look more like the work of termites than that of men. Often half the village — if such a name can be given to these earthen huts — has been washed away by the rains or sapped by the flood; but no great harm is done; with a few handfuls of mud the house is soon rebuilt, and five or six days of sunshine suffice to make it inhabitable.

This description, scrupulously exact, does not give a very attractive idea of a fellahin village; but plant by the side of these cubes of grey earth a clump of date palms, have a camel or two kneel down in front of the doors, which look like the mouths of warrens, let a woman come out from one of them draped in her long blue gown, holding a child by the hand and bearing a jar of water on her head, light it all up with sunlight, and you have a charming and characteristic picture.

The thing which strikes the most inattentive traveler as soon as he steps into this Lower Egypt, where from time immemorial the Nile has been accumulating its mud in thin layers, is the close intimacy of the fellah and the earth. Autochthone is the name that best fits him; he springs from the clay which he treads, he is made out of it, and scarce has emerged from it. He manipulates it, presses it as a child presses its nurse's breast, to draw from its brown bosom the milk of fertility. He sinks waist-deep into its fertile mud, drains it, waters it, dries it, according to its needs; cuts canals in it, builds up levees upon it, draws from it the clay with which he constructs his family dwelling and with which he will cement his tomb. Never was a respectful son more careful of his old mother; he does not leave her as do those vagabond children who forsake their natal roof in search of adventures. He remains there, always attentive to the least want of his antique ancestor, the black earth of Kamé. If she thirsts, he gives her drink, if she is troubled by too much humidity, he dries it; in order not to wound her, he works her almost without tools, with his hands; his plow merely scratches the telluric skin, which the inundation covers each year with a new epidermis. As you watch him going and coming upon that soaking ground, you feel that he is in his element. In his blue garment, which resembles a pontiff's robe, he presides over the marriage of earth and water, he unites the two principles which, warmed by the sun, give birth to life. Nowhere is this harmony between man and the soil so visible; nowhere does the earth play so important a part. It imparts its color to everything. The houses have the earth tint; the bronze complexion of the fellahs recalls it; the trees covered with fine dust, the waters laden with mud, conform to that fundamental harmony; the animals themselves wear its livery; the dun-colored camel, the grey ass, the slate-blue buffalo, the ash-colored pigeon, and the reddish birds all fit in with the general tone.

Another thing which surprises one is the animation visible throughout the country. On the levees along the canals and on those which traverse the inundated portions, there moves a mob of passers-by and of travelers. There is no road so frequented in France, even in the neighborhood of a populous city. Eastern people do not remain much in their houses, and the smallest pretext is sufficient for them to set forth, especially as they have not to think, as we have, of the weather; the barometer is always at set fair, and rain is so uncommonly rare that a man would be glad to get a soaking.

There is nothing more enjoyable, more varied and instructive than the procession of people who are going about their business and who show in succession in the opening of the carriage window, as in a frame in which engravings or watercolors are constantly changing.

First, camels ambling along with a resigned and melancholy look, swinging their long necks, curious animals whose awkward shapes recall the attempts of a vanished creation. On the hump of the foremost is perched the turbaned driver, as majestic as Eleazar, the servant of Abraham, going to Mesopotamia to seek a wife for Isaac; he yields with lazy suppleness to the rough, but regular motions of the animal; sometimes smoking his chibouque as if he were seated at the door of a café, or pressing the slow pace of his steed. Camels like to go in single file; they are accustomed to it, and five or six are usually tied together, sometimes even more; and thus the caravan travels along, showing quaint against the flat lines of the horizon, and for want of any object of comparison, apparently of vast size. On either side of the line trot three or four swift-footed lads, armed with wands; for in the East beasts of burden never lack hostlers and whippers-in. Some of the camels are reddish, others sorrel, others brown, some even are white, but dun is the most frequent color. They carry stones, wood, grass bound with esparto cords, bundles of sugar-cane, boxes, furniture, — in fact, whatever in our country would be loaded on carts. Just now we might have thought ourselves in Holland as we passed along those grey stretches of submerged ground, but the illusion is soon dispelled; as the camel swings along the canal bank, you feel that you are approaching Cairo, and not Amsterdam.

Next come horsemen, bestriding thin, but spirited horses; droves of small donkeys, their masters perched on their cruppers, almost on their tails, their legs almost touching the ground, ready to be used in case the tricky animal falls or jibs, or even indulges, as it often does, in a roll in the dust of the road. In the East the ass is neither contemned nor considered ridiculous as it is in France; it has preserved its Homeric and biblical nobility, and everyone bestrides it without hesitation, the rich and the poor, the old and the young, women as well as men.

Now along the canal comes a charming group: a young woman robed in a long blue mantle, the folds of which fall chastely around her, is seated upon an ass which a man, still vigorous but whose beard is already streaked with grey and white hairs, leads carefully. In front of the mother, who supports it with one hand, is a naked child, exquisitely beautiful, happy and delighted at his trip. It is a picture of the Flight into Egypt; the figures lack nothing but a fine golden halo around their heads. The Virgin, the Child Jesus, and Saint Joseph must have looked like that, and so must their flight have been in the living and simple reality; their equipage was not much finer. What a pity that some great painter, Perugino, Raphael, or Albert Dürer, does not happen to be here.

Damanhûr, which the railroad traverses, looks very much as must have looked the ancient cities of Egypt, now buried under the sand or fallen into dust. It is surrounded by sloping walls built of unbaked bricks or of pisé which preserves its earthy color. The flat-roofed houses rise one above another like a collection of cubes dotted with little black holes. A few dovecotes, the cupolas of which are whitewashed, and one or two minarets striped with red and white, alone impart to the antique appearance of that city the modern aspect of Islamism. On the top of the terraces women, squatting on mats or standing in their long robes of brilliant colors, are looking at us, no doubt attracted by the passing of the train. As they show against the sky, they are wondrously elegant and graceful. They look like statues erected on the top of buildings or the front of temples.

The moment the train stopped, it was invaded by a band of women and children, offering fresh water, bitter oranges, and honey confections to the travelers; and it was delightful to see these brown faces showing at the carriage window their bright smile and their white teeth. I should have liked to remain some time in Damanhûr, but travel, like life, is made up of sacrifices. How many delightful things one is compelled to leave by the roadside, if one wishes to reach the end. A man cannot see everything, and must be satisfied with seeing a few things. So I had to leave Damanhûr and to behold that dream from afar without being able to traverse it. As far as I could see, even through my glass, the land reached to the horizon line, intersected by canals, broken by gutters, shimmering with pools of water, with scattered clumps of sycamore trees and date palms, with long strips of cultivated ground, water-wheels rising here and there, and enlivened by the incessant coming and going of the laborers who followed, on the backs of camels, horses, or asses, or on foot, the narrow road bordering the levees. At intervals there arose, under the shade of a mimosa, the white cupola of a tomb; sometimes a nude child stood motionless on the edge of the water in the attitude of unconscious reverie, not even turning his head to see the train fly along. This deep gravity in childhood is peculiar to the East. What could that boy, standing on his lump of earth as a Stylites on his pillar, be thinking of? From time to time flocks of pigeons, busy feeding, flew off with a sudden whir as the train passed by, and alighted farther away on the plain; aquatic birds swam swiftly through the reeds that outstretched behind them, pretty wagtails hopped about, wagging their tails, on the crest of the levees; and in the heavens at a vast height, soared hawks, falcons, and gerfalcons, sweeping in great circles. Buffaloes wallowed in the mud of the ditches, and flocks of black sheep with hanging ears, very like goats, were hurrying along driven by the shepherds.

The antique simplicity of the costume of the young herds-
men, with their short tunics, white or blue, faded by the sun,
their bare legs, their dusty, naked feet, their felt caps, their
crooks, recalled the patriarchal scenes of the Bible.

At the next station we stopped, and I got out to have a
look at the landscape. I had scarcely gone a few steps when a
wondrous sight met my astonished eyes: before me was the
Nile, old Hapi, to give it its ancient Egyptian name, the
inexhaustible Father of Waters. Through one of those involuntary plastic impressions which act upon the imagination,
the Nile called up to my mind the colossal marble god in one
of the lower halls of the Louvre, carelessly leaning on his
elbow and, with paternal kindliness, allowing himself to be
climbed over by the little children which represent cubits,
and the various phases of the inundation. Well, it was not
under this mythological aspect that the great river appeared
to me for the first time. It was flowing in flood, spreading
out broadly like a torrent of reddish mud which scarcely
looked like water as it swelled and rushed by irresistibly. It
looked like a river of soil; scarcely did the reflection of the
sky imprint here and there upon the gloomy surface of its
tumultuous waves a few light touches of azure. It was still
almost at the height of its rise, but the flood had the tranquil
power of a regular phenomenon, and not the convulsive
disorder of a scourge. The majesty of that vast sheet of water
laden with fertilizing mud produces an almost religious impression. How many vanished civilizations have been reflected for a time in that ever-flowing wave! I remained
absorbed as I gazed at it, sunk in thought, and feeling that
strange sinking of the heart which one experiences after desire
has been fulfilled, and reality has taken the place of the dream.
What I was looking at was indeed the Nile, the real Nile, the
river which I had so often endeavored to discover by intuition. A sort of stupor nailed me to the bank, and yet it was
a very natural thing that I should come across the Nile in
Egypt in the very center of the Delta. But man is subject to
such artless astonishment.

Dhahabîyehs and felûkas spreading their great lateen sails
were tacking across the river, passing from one shore to the

other, and recalling the shape of the mystic baris of the times
of the Pharaohs.

We set out again. The aspect of the country was still the
same; fields of cotton, maize, doora, stretched as far as the
eye could reach. Here and there glimmered the portions of
the ground covered by the flood. Slate-blue buffaloes wallowed in the pools and emerged covered with mud; water
birds stood along the edges, and sometimes flew off as the
train passed, watched by families of fellahs, squatting on the
banks of the ditches. Along the road traveled the endless
procession of camels, asses, oxen, black goats, and foot-passengers, which enlivened to such an extent that peaceful, flat
landscape. I had already noticed when in Holland the additional importance given to figures by a flat country; the lack
of hills makes them stand out, and as they usually show
against the sky they loom larger. I seemed to see pass by the
zones of painted *bassi-rilievi* representing agricultural scenes
which occasionally formed part of the decoration of the halls
of Egyptian tombs. Here and there rose villages or farms, the
lines of whose sloping, earth-grey walls recalled the substruc-
tures of antique temples. Groups of sycamore and mimosa
trees, set off by clumps of date palms, brought out the soft
tones of the walls by the contrast of their rich verdure.
Elsewhere I caught sight of fellahin huts surmounted by
whitewashed dovecotes, placed side by side like beehives or
the minarets of a mosque. We soon reached Tantah, a somewhat important town, to which the fine mosque of Seyd
Ahmed Badouy attracts pilgrims twice a year, and the fairs
of which are frequented by the caravans.

Tantah, from the railway station, — for the train does not
stop long enough to allow travelers to visit the town, — has
an animated and picturesque aspect. Amid the houses in the
Arab style with their look-outs and their awnings, rise buildings in that Oriental-Italian style dear to persons of progress
and of modern ideas, painted in soft colors, ochre, salmon,
or sky-blue; flat-roofed clay huts; over all, the minarets of the
mosque, the white cupolas of a few tombs, and the inevitable
fig trees and palms rising above the low garden walls. Between
the town and the station stretches waste ground, a sort of
fair-ground, on which are camps, huts of reed or of date-palm

branches, tents formed of old rags of cloth and sometimes of the linen of an unrolled turban. The inhabitants of these frail dwellings cook in the open air. The coffee is made, a cup at a time, in a small brass kettle, and on plates of tin are cooked the thin doora cakes. The fuel is camel's-dung. The fellahs suck eagerly the sweetish juice of the sugar-cane cut into short pieces, and the slices of watermelon show within the green skin their ripe, rosy, flesh, spotted with black seeds. Women, as graceful as statues, come and go, holding the end of their veil between their teeth so as to conceal one half of the face, and bearing on their heads Theban jars or copper vases; while the men, squatting on the ground or on small carpets, their knees up to their chins, forming an acute angle like the legs of locusts, in an attitude which no European could assume, and recalling the judges of Amenti ranged in rows one behind another on the papyri of funeral rituals, preserve that dreamy immobility so dear to Orientals when they have nothing to do; for to move about merely for exercise, as Christians do, strikes them as utter folly.

Dromedaries, alone or grouped in circles, kneeling under their burdens, stretch out their long legs on the sand, motionless in the burning sun. Asses, some of which are daintily harnessed, with saddles of red morocco rising in a boss on the withers, and with headstalls adorned with tufts, and others with an old carpet for a saddle-cloth, were waiting for the travelers who were to stop at Tantah to bear them from the station to the town. The donkey drivers, clothed in short blue and white tunics, bare-armed and bare-legged, their heads covered with a fez, a wand in their hand, and resembling the slender figures of shepherds or youths which are so exquisitely drawn on the bodies of Greek vases, stood near their animals in an indolent attitude, which they abandoned as soon as a chance customer came their way. Then they indulged in mad gesticulations, guttural cries, and fought with each other until the unfortunate tourist ran the risk of being torn to pieces or stripped of the best part of his garments. Tawny, wandering dogs with jackal ears, fallen indeed from their old position, and forgetting apparently that they counted Anubis, the dog-headed *Anubis latrator,* among their ancestors, passed in and out among the groups, but without taking the least interest in what was going on.

The bonds which in Europe unite the dog to man do not exist in the East; its social instinct has not been developed, its sympathies have not been appealed to; it has no master, and lives in a savage state. No services are asked of it, and it is not cared for; it has no home and dwells in holes which it makes, unless it stays in some open tomb; no one feeds it; it hunts for itself, gorging on dead bodies and unnamable débris. There is a proverb which says that wolves do not eat each other; Eastern dogs are less scrupulous; they readily devour their sick, wounded, or dead companions. It seemed strange to me to see dogs which did not make any advances to me, and did not seek to be caressed, but maintained a proud and melancholy reserve.

Little girls in blue gowns and little Negroes in white tunics came up to the carriages, offering pastry, cakes, bitter oranges, lemons, and apples, — yes, apples. Eastern people seem to be very fond of that acid Northern fruit which, along with wretched, granulous pears, forms part of every dessert, at which of course one never gets either pomegranates, or bananas, or dates, or oranges, or purple figs, or any native fruits, which are no doubt left to the common people.

The whistle of the engine sounded, and we were again carried away through that very humid and very green Delta. However, as we advanced there showed on the horizon lines of rosy land from which vegetable life was wholly absent. The sand of the desert advances with its waves, as sterile as those of the sea, eternally disturbed by the winds and beating upon the islet of cultivated earth surrounded and stormed by dusty foam, as upon a reef which it endeavors to cover up. In Egypt, whatever lies above the level of the flood is smitten with death. There is no transition; where stops Osiris, Typhon begins; here luxuriant vegetation, there not a blade of grass, not a bit of moss, not a single one of the adventurous plants which grow in solitary and lonely places, — nothing but ground-up sandstone without any mixture of loam. But if a drop of Nile water falls upon it, straightway the barren sand is covered with verdure. These strips of pale salmon-color form a pleasant contrast with the rich tints of the great plain of verdure spread out before us.

Soon we came upon another arm of the Nile, the Phatnitic branch, which flows into the sea near Damietta. It is crossed by the railway, and on the other side lie the ruins of ancient Athrebys, over which has been built a fellahin village. The train sped along, and soon on the right, above the line of green, turning almost black in the dazzling light, showed in the azure distance the triangular silhouette of the pyramids of Cheops and Chephren, appearing, from where I first beheld them, like a single mountain with a piece taken out of the summit. The marvelous clearness of the atmosphere made them appear nearer, and had I not been aware of the real distance I should have found it difficult to estimate it correctly. It is quite natural to catch sight of the pyramids as one approaches Cairo; it is to be expected and it is expected, yet the sight causes extraordinary emotion and surprise. It is impossible to describe the effect produced by that vaporous outline so faint that it almost melts into the color of the sky, and that, if one had not been forewarned, it might escape notice. Neither years nor barbarians have been able to over-throw these artificial mountains, the most gigantic monu-ments, except, perhaps, the Tower of Babel, ever raised by man. For five thousand years they have been standing there, — almost as old as the world, according to the biblical ac-count. Even our own civilization, with its powerful methods of destruction, could scarcely manage to tear them down. The pyramids have seen ages and dynasties flow by like billows of sand, and the colossal Sphinx with its noseless face ever smiles at their feet with its ironical and mysterious smile. Even after they were opened they kept their secret, and yielded up but the bones of oxen by the side of an empty sarcophagus. Eyes that have been closed so long that Europe, perchance, had not emerged from the flood when those eyes beheld the light, gazed upon them from where I am; they are contemporaneous with vanished empires, with strange races of men since swept from the surface of the earth; they have beheld civilizations that we know nothing of; heard spoken the tongues which men seek to make out in hieroglyphics, known manners which would appear to us as strange as a dream. They have been there so long that the stars have changed their places, and they belong to a past so prodigiously fabulous that behind them the dawn of the world seems to shine.

While these thoughts flashed through my mind we were rapidly approaching Cairo, — Cairo, of which I had talked so often with poor Gérard de Nerval, with Gustave Flaubert, and Maxime Du Camp, whose tales had excited my curiosity to the highest pitch. In the case of cities which one has desired to see from childhood, and which one has long inhabited in dreams, one is apt to conceive a fantastic notion which it is very difficult to efface, even in presence of reality. The sight of an engraving, of a picture, often forms a starting-point. My Cairo, built out of the materials of the "Thousand and One Nights," centered around the Ezbekîyeh Place, the strange painting of which Marilhat had sent from Egypt to one of the first exhibitions which followed the Revolution of July. Unless I am mistaken, it was his first picture, and whatever the perfection which he afterwards attained, I do not believe that he ever painted a work fuller of life, more individual, and more striking. It made a deep and curious impression upon me; I went time and again to see it; I could not take my eyes off it, and it exercised upon me a sort of nostalgic fascination. It was from that painting that my dreams started upon fantastic trips through the narrow streets of ancient Cairo once traversed by Caliph Haroun al Raschid and his faithful vizier Jaffier, under the disguise of slaves or common people. My admiration for the painting was so well known that Marilhat's family gave me, after the death of the famous artist, the pencil sketch of the subject made on the spot, and which he had used as a study for the finished work.

And now we had arrived. A great mob of carriages, asses, donkey drivers, porters, guides, dragomans, rioted in front of the railway station, which is at Boulah, a short distance from old Cairo. When we had recovered our luggage, and I had been installed with my friend in a handsome open carriage preceded by a *saïs,* it was with secret delight that I heard the Egyptian providence which watched over us in its *Nizam* uniform and its magenta fez, call out to the coachman, "Hotel Shepheard, Ezbekîyeh Place." I was going to lodge in my dream.

# Ezbekîyeh Square

$A$ few minutes later the carriage stopped before the steps of the Hotel Shepheard, which has a sort of veranda provided with chairs and sofas for the convenience of travelers who desire to enjoy the cool air. We were received cordially, and given a fine room, very high-ceiled, with two beds provided with mosquito-nets, and a window looking out upon the Ezbekîyeh Square.

I did not expect to find Marilhat's painting before me, unchanged, and merely enlarged to the proportions of reality. The accounts of tourists who had recently returned from Egypt had made me aware that the Ezbekîyeh no longer looked the same as formerly, when the waters of the Nile turned it into a lake in times of flood, and when it still preserved its true Arab character.

Huge mimosas and sycamores fill up the center of the square with domes of foliage so intensely green that it looks almost black. On the left rises a row of houses, among which are to be seen, side by side with the newer buildings, old Arab dwellings more or less modernized. A great number of moucharabiehs had disappeared. There remains a sufficient number of them, however, to preserve the Oriental character of this side of the square.

Above the trees on the other side of the square, higher than the line of the roofs, are seen four or five minarets, the shafts of which, built in courses alternately blue and red, stand out against the azure sky. On the right the scarps of Mokattam, of a rosy grey, show their bare sides, on which no vegetation is apparent. The trees of the square conceal the newer buildings, and thus my dream was not too much upset.

Being an invalid, I had to be somewhat careful, and required two or three days of complete rest. If the reader is fond of travel, he will understand how great was my desire to begin exploring that labyrinth of picturesque streets in which swarms a varicolored crowd, but it was out of the question for the time being. I thought that Cairo, more complaisant in this respect than the mountain to the prophet, would come to me if I could not go to it, and as a matter of fact, Cairo was polite enough to do so.

While my luckier companions started to visit the city, I settled myself on the veranda. It was the best place I could have chosen, for even leaving out the people on the Square, the veranda roof sheltered many curious characters. There were dragomans, most of them Greeks or Copts, wearing the fez and a short, braided jacket and full trousers; cavasses richly costumed in oriental fashion, scimitar on the hip, *kandjar* in the belt, and silver-topped cane in the hand; native servants in white drawers and blue or pink gowns; little Negroes, bare-armed and bare-legged, dressed in short tunics striped with brilliant colors; dealers selling kuffiyehs, gandouras, and oriental stuffs manufactured in Lyons, photographic views of Egypt and of Cairo, or pictures of national types, — to say nothing of the travelers themselves, who, having come from all parts of the world, certainly deserved to be looked at.

Opposite the hotel, on the other side of the road, stood in the shade of the mimosas the carriages placed at the disposal of the invited guests by the splendid hospitality of the Khedive. An inspector, blind in one eye, with a turban rolled around his head and wearing a long blue caftan, called them up and gave the drivers the orders of the travelers. There also stood the battalion of donkey drivers with their long-eared steeds. I am told that there are no less than eighty thousand donkeys in Cairo. That number does not seem to be exaggerated. There are donkeys at every corner, around every mosque, and in the most deserted places there suddenly appear from behind a wall a donkey driver and a donkey that place themselves at your service. These asses are very pretty, spirited, and bright-tempered; they have not the piteous look and the air of melancholy resignation of the asses of our own country, which are ill fed, beaten, and contemned. You feel that they think as much of themselves as other animals do, and that they are not the whole day long a butt for stupid jokes. Perhaps they are aware that Homer compared Ajax to an ass, a comparison which is ridiculous in the West; and they also remember that one of their ancestors bore Miriam, the Virgin Mother of Issa, under the sycamore of Matarieh. Their coat varies from dark-brown to white, through all the shades of dun and grey. Some have white stars and fetlocks. The handsomest are clipped with ingenious coquetry so as to make around the legs patterns which make them look as if they were wearing open-worked stockings. When they are white, the end of the tail and the mane are dyed with henna. Of course this is only in the case of thorough-bred animals, of the aristocracy of the asinine race, and is not indulged in with the common herd.

Their harness consists of a headstall adorned with tresses, tufts of silk and wool, sometimes coral beads or copper plates, and of a morocco saddle, usually red, rising up in front to prevent falls, but without any cantle. The saddle is placed upon a piece of carpet or striped stuff, and is fastened by a broad girth which passes diagonally under the animal's tail like a crupper-strap; another girth fastens the saddle-cloth, and two short stirrups flap against the animal's sides. The harness is more or less rich according to the means of the donkey driver and the rank of his customers, but I am speaking merely of asses which stand for hire. No one in Cairo considers it undignified to ride an ass, — old men, grown men, dignitaries, townspeople, all use them. Women ride astride, a fashion which in no wise compromises their modesty, thanks to the enormous folds of their broad trousers which almost completely conceal their feet. They often carry before them, placed upon the saddlebow, a small, half-nude, child which they steady with one hand while with the other they hold the bridle. It is usually women of importance who indulge in this luxury, for the poor fellahin women have no other means of locomotion than their little feet. These beauties, as we may suppose them to be, since they are masked more closely than society ladies at the Opéra ball, wear over their garments a *habbarah,* a sort of black taffeta sack, which fills with air and swells in the most ungraceful fashion if the animal's pace is quickened.

In the East a rider, whether on horseback or on an ass, is always accompanied by two or three footmen. One runs on ahead with a wand in his hand to clear the way, the second holds the animal's bridle, and the third hangs on by its tail, or at least puts his hand on the crupper. Sometimes there is a fourth who flits about and stirs up the animal with a switch. Every minute Decamp's "Turkish Patrol," that startling painting which made such a sensation in the Exhibition of 1831, passed before me, amid a cloud of dust, and made me smile; but no one appeared to notice the comicality of the situation: a stout man dressed in white with a broad belt around his waist, perched on a little ass and followed by three or four poor devils, thin and tanned, with hungry mien, who through excess of zeal and in hope of backshish, seem to carry along the rider and his steed.

I must be forgiven all this information about the asses and their drivers, but these occupy so large a space in life at Cairo that they are entitled to the importance which they really possess.

# Ancient Egypt

*T*he solemn title must not terrify the reader. M. Ernest
Feydeau's book is, in spite of its title, most attractive reading.
In his case science does not mean weariness, as happens too
often. The author of "Funeral Customs and Sepulture among
the Ancient Nations" desired to be understood of all, and
everybody may profit by his long and careful researches. He
has not sealed his work with seven seals, as if it were an
apocalyptic volume, to be understood by adepts only; he has
sought clearness, distinctness, color, and he has given to
archæology the plastic form which it almost always lacks.
What is the use of heaping together materials in disorder,
stones which are not made to form part of a building, colors
which are not turned into pictures? What does the public, for
whom, after all, books are meant, get out of so many obscure
works, cryptic dissertations, deep researches, with which
learned authors seem to mask entrances, as the ancient Egyptians — the comparison is a proper one here — masked the
entrances to their tombs and their mummy pits so that no
one might penetrate into them? What is the use of carving
in darkness endless panels of hieroglyphs which no eye is to
behold and the key to which one keeps for one's self? M.
Ernest Feydeau is bold enough to desire to be an artist as well
as a scholar; for picturesqueness in no wise detracts from
accuracy, though erudites generally affect to believe the contrary. Did not Augustin Thierry draw his intensely living,
animated, dramatic, and yet thoroughly true "Stories of the
Merovingian Times" from the colorless, diffuse, ill-composed
history of Gregory of Tours? Did not Sauval's unreadable

work become "Notre-Dame de Paris" in Victor Hugo's hands? Did not Walter Scott, by his novels, Shakespeare by his dramas, render the greatest services to history by giving life to dead chronicles, by putting into flesh and blood heroes on whom forgetfulness had scattered its dust in the solitude of libraries? Does anyone suppose that the chroniclers of the future will not consult Balzac to advantage, and look upon his work as a precious mine of documents? How great would be the interest excited by a similar account, domestic, intimate and familiar, by a Greek or a Roman author? We can have some idea of this from the fragments of Petronius and the Tales of Apuleius, which tell us more about life in the days of antiquity than the gravest writers, who often forget men while dwelling upon facts.

In an essay on the history of manners and customs which forms the introduction to his book, M. Ernest Feydeau has discussed this question of color applied to science with much spirit, logic, and eloquence. He proves that it is possible, without falling into novel writing, without indulging in imaginativeness, and while preserving the gravity and the authority of history, to group around facts, by the intelligent reading of texts, by the study and the comparison of the monuments, the manners, the customs, the books of vanished races, to show man at a particular time, to put as a background to each event the landscape, the city, or the interior in which it occurred, and in the conqueror's hand the weapon which he really carried. Ideas have forms, events take place amid certain surroundings, individuals wear costumes which archæology, properly understood, can restore to them. That is its proper task. History draws the outline with a graver, archæology must fill it in with color. Understood in this way, history makes the past present. The innovating archæologist, by an apparently paradoxical inspiration, has asked of death the secret of life; he has studied the tomb, which has yielded up to him not only the mysteries of destruction, but the customs and the national life of all the nations of antiquity. The sepulcher has faithfully preserved what the memory of man has forgotten and what has been lost in scattered libraries. The tomb alone, opening its somber lips, has replied to the questions of today; it knows what historians do not know; it is impartial, and has no interest in lying, apart from the innocent imposture of the epitaph. Each generation, as it sinks forever under the ground, after having lived and moved for a few moments on its surface, inscribes upon the walls of its funeral dwelling the true expression of its acts, its beliefs, its customs, its arts, its luxuries, its individuality, all that was seen then and that shall never again be seen, and then the hand of man rolls boulders, the desert heaps up sand, the waters of the stream deposit mud upon the forgotten entrance to the necropolis. The pits are filled up, the subterranean passages are effaced, the tombs sink and disappear under the dust of empires. A thousand, two thousand, three thousand, four thousand years pass by, and a lucky stroke of the pick reveals a whole nation within a coffin.

The ancients, differing in this respect from the moderns, spent their life in preparing their last dwelling. The history of their funerals contains, therefore, the germ of their whole history. But that history, full of intimate details, mysterious facts, and documents at times enigmatical, is not to be written like the other form of history which men are satisfied to repeat from age to age. It is amazing how many years the author had to spend in study and research in order to write his book, to bring together his materials, to analyze and to compare them.

After having clearly defined what he means by archæology, the author enters upon his subject. Going back to the beginnings of the world, he depicts the amazement and the grief of man when for the first time he saw his fellow-man die. The entrance on earth of that unknown and terrible power which has since been called death is solemn and tragical. The body is lying there motionless and cold amid its brethren, who are amazed at the sleep which they cannot break, at the livid pallor and the stiffness of the limbs. Horror succeeds surprise when the signs of decomposition become visible. The body is concealed under leaves, under stones heaped up within caverns, and each one wonders with terror whether that death is an exceptional case, or whether the same fate awaits everyone in a more or less distant future. Deaths become more numerous as the primitive family grows older, and at last the conviction comes that it is an inevitable fate. The remembrance of the ancestors, the apparition of their ghosts in the wonders of dreams, the anxiety as to the fate of the soul after the destruction of the body, give rise, along with the presentiment of another life, to the first idea of God. Death teaches eternity and proves irrefragably the existence of a power superior to that of man. The belief in metempsychosis, in the migration of the soul, in other spheres, in reward and punishment according to the works done by men in the flesh, arose among nations in accordance with the degree of civilization which they had attained. Among the least civilized these doctrines exist in a state of confusion, remain vague, uncouth, surcharged with superstition and peculiarities. Nevertheless, everywhere the mystery of the tomb is venerated.

It may be affirmed that no nation was so preoccupied with death as ancient Egypt. It is a strange sight to behold that people preparing its tomb from childhood, refusing to yield up its dust to the elements, and struggling against destruction with invincible obstinacy. Just as the layers of Nile mud have overlaid one another since the birth of time, the generations of Egypt are ranged in order at the bottom of the mummy pits of the hypogea and the pyramids of the necropolis, their bodies intact — for the worm of the tomb dare not attack them, repelled as it is by the bitter bituminous odors. But for the sacrilegious devastations of man, that dead people would be found complete, and its numberless multitudes might cover the earth. Imagination is staggered when it attempts to calculate the probable numbers; if Egyptian civilization had lasted ten centuries longer, the dead would have ended by expelling the living from their native land. The necropolis would have invaded the city, and the stark mummies in their bandages would have stood up by the wall of the hearth.

You cannot have forgotten the marvelous chapter on "A Bird's-eye view of Paris," an amazing restoration by a poet, in which archæology itself, in spite of the progress it has made, would find it difficult to discover a flaw. Well, what Victor Hugo has done for mediæval Paris, M. Ernest Feydeau has attempted for the Thebes of the Pharaohs, and his restoration, as complete as it is possible for it to be, and which no historian had attempted, stands out before us as sharply as a plan in relief, and with all the perspective of a panorama. Thebes of the Hundred Gates, as Homer called it, — antiquity has told us nothing more about this ancestress of capitals; but M. Ernest Feydeau takes us walking with him through the city of Rameses; he shows us all its monuments, its temples, its palaces, the dwellings of the inhabitants, the gardens, the harbor, the fleet of vessels; he draws and colors the costumes of the people; he enters the harems, and shows us the traveling musicians, the dancers, the enslaved nations which built for the Egyptians, the soldiers maneuvering on the parade ground, the processions of Ammon, the foreign peoples which come seeking refuge and corn, the caravans of thirty-five hundred years ago bringing in the tribute. Then he describes the colleges of priests, the quarters inhabited by the embalmers, the minutest details of the embalming proc-esses, the funeral rites, the construction of the thousands of hypogea and mummy pits which are to receive the mummies. Finally he shows us, passing through the streets of that strange city, the funeral procession of a royal scribe upon its cata-falque, drawn by oxen, — the numberless mourners, the hosts of servants bearing alms and offerings. I regret that the length of that passage does not allow of my quoting it in full and enabling the reader to mark the union of a beautiful style with scientific knowledge. Unquestionably no modern trav-eler has ever given a more picturesque description of any existing city, Constantinople, Rome, or Cairo. The artist seems to be seated upon the terrace of a palace, drawing and painting from nature as if he were a contemporary of Rame-ses, and as if the sands had not covered with their shroud, through which show a few gigantic ruins, the city forever vanished. And yet he indulges in no chance supposition, in no rash padding. Every detail he gives is supported by the most authentic documents. M. Ernest Feydeau put aside every doubtful piece of information and all that appeared suscep-tible of being interpreted in more than one way. He seems to have been anxious to forestall the suspicious mistrust of scholars, who object to having the dry results of erudition clothed in poetic language, and who do not believe that a treatise on archæology can possibly be read with as much interest as a novel.

As I have said, the Egyptians have left us no books, and had they done so the art of deciphering hieroglyphics or even phonetic or demotic writing is not yet assured enough to allow of absolute trust being put in it. Happily the Egyptians performed a work of such mightiness that it amazes the beholder. By the side of the hieroglyphic inscriptions they carved on the walls of palaces and temples, on the sides of pylons, the faces of the corridors and the bays of funeral chambers, on the faces of the sarcophagi and on the stelæ, on the covers and the interior cartonnages of the mummies, — in short, on every smooth surface of rock, whether sandstone or granite, basalt or porphyry, with an ineffaceable line colored with tints that the long succession of ages has not faded, — scenes in which we find in detail the habits and customs and the ceremonies of the oldest civilization in the world. It seems as if those strange and mysterious people, foreseeing the difficulty which posterity would experience in deciphering their hieroglyphics, entrusted their translation to drawing, and made the hypogea tell the secret kept by the papyri.

Royal ceremonies, triumphal entries, the payments of tribute, all the incidents of military life, of agriculture, sport, fishing, banqueting, dances, the intimate life of the harem, all is reproduced in these endless paintings, so clearly drawn, with the difference in races, variety of types, shape of chariots, of weapons, of arms, of furniture, of utensils, of food, of plants, still clearly visible today. A maker of musical instruments could certainly make a harp, a lyre, or a sistrum from the pattern of those upon which are playing the female musicians at the funeral repast represented in one of the tombs of the necropolis of Thebes. The model of a dog-cart in a plate of modern carriages is not drawn more accurately than the profile of the chariot seen in the funeral procession of the ecclesiastical scribe of Amenoph III, a king of the eighteenth dynasty.

The author has not confined himself to these purely material details. He has examined the funeral papyri which, more or less valuable, are found with each mummy; he has

carefully studied the allegorical signs which represent the
judgment of the soul, the good and evil deeds of which are
weighed before Osiris and the forty-two judges, and thus he
has mastered the mysterious beliefs of the Egyptians on the
question of the future life. The soul, whether it was conducted
to Amenti or driven into the infernal regions — that is,
towards the West — by the dog-headed monkeys, who appear
to have been a sort of dæmons charged with the carrying out
of sentences, — the soul was, nevertheless, not freed from all
connection with the body; its relative immortality depended
in some sort upon the integrity of the latter; the alteration,
the deprivation of one of the limbs was supposed to be felt
by the soul, the form of whose impalpable specter would have
been mutilated and could not have traversed, wanting a leg
or an arm, the cycle of migrations or metempsychoses. Hence
the religious care taken of the human remains, the infallible
methods and the minute precautions of the embalmers, the
perfect solidity and the secret location of the tombs, of which
the priests alone possessed the plan, the constant thought of
eternity in death which characterized in so striking a manner
the ancient Egyptians and makes them a nation apart, incomprehensible to modern nations, which are generally so eager
to give back to the earth and to cause to disappear the
generations which have preceded them.

During his long and intimate acquaintance with Egypt, M.
Ernest Feydeau, who is not only an archæologist but also a
poet, after he had sounded the mysteries of the old kingdom
of the Pharaohs, became passionately attached to that art
which the Greek ideal — which nevertheless is indebted to it
for more than one lesson — has caused us to despise too much.
He has understood, both as a painter and a sculptor, a beauty
which is so different from our own standard and which is yet
so real.

Hathor, the Egyptian Venus, seems to him as beautiful as
the Venus of Milo. Without entirely sharing that feeling, I
confess to admiring greatly the clean outline, so pure, so
slender, and so full of life. In spite of the hieratic restrictions
which did not allow the consecrated attitude to be varied, art
shows out in more than one direction. There is a beauty of a
strange and penetrating charm foreign to our own habits in

the heads with their delicate profiles, their great eyes made larger by the use of antimony, the somewhat thick lips with their faint, dreamy pout, or their vague smile resembling that of the sphinx, in the rounded cheeks upon which hang broad discs of gold, in the brows shaded by lotus flowers, in the temples framed in by the narrow tresses of the hair, powdered with blue powder, which are shown in funeral processions. How youthful, how fresh, how pure are the tall, slender bodies, the swelling bosoms, the supple waists, the narrow hips of these dancers and musicians who beat time with their long, slender fingers and their long, narrow feet. The Etruscans themselves have never produced anything more light, more graceful, and more elegant upon the bodies of their finest vases, and in more than one famous Greek bas-relief can be recognized attitudes and gestures borrowed from the frescoes of the necropolis and the tombs of Egypt. It is from Egypt also that Greece took, while diminishing their huge size, its Doric and Ionic orders and its Corinthian capital, in which the acanthus takes the place of the lotus flower.

www.ingramcontent.com/pod-product-compliance
Lightning Source LLC
Chambersburg PA
CBHW032147020726
47496CB00003B/758